JACQUES OSCAR LUFULUABO

SHADOW
OF
PUNISHMENT

TRANSLATED FROM THE ITALIAN BY

Cecilia Negri
Traduzione Vincente Agency

Revised Edition 2019
Edited by Shaun Rhodes Bsc. (Hons)

Original title: L'ombra del castigo
Copyright © 2014 by Jacques Oscar Lufuluabo

Translated from the Italian by
Cecilia Negri – Traduzione Vincente agency

Edited by Shaun Rhodes Bsc. (Hons)

For information contact **info@joloscar.com**
or visit author's website **www.joloscar.com**

ISBN: 9781976874116

"The mind is its own place, and in itself can make a heaven of hell, a hell of heaven."

John Milton

"There is nothing either good or bad, but thinking makes it so."

William Shakespeare

CHAPTER 1

Rosa's words had tormented him the whole day. Echoing in his brain like demons in the night, they had struck him to his breaking point. He had spent his afternoon in the attempt to calm that untold rage impulse, but nothing had served its purpose. Franco realized that the only way to stop it was by doing something, so without further ado, he ran out of the house, got into his car and in a few moments was streaming away into the evening traffic.

Rosa lived on the other side of the city. It took him almost a whole hour to get to her place. An hour in which anxiety finished consuming him completely. The flooded streets of cars that had at first occupied his vision, slowly dispersed under his eyes and by the time he arrived at destination, the streets were close to deserted. Only the headlights of his ramshackle Beetle lit the area.

Wrapped in the silence of the night, unsure whether she would let him in, he felt seized by negative thoughts but the sight of an old man leaving the building broke through his thoughts. Putting an end to all hesitation, ignoring he had double parked, he ran to the door of the building only to find it shut just after he got there. "Damn it!" he yelled, feeling his rage rising once again.

He would have liked to kick that door down. He raised a fist to punch it but the man was still there, not far from him, staring right at him. He therefore restrained himself, clenching his teeth and tensing his neck and arm muscles. He could feel all the tension that was reverberating through his soul in his fist and so, as to let it out, he tightened his hand even more.

"What an idiot!", he thought to himself. He had in fact lived in that building for a whole year. He had just broken up with Rosa some months before but hadn't yet got rid of his keys. He took them out of his pocket and opened the door.

Before entering, his gaze fell upon the apartment intercom panel. He noticed that apartment number five's label showed "Franco Mezzana – Rosa Fogliani" on it. Surprised to see that his name was still written there, he wondered why Rosa hadn't removed it. Not that he minded, not at all. She had clearly expressed the will to completely erase him from her life, and to read his name next to hers seemed to leave a glimmer of hope. But that thought faded fast as he remembered the reason why he was there. He was there for the truth and, one way or another, he was going to get it. So he swung the door open and went upstairs.

Everything was how he left it. The lighting in the entrance hall was still out of order. The same went for the lights on the landings that now only stood there for decoration.

Franco continued carelessly up to the second floor until where, upon reaching the door, he felt his anxiety suddenly increasing. A slight noise behind him was enough to make him jump. He had the strange feeling of being observed and turned around and looked into the darkness enshrouding the entire floor, but didn't see or hear anything. He turned back round, took out the key to the apartment and inserted it in the keyhole and, realizing it didn't fit, he understood that Rosa must have changed the lock. It suddenly came to him that his name on the intercom panel was just a trivial matter and, in an impulse of rage, he started banging violently on the door.

"Rosa!" he screamed furiously, "Open up!"

When the door opened, he instinctively raised an arm to

***

Rosa was twenty-eight. She was unique in her way. She had a pleasant face that would stand out with that amazing contrast created by her green eyes and her beautiful red hair. She was a merry and lively person, but that night she was all out of sorts and her mood was terrible.

"I'll report you, you jerk," she had yelled at Franco furiously, slamming the door in his face.

Once alone, she continued swearing at him as if he was still there to receive her insults. That lunatic had turned her house upside down. He had finally left, but, behind him, he had left devastation. Seeing the room in such a mess, she raised her hands to her head and took a deep breath, feeling relief and despair at the same time. Pieces of glass were scattered all over the living room. Of the four chairs that had been set around the table, only one was still in its place. On the floor were the fragments of the vase, wedged between the pieces of glass from the mirror and, not far from that, was what was left of the plant. With its wire torn off, the phone was lying idle and mute on the sofa, while the other objects, big and small, were lying around all over the floor, in the most absolute chaos.

"Bastard!" Rosa said once again, before heading towards the entrance. She took a broom and an old bucket from the closet. When she came back to the living room, and the disorderly sight appeared in view, her breath was caught in her chest. She would have wanted to call the police, report him, but her gaze fell upon the now useless device lying helplessly on the sofa. Her cell phone might have survived the disaster, but just the idea of looking for it in all that mess, convinced her to forget about it. That night had already been tiring enough. With a sign of resignation, she bent down to collect what hadn't been destroyed.

She lifted the chairs and put them back into place. While picking up the mess of broken glass, she heard knocking on the door. She thought that, unlike her, that bastard still hadn't had enough.

"Get out," she said. She was determined not to let him in.

But the bell went on ringing repeatedly. With her nerves on end, she felt like she was going to go insane. The only solution was to open the door. Without even turning the light on, she crossed the room to the entrance, with the worst of intentions. Once she had opened the door, she would have started screaming like crazy and maybe somebody else would have called the cops.

Unfortunately, she didn't have time to utter a single word. In unlocking the door, she could only see a reflection glittering in the darkness. She glimpsed a hand brushing her face and in it a metallic object that she didn't recognize. A fraction of a second later, she felt a stabbing pain creeping up from her neck. She felt the air knocked out of her lungs. She brought her hands to her throat in pain, and was shocked to realize there was a warm and dense liquid rippling over her arms. For a few seconds, she stood like that, swaying on the spot. She opened her mouth wide in a last desperate attempt to breathe, but, emitted a guttural sound. Then, she collapsed on the floor, drained out. Only then, an icy-cold feeling passing through her body, she realized that death was close.

CHAPTER 2

Some months before...

"Dr. Giliberti! I've finally reached you," Lisa said. "I've been trying to contact you for two days."

"I'm sorry," the voice on the telephone replied. "I have been busier than usual."

"I would like to know your decision regarding the conference. Will you be attending?"

Before Dr. Gilberti was able to answer, the telephone emitted a beep and a reddish light started blinking. Lisa wouldn't have wanted to put off that call any further, but she apologized to the professor and put him on hold. The voice of the secretary rang from the speaker phone announcing a call from Miss Fogliani on the other line.

"I'm busy, Stefania," she replied. "Tell her to leave a message."

"This is the third time she's called."

"I can't speak to her right now!" retorted Lisa sharply, going back to her previous call.

"I'm sorry for the interruption," she said.

"Don't worry. I can only imagine how busy you are these days. I've checked my schedule by the way. I don't have any appointments that can't be postponed on that day so consider my participation."

"Oh! Thank you, Professor. Then, I confirm that the conference will be held next week, as planned."

After exchanging a few words, the two said goodbye and, when the call ended, she leaned back in the chair feeling relieved.

Lisa Colasanti was forty-three and belonged to high society. Proud of her name, she had never taken on that of her husband, Vincenzo Della Torre. For six years now, she had been managing *VitaNuova*, an organization for drug addiction rehabilitation with several centers in different areas of the country. She had been kept on the phone all morning. Headquarters had decided to host a new rehabilitation support symposium and somebody had had the brilliant idea of putting her in charge of its preparation. She had obviously delegated most of the legwork to her assistants, but she had decided to contact the most prominent spokesmen personally, in order to explain the theme of the symposium accurately and the important role it took on from a social-healthcare point of view.

Of the ten expected to attend the conference as lecturers, only six had confirmed their availability. Two were unable to participate, while the other two were unreachable. Just to be sure, she would have contacted them during the following days, but by now the matter was expendable. After all, she had been able to confirm the presence of the most important contacts and she could deem herself satisfied.

As it often happened when she reached a professional goal, she started thinking back to when, she had first started working at the center seven years earlier. After only one year, they had promoted her to director, and she had always wondered if it had been because of her skills or for her high position in society. She knew perfectly well what influence her nomination had brought to the organization. Apart from increasing its prestige and credibility, she had enabled financial support to expand substantially. Not so much as for the extended state benefits, but it was thanks to the charity dinners that she would organize that were attended by many relevant personalities from high society. All in all, she felt content with her work, but that unanswered dilemma had never allowed her to really feel fully satisfied.

Anyway, it was nearing 12, and soon her husband would be there to pick her up for lunch. So she let go of all her unanswered questions, gathered her stuff and was about to get up to leave, when she remembered her last call. Bothered, she sat back down and dialed Miss Fogliani's extension number but her telephone seemed to ring unattended. She waited a little longer, until after what seemed the umpteenth unanswered ring, after which she hung up, irritated.

When she was about to stand up, she heard a knock on her door and, before she was able to say to come in, she saw her door being thrust wide open. Rosa Fogliani darted into her office shaking a handful of papers into the air.

"Well?" Lisa said, irritated. "Has asking for permission to enter died out?"

"I've been waiting for your call for almost half an hour and…"

"And I've had a morning full of appointments. I didn't think I had to report to you. Anyway, what is it? What's so urgent for you to burst in like this?"

"It's about the personnel management."

"What about it?"

"I finished coordinating the team last week, but from the papers I can see you've brought in a new member without informing me."

Rosa was a psychologist, and she had the role of therapeutic coordinator. Although it was Lisa who was to be in charge of the team, Rosa was the mediator between Lisa and personnel as for management and from a technical point of view. She could not be kept in the dark about matters concerning the wellbeing of the center.

"You are right. I apologize," Lisa said, feeling momentarily dazed. "I had completely forgotten about it."

Rosa didn't say anything. She just hinted a little expression of surrender.

"I know I should have informed you sooner," Lisa continued. "But I was only just told. Last month I communicated to headquarters that ours is the only division that hasn't introduced art therapy as a healthcare support. So it was only last week that they informed me that my request had finally been accepted. The new health provider should be arriving tomorrow."

"It would have been great news if you had kept me updated. Now I have to get back down to work!"

"I am very sorry, Miss Fogliani, it's just that this conference…"

"Am I disturbing you?" somebody said, interrupting her.

"Oh! Vincenzo! Sorry for being late," Lisa said when her husband appeared. And turning to Rosa, she said: "I hope we can consider this matter closed."

"Of course. No worries," Rosa answered, with a look on her face that was all but convincing.

"Speaking about which… Here is the report of the new team member. You will find all the necessary details there."

Vincenzo Della Torre was waiting at the office's threshold and Miss Fogliani, on leaving, stared at him with an overbearing look. Lisa noticed the provocative look, yet, feeling uneasy for the unpleasant situation, and kept silent. She wondered what was Rosa's problem, and only when she had left, did she go away with her husband.

While doing so, she informed her secretary that she would be back in the afternoon and the woman wished her an enjoyable lunch.

***

Franco Mezzana was on his way out of the corridor when he saw Rosa leaving management. Anxious to talk to her, he turned on his footsteps and approached her, still unsure on what to say. After a few moments' silence, he was about to say something, but

Rosa's behavior – a nervous shuffling of papers – were a sure sign that nothing good would come of it. Then Franco noticed Mrs. Colasanti leaving with her husband and understood. There had been no love lost between the two, for months now. Their squabbles were now on a daily basis. Understanding that they probably had had another argument, he put a hand on Rosa's shoulder and said: "What happened this time?"

She obviously hadn't noticed him coming. Seeing him, she shook his hand off vigorously. "Nothing!" she replied sharply. "Nothing happened. And anyway, it's none of your business."

"Don't you think it's time to drop the act?" he said. "You're being ridiculous."

"If being ridiculous means not having you around, I definitely prefer it."

"Can you tell me what the hell you expect from me?"

"I just want you to disappear. And, unless it's work related, don't look for me. Don't talk to me. Don't think about me. I do not exist for you. Do you get it now? I do not exist."

"You're just a dork," he striked back, snatching the papers from her hands. "Talking with you is pointless."

Without adding anything else, he threw the mass of papers in her face and went away, irritated.

Franco Mezzana was responsible for the forensic department. He had had that role for three years and, heading towards his office, which was twenty meters away, he wondered whether it was time to change his environment.

He opened the office window and pulled himself close to his desk. With no urge to do so, he turned on his computer to check his e-mail. Waiting for the processor to start running, he started fiddling with an old razor he used as a letter opener. It was a *Globusmen Solingen* with an ivory handle and a *Focus High Class* blade.

It was a collector's item he had inherited and that, each time, would bring him back to his childhood days. He remembered when his grandfather had removed the first moustache, making him feel like a man, and the day he had given him with such a beautiful object. "One day you'll be the one taking my place here," he had told him on that occasion. And he had imagined himself there, with a nice barber's uniform and tools in his hands. Then time had dealt its cards and with his grandfather's death, those childish dreams had then disappeared.

With his past in mind, he opened a drawer in his desk and took out a leather band. He passed the blade over it on both sides repeatedly until it was perfectly sharp. Then he took a sheet of paper and folded it in two perfectly. He passed the blade along the fold. Seeing how the cut was precise and linear, he felt satisfied and put the strap back in its place.

Before working on his computer, he checked his messages on the answering machine. There was only one, from his ex-wife, reminding him of his fatherly duties. On the contrary, his in-box was flooded with dozens of e-mails. He took a quick look and noted one by SerT, the public service against drug addiction, and decided to open it. It was a simple confirmation notice regarding the shipping that would be followed by the delivery of the relevant papers. The administration was informing him that they were starting the process for the arrival of a convict to the center. In fact, the SerT, apart from having an agreement with the local health authorities and universities, therapeutic communities, alcoholic associations and other health-care structures, was also connected to the prefecture, the Court House and different detention institutions.

In the e-mail "hepatitis B" had been underlined and in the attached dossier were listed all the detainee's pathologies as well as the requested administration therapy.

VitaNuova was an organization that was fully compliant for the reception of those users. From the beginning, the center had been created to answer to all needs in the best way possible. Patients affected by hepatitis, or HIV-positive, who accounted for the majority of cases, were hosted in separate buildings. The complex then provided for a specific separation for minors, and, of course, a division for male and female accommodation. Finally, a last department was dedicated to those who needed further medical support once they had finished their therapeutic program.

With his eyes lost on the screen, Franco felt a feeling of bitterness grab hold of him. A frequent feeling despite having worked there many years. He was against any sort of hierarchy. He believed that everybody was free to do whatever they wanted with their life. But he had always been against the use of drugs. From his point of view, they were a limitation of one's freedom and to see those people, who had ruined their lives, every day, made him feel sad.

To feel better, he tried to imagine himself in some lost place, at the other side of the world. In turn, Rosa came to his mind. He still kept the picture showing them hugging, the Mexican Sea behind them. The one summer they had spent together, made unique by the awareness that they would never share those moments again. They had met at the rehabilitation center and, from the very first moment, they had been attracted to each another. Then, with the passing of time, they had found something in common. Both anarchic, each in their own way, they had created a world of their own. A fairy tale that had lasted a whole year, but that had finally crashed against an invisible rock. At least for him. He still couldn't understand why she had broken up with him.

Thinking back to the argument they had just had in the corridor, he regretted his last gesture. He had thrown those papers in anger, and this had probably something to do with the end of their relationship. He had always been too irascible, ready to lash out in response to a wrong word. And she couldn't stand it. Feeling like an idiot, he felt powerless at his lack of self-control. But then he thought that maybe all wasn't lost. He could still change. He would do it for Rosa. And maybe she would give him a second chance.

CHAPTER 3

Lisa and her husband had been invited to lunch by a couple of friends. Riccardo Monti was a famous Chief physician of a private clinic and his wife Elena, was Lisa's best friend.

The two had known each other since university. They had been together throughout their studies and, even though they had taken different paths since, they had never stopped seeing each other. They were both busy women. They had last met at least a month earlier. Elena was a well-known journalist and, as for her friend, her job took up the best part of her time.

While their husbands limited themselves to a friendly handshake, the two old school mates hugged one another affectionately.

"You have to tell me your secret," Lisa said. "Each time you seem younger than the time before."

"Oh, stop kidding!"

"Kidding? It seems like you'll never get old. You've been the same since school."

"Oh my God! I hope not. I was nothing more than a stupid little girl."

"Dear Ladies, you're both beautiful," interrupted Riccardo.

"But what do you think about continuing our conversation at the table?"

As the good host he was, the man showed them the way and they all followed suit without a word.

As it was a sunny day, lunch had been served outside, on the ample terrace that led off of the living-room. Even though it wasn't a gala lunch, everything had been meticulously arranged. The table was dressed with a lively colorful tablecloth, decorated with a flower central piece that matched the plates perfectly. Glasses and silver cutlery were also placed with utmost care. Lisa was hoping for a friendly lunch, without formalities and she felt uneasy by that kind of reception. Knowing that it wasn't Elena's fault, let alone Riccardo's, she gave her husband a reproachful look. The reason everything had been prepared to perfection was only to avoid hurting his sensibility. As he was a fanatic of luxury, Vincenzo didn't hesitate in snobbing anybody who wasn't able to give their quality of life a certain style.

As soon as the four of them had taken their seats, a young waitress showed up holding a food trolley and, one at a time, she put a cup of hot broth in front of each person.

"What about dear old Gina?" Lisa asked, referring to the previous waitress.

"Unfortunately she retired," her friend answered. "She was getting of a certain age now."

"I'm sorry," she replied.

Still uncomfortable because of her husband, she remained silent for most part of the lunch, making an effort to speak in answering only when asked a question.

When the fish was served, the waitress was about to pour some wine into her glass, but she hurriedly waved her hand in refusal.

Elena gave the girl a severe look.

"You must forgive her," she apologized, feeling sorry. "She's new and…"

"Don't worry," Lisa said, understanding that the girl hadn't received any instruction about it.

To reassure her friend, she smiled a little to belittle what had happened. Despite this, an oppressive silence took hold, and a feeling of embarrassment replaced the lively spirit of a few moments earlier.

Lisa had been an alcoholic. Anybody who knew her well was aware of it. Back then, her story had been a scandal. Her nightmare had started when at nineteen, her boyfriend at that time, Enrico, had raped her. Getting back on her feet hadn't been easy. Elena had been a lifeline for her. She had been the only one who had really been able to understand her. And this was what made their friendship so special. Notwithstanding, Lisa's life had become grey. She had not been able see a future in front of her anymore, and she had slowly found a refuge in alcohol. Only in drunkenness, was she able to escape a reality she didn't want and couldn't accept. Then, during her recovery she had had many relapses. She had already been married to Vincenzo for a couple years when she fell back into it the last time. At thirty-one, bottle in her hands, she had been once again ready to destroy everything she had built.

That time, her husband had had her admitted to a specialized clinic, where she had finally been able to leave everything behind her. Or maybe so. She was well aware of her relapses. Fearing the return of the uneasiness, she had commissioned an armored bar cabinet for their home, to which only Vincenzo had the key.

Obviously, this was just the eccentric behavior of a victim, because had her discontent ever come back, she would have been able to find the antidote at any corner of any street. But, just seeing that bar made her feel protected from her insecurities and herself.

In short, Lisa hadn't had an easy life, and she identified with the people in the center. She had lived the path of addiction. She could fully understand the existential tragedies of the people who came and went. With them on her mind, she looked at her watch. Even though their lunch wasn't over, she decided it was time to get back to work. Thinking about her past had depressed her. She wouldn't be of good company anyway.

"Please forgive me," she said. "But I must be off."

"What?" Vincenzo replied. "You don't want to leave in the middle of lunch."

"Don't worry, Vincenzo," Elena said.

Lisa looked at her friend and, feeling relieved, smiled at her. As always, she had understood her.

CHAPTER 4

Ivano had struggled to sleep all night; he was so excited about what was going to happen the following day he'd found it difficult to drift off. He'd eventually managed a couple of hours and then woke in a state of euphoria.

After an abundant breakfast, he had taken his time to dress (he wanted to give a good impression) and then he had waited, impatient, for the morning to come to an end. It was a special day. He had been hired to work in a rehabilitation community and today would be his first day. He didn't remember ever having sent his curriculum to that specific structure, but he had sent so many, he couldn't be sure. Luckily for him the center was urgently looking for an art therapist and his application had magically appeared.

When it was time to leave, he rushed out, not wanting to be late. Experiencing a mixture of nervous apprehension he felt as if his heart was in his mouth.

Ivano Terravalle was thirty-three, but his past experiences definitely exceeded those of many other people. The first time he had smoked hashish, he had just turned twelve. Like many young teens, he had never thought it would be dangerous. "A couple of joints aren't going to ruin my life", he had always thought to himself. And he had continued saying this same old line, over and over again, from when, after soft drugs, he had crossed over to hard ones. Opium, morphine and crack, cocaine, heroin and LSD, he had really tried them all. Going in and out of rehab centers, he had seen his life change only when at twenty-six, he had decided to get it over and done with, and had attempted suicide. His mother had found him in the bath, his veins cut, lying in a pool of blood, but still alive. Just in time to ask for help. Doctors were able to save him by a hair.

Stopping to start once again had become a habit. But that time Ivano's was a true cry for help and he had really let others help him. Learning to value things he had never given importance to, including himself and his art, he discovered that art, which nobody appreciated, could be a cure for many. So, after a hard fight from the road of drug addiction, he had ended up specializing in art therapy.

But the number of jobs were little in that field. There had never seemed to be any room for him. Yearning to put into practice what he had learnt, he had had to withstand three years of waiting, three full years in which he had been in and out of occasional and badly-paid jobs, but now his moment had finally come.

In getting out of his car, he glanced at his watch. He had arrived a little early, so he took his time in walking to the building. He had already been there two weeks earlier to talk to HR, a Mr. Bernini. Knowing that this time, he would be received by the director, he tried to imagine what kind of person would be sitting in front of him. He imagined it would be a bulky sixty-year-old man, wearing lenses over his nose, studying him suspiciously. He then remembered the day of his first interview. The HR person had given him a name. He couldn't remember it, but he was quite sure it was that of a woman. He took out the paper where he had jotted everything down, and realized he was right.

Once past the entrance, he walked the short corridor leading to the main lobby. On the front wall was a panel showing the floor plan of the entire building. An arrow at the top pointed to the Managing Director's office and he went on, until he reached the secretary's room. In the room he found a woman behind her desk busily working on her computer, and a door on the back wall with a Managing Director plaque on it.

"Good morning," the secretary said, as soon as she realized he was there. "May I help you?"

"I'm Ivano Terravalle. I have made an appointment with Dr. Colasanti."

"Just a moment, please," she answered. After having announced him, she motioned to him to go in.

As soon as he entered, he realized that the director was actually a beautiful woman. Classy too. He wondered what a woman like that had to do with such a place. He thought that, all in all, it had nothing to do with him. And anyway, he had learnt to go beyond appearances.

"Good morning, Mr. Terravalle," Lisa said, approaching him. "It's a pleasure to meet you."

"My pleasure," he answered, giving her his hand.

Strangely, she stood still. Understanding she wasn't going to respond to his greeting, he felt a wave of discomfort.

"I must say you're not the type of person I was expecting," he then added, in order to shake off that feeling.

But he regretted it immediately, because the sentence could have been interpreted as much as a compliment, as well as an insult. He didn't know yet who he was dealing with, and his fear of having just made a mistake unsettled him. He wondered how she would interpret his words.

"Why, what type of person were you expecting?"

"Uhm, no, I didn't mean to say anything in particular. It was just a figure of speech," he answered, trying to make up for his mistake.

A hint of a smile appeared on Lisa's face and she invited him to take a seat.

"Has someone already shown you around the building?"

"Yes. Mr. Bernini gave me a tour."

"Good. In any case, take this information. It will surely be helpful," she said, placing a file on the desk.

"Absolutely!" he answered. "You can rest assured that by tomorrow I'll know everything that needs be known about this place."

"Don't worry! We are strict here, for obvious reasons. I'm sure you can understand. But it's not like we're in a police state."

Ivano felt relieved. The person in front of him, was a person you could talk to. There was no need to feel distressed. But in turn, when the director asked if he had any specific questions, he shook his head in reply. He thought it was best to keep his doubts to himself for the moment.

"Then, I only need to introduce you to the person supervising personnel." she said, while pushing the interphone button. "It's the person you'll be referring to."

Lisa asked her secretary to put her through to Miss Fogliani, but she answered that her colleague had just left.

"Well...! It seems like we have to postpone this meeting 'til tomorrow," she said.

"Don't worry, no problem."

"Maybe in the meantime you can have a look at the papers I gave you."

"OK," he replied, a little annoyed.

When the director stood up and showed him to the door, he followed in silence. But, before leaving, he turned back with his hand outstretched. Accidentally, he hit the furniture on his side and his arm jumped forward, brushing the woman's shoulder. Her reaction stunned him, seeing her jerk back as if to dodge a poisonous snake. He then thought that he must have misjudged her. If she was terrified of a simple handshake from a former drug addict, then maybe she wasn't the best person to cover that position.

"I'm sorry," he said, now more uncomfortable than ever. "I didn't want to..."

"See you tomorrow," she interrupted, ending their

conversation.

***

Distressed by what had just happened, Ivano hurried off to leave the place. The director's awkward behavior had made some of his long-gone insecurities re-emerge. He took deep breaths to calm his nerves. He wondered where he had possibly gone wrong. However, unable to find a meaning to her illogical behavior, he surrendered to keep his doubts.

Once he reached his car in the parking lot, he noticed two women chatting further on. One had her back to him, but he would have recognized her in a thousand. The red of her hair was as unique as a fingerprint or the mapping of an iris.

"Hey, Giada!" he shouted, waving an arm in the air.

She turned around a moment later and looked at him, puzzled.

Then, with a complete and total indifference, she turned her back to him once again.

She hadn't recognized him.

After all, it was understandable. It had been well over eight years since the end of their relationship and they hadn't been in touch after that. So, without thinking too much of it, he walked in her direction. He was curious to see the expression on her face once she realized who he was.

But unfortunately, just after a couple of strides, he saw the two women say goodbye to each other. Without giving him any consideration, she got into her car and left. When the car passed within a few meters of him, Ivano made to say something, but, in an instant, the vehicle was too far for her to hear him. Disappointed, he stood there, following the car with his eyes until it passed the iron gate around the parking lot and took to the road, disappearing from sight.

"Excuse me Miss," he then said to the other woman, who in the meantime had started walking in his direction. "Does your friend work here?"

"Who?" she asked perplex.

"The lady you were talking to a while ago."

"Oh, yes. But we're not friends," she answered, not stopping. "She is a psychologist of the center."

"A psychologist?!" he exclaimed, dazed.

The girl, though, seemed to be in a hurry and didn't bother to give him anymore details.

CHAPTER 5

Giada Rubini worked for a cleaning company. It was the only job she had found when her father died and things had never changed since. That morning the elevator was going slower than usual. When it finally decided to open its doors, after a repeated up and down, she pushed her cart inside and pushed the top floor button, from where she would go back down every floor, one by one.

As soon as she stepped out, she realized the corridor was almost empty. Apart from the four or five employees, she'd usually find there chatting every day, there was no one else around. More than once Giada had wondered what position those people occupied within the company. Over the years she had ever only seen them deeply concentrated in conversation, never busy in anything that would make you think it had anything to do with work. She had never dared ask. Even though so familiar to her, those faces belonged to absolute strangers. None of them had even ever deemed her worthy of a glance.

Now used to being unseen, she went about her own business as it was. After having filled the bucket with water, she added the floor cleaner and went to the far end of the corridor. As every other day, she would have had to clean a hundred and eighty-eight steps. After all, those were her true friends. Indeed, with nobody to talk to, one day she had found herself talking to them, finding she could tell them anything at all, without feeling judged.

She had learnt to tell one stair from another, and had even given each one a name. Just some silly game she would play to kill time and not feel lonely.

While mopping, she put her headphones on, and listened to the daily news. She heard somebody had won an incredible lottery prize. Having guessed the correct set of five winning numbers, he had hit the jackpot and had been covered in money. The radio speaker was saying that the win had occurred in a little village, with just a few hundred inhabitants. Surely, it wouldn't be that hard to find the new millionaire. Anyway, Giada cared little or nothing about who he was. The only thing she was certain of, was that she, differently from this guy, would have had to keep sweating her guts out to earn her miserable salary. Unfortunately, that morning she had received the electricity bill, whilst a week earlier she had received the gas one. Furthermore, with the increase in her apartment rent, she would have had to scrape the bottom of the barrel of what was left of her bank account that month.

With those bad thoughts in her head, she took off her headphones and passed a hand over her sweaty forehead. She stopped for a moment to rest and tried her best to calm her nerves. Sighing, she leaned back on the wall. She raised her head up. She wanted to cry, and was about to. Only the noise of steps coming from the staircase above, kept her from doing so. A young girl passed in front of her, not bothering where she was putting her feet, and Giada felt the anger repressing all her other feelings. She hated the people who left their footprints behind them, without showing any respect for her job. In that moment, she would have liked to scream out of anger but, as she was used to doing, she put up with it in silence.

The girl ran down some other steps, and stopped suddenly. Turning towards her, she observed her with curiosity.

"Do you need anything?" Giada asked, feeling her eyes on her.

"No, nothing. I was admiring your hair. I really like it! I wanted to dye mine, but I didn't know how. Now I think I'll color it red like yours."

"For all I care, you can dye it green," she replied back, irritated.

Taken aback by her answer, with a look of disappointment on her face, the girl turned around and continued going down the staircase. And, in hearing her steps fade into the distance, Giada returned to her thoughts.

CHAPTER 6

Co.S.Mic was listed in the stock exchange as one of the country's top multinational companies. It had originally been founded with the name *Co.S.Class*, and opened to the public in 1932. Its founder had been Alberto Colasanti who, investing in the shoemaking production, had been able to obtain an important position in the international market. Upon his death, Vincenzo Della Torre, who had been married to Lisa for some time already, succeeded Colasanti as president, and found himself managing the majority packet of actions. With the support of almost all of the shareholders, he had been able to have his trusted man, Guido Marinelli, elected as Managing Director. He had then started the acquisition of other companies at an ever-increasing rate. *Co.S.Mic*, now, had participation shares in thirty-four companies.

Della Torre was a rugged man. The size and height of his body could instill a bit of fear, but still, he had a pleasant appearance. His grizzled hair and well-defined face gave him an undeniable touch of class. He had all he had ever wished for in life. He was now a powerful man. But back in the past, he had experienced being poor, first-hand. His father had died a little after he was born, and he had just turned eighteen when his mother's premature passing had forced him to deal with life's difficulties. He had made tremendous efforts, to pay for his studies in Business and Economics, waiting on tables by day and studying by night. It had taken him eight years to get his degree, but, in the end, he had done it. He had earned that piece of paper which then had opened the doors for him. In fact, after a few months, he had been able to find a good job at a big marketing company and his life had changed at once.

He and Lisa had met at a party. On that occasion, Vincenzo hadn't felt so attracted to her even though she was an attractive woman, she wasn't his type. His interest for her came only a few weeks later, when he discovered who she really was. Since then, he had done everything he could to seduce her and, at the early age of thirty-two, thanks to a fairy-tale wedding, he had finally entered high society.

He was examining some documents, when he took a glance at his watch. It was already a quarter to five and the Board of Directors' meeting was scheduled at five.

"Vilma..." he said, pushing a button on the phone. "Have the others arrived yet?"

"Yes, Mr. President. They're all in the meeting room," the secretary answered.

"Why didn't you tell me?" he reproached her.

"I'm sorry, you didn't tell me..."

"It's not my job to teach you yours," he retorted, silencing her, ending the conversation.

Inefficiency was something he couldn't tolerate at all, especially when it came from his subordinates. Annoyed, he gathered the documents on his desk, opened a drawer and put everything in it. He would finish examining them the next day.

In the meeting room, the members of the Board were discussing some of the matters of the agenda rather heatedly. Each of them was trying to make their own opinion prevail, Vincenzo's entrance went unnoticed. A moment later, a woman turned around and, upon seeing him, she approached him.

"Hi, Sabrina," he said, a sarcastic smile on his face. "You always surprise me. I would have sworn that today you would have delegated somebody else and wouldn't have shown up.

"And why should I have?" she answered. "To give you another satisfaction?"

"Come on! Don't take so badly. After all, we're on the same side."

"Us? You and I… on the same side? What do you mean? Are you trying to make me laugh?"

"I'm only doing the company's best interest. I do what you don't have the courage to do."

"You do what's best for you. That's the truth."

"Well…! You think what you want," concluded Vincenzo, moving away from her.

Sabrina Colasanti was Lisa's younger sister and, unlike her older sister, she was a very determined woman. She was the second majority shareholder and was feared and respected by her colleagues. But, along with that esteem, they felt some intolerance towards her ideas about the company's management. Unlike other members of the Board, she didn't agree with her brother-in-law's decisions and, in a never-ending fight for power, she looked for new alliances in order to secure her position.

Vincenzo greeted all the people in the room, shaking their hands vigorously. They each took their place so as to start the meeting. The agenda at hand included points regarding the management and the approval of a new business plan.

Vincenzo was aware Sabrina didn't agree on this last point and, knowing that each matter would be approved by the majority, he looked at her, feeling satisfied. She looked at him too, with a challenging expression. She seemed to want to suggest that the game wasn't over yet. He smiled, amused and observed her for a few more moments, until Marinelli started talking, meaning the meeting had started.

CHAPTER 7

It was early evening when Ivano finally arrived home. Disappointed by the events of the day, he had wandered around the city with no purpose. Once he had got rid of the image of the Director from his mind, he had spent the rest of his time thinking of Giada. The fact that she hadn't recognized him had really upset him.

Ivano hadn't eaten anything all day, and now his appetite had started to build up. But his mind was elsewhere. Cooking was out of the question. So, in an effort to satisfy his hunger, he took a cold beer out of the fridge and prepared himself a sandwich. He sat in his living room and ate, greedily. After having swallowed his last bite, he took up his can, took some sips and then wiped his lips with his hand.

Feeling satisfied, he let himself relax into the armchair. On the wall facing him were paintings he had created when Giada was still part of his life. Paintings put there to preserve precise moments of his life, evoking far-off memories. Ivano remembered how much she had meant to him. She had helped him overcome terrible times. Days in which he wouldn't have survived, if it hadn't been for her. At that time, they both had a difficult life. Understanding each other was a necessity at the very least. And even though she only sporadically used drugs, she had been his companion of adventure.

To wait a whole night to see her again seemed too much.

Just a glimpse of her had reawakened a feeling in him that he thought was gone, and he could feel the fretful impatience growing inside him. He thought he must still have her telephone number somewhere. If she hadn't changed it, he could at least talk to her.

Looking for that number, Ivano started searching through all the drawers in his apartment. He could not remember where he had put it. Thinking about it, he figured out that his old telephone book had to be in the entrance cabinet. The *surplus cabinet*, as he had renamed it after dumping a ton of useless things in it. Now rummaging through the stuff inside, he took out all kinds of things. He even found Giada's old diary. He remembered how, at the time, she had needed to write the great facts of her life down on paper. He remembered the day when her obsessive mania had ended and she had handed it to him, giving him the task of getting rid of it once and for all; he never did. More than once during those early years after they had parted he had leafed through it, until he had put it in the cabinet, out of his mind. Letting the papers play in his fingers, he smiled a little. After all, it was funny the way the past had come back to him after years.

He put the diary back where he had found it, like it was an old relic to be treasured. He then continued his rummaging before finally uncovering the telephone book. Skimming the worn-out pages, he realized that many of the names were faded with age and impossible to read. Luckily, Giada's number was still readable. So, without waiting any longer, he took out his phone and called. The phone rang out hollow. Convinced that the number was unserviceable, he was about to hang up when finally somebody answered.

"Hello?" the voice at the other end said.

Filled with excitement, he found himself speechless.

"Hello?" the voice said again.

"Giada…" he finally said. "Is it you?"

"Who is it?" she asked.

"It's me, Ivano."

There was a pause on the other end of the line.

"Ivano?" she asked, surprised.

"Yes, Giada. It's me. How are you?"

"And what do you want after all this time?"

"Sorry if I'm bothering you, but I couldn't wait any longer."

"Waiting for what?"

"You know, today I saw you. I said hello to you, but you didn't recognize me."

"And you call me after all these years only to tell me you saw me in the street?"

"No, no. I saw you at work. I couldn't believe it! I would never have imagined you would become a psychologist."

"A psychologist? What the hell are you talking about?"

"Why, isn't it so? The girl you were talking to in the parking lot told me. Is it not like that?"

On the other side, a long silence.

"I need to see you," she finally said, now showing some interest.

"Sure. I can't wait for tomorrow. So we can meet and…"

"No, no! It's urgent," she replied. "I must see you now. We need to talk."

Ivano was puzzled. He was about to speak but she didn't give him the chance to.

"Have you moved or are you staying at your old place?" she asked.

"I'm where you left me."

"Then I'll be there in a half hour."

She hung up without adding anything else. Shocked but pleased, he sunk into his armchair, waiting for her to arrive.

***

Giada raced around, leaving her dinner half eaten finding her shoes and bag and, not even bothering about turning the lights off, she had grabbed her car keys and rushed out.

The evening was giving into night and there were only a few cars on the street. With her hands on the steering wheel, her mind somewhere else, she was speeding away, almost as if taken by a sudden rapture. At first, Ivano's words had appeared as complete nonsense. Then a thought had crossed her mind, and she had understood. He had had to mean Rosa, her twin sister. When they were kids, people often mistook them for one another. Sure, the same woman, Silvia Fogliani, had given both of them life, but while Rosa could consider her a mother, Giada couldn't say the same. She remembered the day their parents decided to separate perfectly. They agreed consensually on the destiny of their two daughters, deciding to take one each. Rosa had remained with her mother, while Giada had had the misfortune of growing up with her father, Sergio Rubini. He had raised her living in fear and humiliation, filling her with doubts which made her feel undeserving and inadequate. So she had grown up hostile towards her mother, who, instead of fighting for her, had let her go. Her love for her had turned into resentment, then into hate. Giada had always blamed her sister for their parents' divorce, considering her the true reason for the separation. She had always been the reason for those continuous quarrels which always ended up being nasty fights. Adding to this, she also felt incredibly envious. Rosa had had the luck of growing up with the love of a mother. And Giada had never forgiven her for this.

It had been years since she had erased both from her memory. Since the day she had written a letter without receiving any answer. She had waited a week and then another, and yet another. When she had finally asked her father for an explanation, he had told her that they had died in an accident. In truth, they had just moved. She hadn't been told, but on that occasion, Giada chose to believe her father's words. She would rather think of them dead than have continued suffering for them.

Since then, she hadn't received any news about them and she hadn't thought about them anymore. However, Ivano's words had resurrected her past and everything that she thought she had left behind was now cruelly returning.

***

As soon as she reached the house, Giada rang the intercom until the door popped open. The building didn't have an elevator, so she ran up all six floors without stopping. When she arrived, she found Ivano waiting for her at the entrance to his apartment. Out of breath, she wasn't able to speak; those stairs had nearly killed her.

He hugged her for a long time before inviting her in. Without hesitating, she moved into the living room, and flung herself into the armchair. Bending forward, she lent her elbows on her thighs, holding the weight of her chest. Because of her ragged breathing, her agitation and fatigue from racing up the stairs she could hear her heart hammering in her chest. To combat this, she breathed deeply to get her breath back. "Where is it that you saw me?" she asked Ivano.

"What?, what's the matter with you? After so many years, this is the first thing you want to ask me?"

"I'm not here for small talk," she replied. "Tell me again what you told me on the phone. Where did you see me?"

Ivano seemed annoyed by her behavior, but he answered without any further objection.

"At the rehab center," he said. "Today was my first day of work there. I had high expectations, but I wasn't expecting to find you there."

Giada didn't understand what job he was talking about, but anyway, she didn't care. "Are you sure it was me?"

"Sure. Seeing your hair was enough for..."

"So you didn't see my face, did you?"

"Sure I did. While you were talking in the parking lot. You turned to look at me, but you didn't recognize me. If I must be honest, I felt hurt."

Giada pondered for a few moments in silence. If even Ivano

had been misled, it had to be Rosa for sure.

"So, what's the mystery?" Ivano asked, his curiosity rising.

"It's not me you saw, but my sister."

"What are you saying?" he replied. "You don't have any sisters."

"Believe me, it's the truth."

"What? Are you kidding me?"

"Absolutely not. I swear it's true."

"And why did you never tell me about her?" he asked, ever more skeptical.

"I believed she was dead."

"Do you think I'm an idiot? I don't know what game you're playing at, anyway tomorrow..."

"No!" she exclaimed, jumping from the armchair and grabbing at his shirt. "You mustn't talk to her about me. Promise me. You have to promise me."

"Hey, fine! I'll do it your way. But calm down."

Despite the fact that he had just agreed, Ivano's sullen face clearly showed his disappointment. Giada understood she had acted too hastily. Plagued with anxiety, she hadn't cared at all about Ivano's reactions. That she wasn't there for him, was now clear. And this wouldn't come to any good.

"But what did you hope to achieve by coming here?" Ivano asked, deeply annoyed.

She approached him without saying anything. She started caressing his face, and ruffled his hair gently. Unbuttoning his shirt, she put her hands on his chest, moved her mouth to his ear and in a whisper, she said: "I don't know how yet, but now that I have found her, I'll have my revenge. And you'll have to help me."

Ivano looked at her, puzzled. He opened his mouth to talk but, before he was able to say a single word, she placed her lips on his, suffocating any further questions.

CHAPTER 8

The noise of machinery was unbearable. Disturbed by the racket, Rosa woke abruptly. Glancing at the clock on the night stand, she thought somebody had gone crazy. To start work at that time of the morning was barking mad. She rubbed her hands over her face and eyes and, propping herself up on her elbows, looked out the window. Immediately in front of her apartment a new building was being constructed. It had been going on for months now, but she had never gotten used to it. She couldn't cope with the noise anymore, depriving her of hours of sleep each day. The stress of it would end up killing her she thought.

The workers had already been at it for some time, but they were just doing their job, she surely couldn't take it out on them. In truth, what she really hated was that grayish skeleton made of columns and floors, which were yearning a covering. Her bedroom was very bright, she had chosen the room because she loved the morning light. She adored waking up to the feeling of the sun on her face. But once the walls of the new building would have been pulled up, she would have seen her beautiful sunlight stolen away from her. She couldn't do anything about it anyway. She knew it well. So, resigning herself, she got up, still half asleep, and went to the bathroom to take a shower.

Once showered, Rosa dressed in the clothes that she had prepared the night before and having brushed her hair she went to prepare breakfast. She put the coffee pot on the stove and took the milk out of the fridge along with some butter and marmalade. Then she opened the kitchen cupboard to get the bread and a melancholic smile spread over her face. Inside the cupboard door, she had stuck a picture. It was the only one left of her with her mother and sister. She had put it there so she would be able to see it every day, and so that the memory she had of them would never fade. At first, she had thought of having it framed and hanging it somewhere in the house, but she had found the idea too banal. Instead, keeping it inside a cupboard was a nice way not having to share them with anybody else.

The coffee pot was hissing, and released its vapor into the air along with the aroma of the blend. The milk was hot enough now too. After pouring it into a cup, Rosa streamed some coffee in as well, pouring what was left into another little cup.

She had just started eating when she heard her stomach growling. Caught by a wave of nausea she thought of the dinner of the day before. She had come home irritated by how things had gone at work and to take her mind off of it she had eaten everything she had found, until Franco and Miss Colasanti's images had been swallowed away. But now, she was paying dearly for that feast. Feeling like she was about to vomit, she ran to the bathroom but nothing came out.

The day had started badly and seemed to be getting worse for Rosa. She began thinking about the previous day and it reminded her of what was awaiting for her at work. She would have to reorganize many of the shifts and she didn't want to. While trying to think about something else, she sipped some more coffee, without really enjoying it. Her stomach was still in turmoil so she emptied the cup into the sink, took an antacid, swallowed it and hoped that it would settle her churning stomach quickly.

***

Getting to work hadn't been easy. The continuous stomach upturns had tormented her the whole way. Rosa sat at her desk, trying to ignore them. Maybe focusing on work would help her to not think about it.

She checked the weekly program time schedule to be sure that inserting the new operator wouldn't affect the others' jobs. She knew perfectly well that it was a useless exercise. The shifts were already distributed and in order to insert a new person, she was obliged to reduce the duration of some other activity. This meant she had to decide which one was more and less important. She didn't like it at all, but it was her job and it was up to her to do it.

Rosa had been concentrating on this task for twenty minutes or so when her telephone began to ring. It was the director, asking her to her office and, for once, Rosa was happy to hear her voice. She put aside what she was doing and headed to see her.

"You wanted to see me?" she asked, as soon as she got in.

"Come in, Doctor Fogliani," Mrs. Colasanti said. "I want to introduce you to our latest recruit, Ivano Terravalle."

"Nice to meet you," she said.

"We finally meet," Ivano answered, looking at her, goggle-eyed.

"Finally? What do you mean?"

"Oh, nothing." Lisa intervened. "It's just that he was meant to start yesterday. But you had already left, so I preferred to postpone his starting day until today."

"Oh, I understand."

Rosa noticed that the man continued to stare at her. He hadn't moved his eyes from her since the moment she had entered. It was starting to bother her. Staring at him carefully, she tried to fathom what kind of person he was and what he was thinking. From what she had read in his dossier, he was a former junkie, but seeing the expression on his face, she wondered if that was really true. Looking at him now, she wouldn't be surprised to discover he had just got a fix.

"So Doctor, I'll leave him to you," Lisa said.

"Yes, of course," she answered.

The two walked down the corridor and Rosa showed the newcomer the various administrative departments, among which was her office. With the excuse of a coffee, she showed him to the cafeteria dedicated to personnel and then she took him on a tour of the building, introducing him to his new colleagues as they went. Despite the fact that his job didn't require it, she decided to bring Ivano to the area which was used as a stay for patients. They had just arrived when three staff members entered, wearing latex gloves, and arrogantly entered a resident's room. Taken by surprise, Rosa and Ivano remained still, observing them.

A young guy was standing in the middle of the room, while the three men started a search. They began with the night stand, then pulled apart the bedsheets, looked under the bed and in any containers that may be hiding contraband.

"It's a simple check," Rosa said, trying to lighten the situation. "Sometimes it's necessary."

"Sure," he agreed without showing much surprise.

"Ok! Everything here is fine," one of the men said. "But you have to come with us. Today it's your turn."

Rosa knew perfectly well what the problem was. Clearly, they were concerned that the guy had taken drugs unnoticed. He would have to perform a supervised urine test. Looking at Ivano, she thought about it being his first day and so, to avoid demotivating him before he had even started, she was about to explain to him what the issue was, but then stopped. She remembered what she had read in his dossier. Terravalle had been in and out of rehab centers himself and would know of this procedure all too well.

"Urine test, huh?" he said, as if reading her mind.

"I think so," she limited herself to answering.

When things went back to normal, the pair continued on their tour. They retraced their steps until they reached a room that was still in need of some preparation for it to become a workplace.

Rosa informed Ivano that that was the room he would be using for his activities and, despite the area looking a little limited, he seemed satisfied.

"We should define the therapeutic model to follow together," she said. "But right now I have to go. We can discuss it later."

"That's fine. See you later."

Rosa was about to leave when she felt that the man's face was somehow familiar to her. She had noticed it earlier but until that moment her memory had refused to suggest any recognition. Then suddenly, she remembered.

"Was it you shouting in the parking lot yesterday?" she asked.

"I'm sorry?" he replied, slightly agitated.

"I thought I had already seen you! It was you in the parking lot, wasn't it?"

"Oh, yes! I mistook you for someone else."

"Oh, I see."

"Thank you for the tour," Ivano said.

Rosa saw him offer her his hand, almost as if to push her. She had the clear impression he wanted to finish the conversation as quickly as possible.

"Goodbye," she answered, shaking his hand. "Have a good day."

CHAPTER 9

Lunch time had passed, and Rosa hadn't arrived. Giada, waiting near the center, was expecting her to appear, and had remained in her car all morning. The night before, Ivano had given her directions to reach the center and, following his suggestions, she had stopped on the road next to the parking lot. From that position, and despite the iron fence, the view was perfect. In the grip of impatience, she continued to cast her eyes at the dashboard clock while vigorously clinging to the steering wheel and squeezing it like it was a cloth being wrung out. When Rosa finally came out, Giada immediately identified her. Distance was insignificant. She would have recognized her sister from miles away.

She realized how time had made them even more incredibly similar and could see the mirror image of herself. She felt an emotion she wasn't able to explain, even to herself. A mix of satisfaction, hate, anger and happiness... and, who knows what else. Feeling agitated, her body started to tremble. An unbearable fire was burning inside her, and an incessant shaking gripped her from head to toe. Feeling her hands become clammy on the steering wheel, she realized they were sweating, as was her forehead. She passed her fist over her face and tried to remove the damp sensation by ungracefully rubbing her hands against her trousers. Finally, her breath short, she said harshly: "I found you, wretch. Now you'll pay for it."

While pronouncing those words, she started to squeeze a paper bag on the seat next to her. She had brought it from home without a precise goal. On her way out, she had unconsciously grabbed a kitchen knife, and put it in the bag. But she had acted without any particular reason. Nothing had been planned. It had simply happened.

In reality, she hadn't known what her real intentions were until a few moments ago. Now she understood what they were.

Feeling the knife cut into her hand, she became aware of the true task awaiting her. The idea of eliminating her sister had crossed her mind a thousand times in the past, but she had never expected her fantasy to become a reality.

Rosa was still in the parking lot, calmly walking between the various cars, aiming for her destination. Just by looking at her, Giada felt the instinct to jump out of her car, grab her from behind and finish off her work. But she wouldn't do such a foolish thing. Doing it that way wouldn't be a satisfactory method of revenge for her. She wanted to be seen, recognized, if only for a moment. Rosa was supposed to die while being aware of who her executioner was. Only then, would Giada be freed from the torments of her past.

Breathing deeply, she tried to relax. She let the paper bag containing the knife fall onto the passenger seat and closed her eyes for a few moments. Her plan required concentration and self control; it was absolutely essential that she calmed herself down. She needed at least thirty seconds of deep breathing to regain control over herself. Finally, when she opened her eyes again, Rosa had disappeared from her view. She felt overcome with frustration. But it only lasted a moment. She just had to turn her gaze to see her sister a little further away, still in the parking lot. Rosa had turned and was talking with a man who had arrived during the short time Giada had had her eyes closed. The man looked tall and strong, his hair a little grizzled. Giada had the impression that she knew him. But from that distance, she couldn't quite see his face. And, of course, it was quite unlikely that she and the man would somehow know each other, she mused.

Another couple of minutes passed before the conversation came to an end and the two said goodbye. As soon as Rosa went to her fuchsia colored car Giada started up her own vehicle; she needed to be ready to cautiously follow her sister. Giada needed to discover every detail of Rosa's life, starting from where she lived.

Rosa drove to the exit and then on to the road that ran parallel to the parking lot. She passed Giada who immediately stepped on the gas and set off in pursuit; a mission made more difficult owing to the traffic congestion on the street. Many vehicles came between them. A pedestrian in the way or a red light would be enough to upset her quest. On more than one occasion, she had lost sight of the car and was thankful that its gaudy color helped her recognize it from a distance.

After thirty minutes or so, travelling on the main roads, Rosa finally steered into smaller side roads. Trailing her became easier and, without any further obstacles between them, Giada would be able to park up nearby and keep an eye on her, avoiding any risk of being seen. Despite this Giada began feeling impatient; the journey seemed endless. The fear of being caught became paramount in her mind, but her uncertainty disappeared before it could take root as a few moments later, Rosa's car stopped, reversed and finally parked. Giada continued for a few more meters and then parked close by. She saw her sister heading to an adjacent building, where she stopped in front of an opaque glassed main door.

Realizing she had arrived at where she wanted to be, Giada remained seated in her car, observing the building and filled with envy. The area was one of the richest in the city and houses there cost the earth. To live there meant you lived like a lord, that you were rich and that you had a good life. That destiny should have been hers, she thought, sadly.

Rosa was about to enter the building when a vehicle arrived from the other side of the road. The driver honked to her. She turned around and greeted him with a wave of acknowledgment. The car stopped immediately next to Giada's causing her to hunch down inside, making sure she wasn't seen or noticed. She recognized the man getting out of the car as the one she had seen half an hour earlier in the parking lot. To now see his face close-up she confirmed to herself the impression of familiarity that she had had. He had frequently been on television and in the newspapers; she knew who he was. Searching her memory for his name it finally came to her. Della Torre. That was his name. She wondered what on earth Rosa was doing with this influentially rich man. Raising her head a little she saw him leaving his car and head towards her sister, who was still standing at the main entrance to prevent the door from closing. As they entered the building, the two slowly disappeared behind the opaque glass but, before their image could completely disappear, she was able to see them in each other's arms, kissing.

Giada's feelings of envy and bitterness now steadily grew out of proportion. Rosa had had all the luck; even to the extent of having a rich and powerful man in her life. Consumed with jealously, Giada let herself fall back into the seat. She felt low in spirits, angry and dissatisfied with the life-cards that had been dealt to her. She turned her gaze to a building under construction not far from her. Sensing a feeling of vulnerability and incompleteness emanating from the edifice, she realized it perfectly mirrored her soul; empty and devoid of life. She remained there, staring at it in silence, clearing her sister's image and feelings of revenge from her mind. The only thing she could think of at that moment was the sense of pity she felt for herself.

Then a light on the second floor of Rosa's apartment block illuminated one of the windows. Another one was then lit up on the adjacent side of the building, directly in front of the building that was under construction. It had to be Rosa's apartment. It wasn't possible to see or hear anything from below, so, without hesitating any further, Giada started her car and headed back onto the road.

CHAPTER 10

Climbing up the stairs, Rosa instructed Vincenzo to be silent, but he continued to ignore her reproaches. Once they reached the apartment, she hurried him in, pushing him inside and closing the door behind her.

"It's the millionth time I've warned you," she said, suppressing a smile. "The old lady living upstairs is a true nosy neighbour. Remember, it's you that will have problems. I don't care if we get discovered."

"Yes, yes, I know. But I couldn't wait any longer."

"Huh?"

"You know what I mean. Don't feign innocence with me. Come here."

Vincenzo raised his arms to hug her, but she immediately freed herself. She ran behind the sofa and started laughing.

"If you want me, catch me," she teased.

"What? Do you want to play? You're a naughty little girl."

"That's why you like me."

"That's it! And now I'm dying to hold you."

With his words hanging in mid-air, he jumped up to catch her. She began sneaking around the room like a leveret on the run.

Chasing each other around the living room, they prolonged the experience of their foreplay, enjoying the pleasure of expectation. Rosa was fully aware of the risks Vincenzo was taking. Knowing how much he was prepared to risk seeing her made her feel important. She would do everything she could to give vent to that passion too. Borne as a simple attraction, their relationship had slowly turned into a kind of mutual dependence, a true need to be satisfied day by day. Being apart had become impossible for both of them. They needed each other in the same way they needed to breathe. They belonged to each other. They felt like they always had, and, even though he was married, Vincenzo's relationship with his wife was artificial. Rosa was certain that his being married would never affect their special bond.

They prolonged their pleasurable role-play for a little while longer before the gazelle made her fierce lion follow her into the bedroom, allowing him to satisfy his voracious sexual appetite. Knowing how he adored admiring her body, Rosa immediately divested herself of her clothes. Her black lingerie trimmed with lace set off her figure exquisitely, but she removed these items too. She gracefully slipped onto the bed, propped herself up on one side and crossed her legs, provocatively.

Hypnotized by her charm, and keeping quite still, he stood before her, appreciating her beauty. She raised a hand and, with a mischievous look, she began motioning with her index finger, inviting him to come closer. Vincenzo hesitated for a few more seconds, afraid to ruin this perfect moment. Then, sitting down next to her, he started to delicately caress her, tracing every line of her body.

Feeling pleasure under his touch, she remained still and let him continue. When she felt his hands grasping her hair, she leaned towards him and clung to him. Item by item, she undressed him and soon they were naked on the bed, one on top of the other.

He was inside her when Rosa, panting, felt her body becoming hot and wet, as a sense of excitement and emotion started to take over.

***

Later when she woke up, Rosa could feel her sheets still damp with sweat from their frenetic lovemaking. Vincenzo was still sleeping peacefully. Turning onto one side, she rose a little on her elbow and, bending her other arm, she placed her hand under his chin. Delicately, she moved away the part of the sheet that was covering her lover, admiring him. She loved to observe him while he was sleeping. Despite his size, he looked like a helpless child. Passing a hand over his face she gently removed the hair stuck to his forehead and, with an imperceptible touch, she caressed his chin.

Vincenzo had arrived into her life like a meteorite. Before meeting him, she had never realized what she was really looking for in a man. His coming had opened her eyes, triggering in her an understanding of how meaningless her relationship with Franco had been. She was looking for a father figure, a person who would give her security and a sense of protection, and with whom she could share everything. And she had found all of this with Vincenzo.

Staring at the wedding ring on his finger, she thought fleetingly about what the ring represented. She felt a strange sensation, but it wasn't jealousy. It had something to do with her only and her own ideologies. She saw herself as a child, sitting in the Church pew, listening to the Sunday Mass and she remembered how her mother had tried to instill Christian faith into her.

"How can I even know that God exists?" she had asked once.

"Think of it as a nice game where you talk and He listens. You will realize how in the end you won't need to ask useless questions," her mother had answered her.

And since then that trick had worked because, despite not believing in things that she wasn't able to see or touch, something of her mother's remark had remained inside her. Uncertainties she would never be able to answer often cornered her. Exactly as in this moment. The thought of dating a married man had made her feel dirty. There wasn't a precise reason why besides the teachings that her mother had repeated to her a thousand times. Rosa didn't believe in them. She never had. But she still felt like she was doing something wrong. So wrong. However, regardless of her misgivings, her feelings for Vincenzo were too strong to ignore, too strong for any past teachings to have any impact on her actions.

CHAPTER 11

That night Lisa got home sooner than usual. She lived with her husband in a wonderful villa in the hills, just outside the city. A tall stone wall marked the boundary of the property, while a well-tended garden encircled the large building. On the second floor, an enormous terrace allowed them to observe Rome in all its magnificence and, at that time of the afternoon, the sunset's colors usually offered some amazing visual effects.

It had been Lisa's father, many years earlier, who had bought the house, and she had always refused to consider moving anywhere else. Vincenzo would have preferred to live in the city itself, to better manage his business, but she would never approve that idea. To live in the house where she had grown up made her feel protected, safe against everything and everybody.

Her husband was due to arrive home around dinnertime, or maybe even later. Lisa decided to make some phone calls. She still needed two more speakers for the conference and she thought this quiet time would be a good moment to try and make contact with them.

Using the telephone in their living room, she dialed the first number to call Dr. Tursi, but, as in the previous days, the call went straight to voicemail. She had left messages on previous occasions and hadn't had a response so she hung up, irritated and decided to eliminate him once and for all from the list. She unwillingly moved to the second contact, but when a voice answered on the other end of the line, her feeling of apathy swiftly disappeared.

"Can I speak to Dr. Parisi, please?" she asked, faking enthusiasm.

"It's Dr. Parisi speaking. Who's this?"

"It's Lisa Colasanti. I'm the director of a rehab center, *VitaNuova*. I'm calling you because we are organizing a conference and we'd be pleased if you'd participate."

"A conference about what?"

She explained every detail to him and gave him her number, should he wish to confirm.

When the conversation was over, she felt relieved. Finally, she had finished the detestable task. Stefania would have to take care of the rest; it wasn't Lisa's responsibility anymore. Sure, she would have to attend the conference, but in terms of preparation, she was done.

Letting herself relax in the armchair, she realized how exhausted she felt and wished she could sleep for two days straight. But the stresses she had accumulated during recent weeks wouldn't allow her to rest. She decided that maybe reading a book would be a good way to unwind.

At the end of the living room a large bookcase occupied almost the entire wall. Lisa gazed over the titles, looking for something interesting. An old and battered book grabbed her attention. The heading, *Walking the World,* radiated a sense of freedom, she took it and returned to her armchair. She was sure that the book reminded her of something, but she didn't know what. As she began to leaf through it, she saw wonderful landscape pictures that she could escape into. As Lisa continued flicking through the pages an old snapshot unexpectedly fell out of the book, breaking the spell. Her body went rigid and a feeling of terror imprinted itself on her face. The picture, taken many years earlier, portrayed her and Elena with a guy. The dedication read: *"To Lisa, my eternal love. Enrico."*

She had been nineteen at the time and Enrico had been her first boyfriend. The two had met during their first year at the university; a time when Lisa believed in true love. She had continued to believe until one day Enrico, drunk, had raped her.

An event that had changed her life forever.

It was after this that she had started drinking excessively. Memories felt too burdensome for her to carry and she had found in alcohol a remedy that helped obliterate these for a while. Enrico had been reported and arrested, but it hadn't been enough to cancel the awful episode from her mind. She had destroyed everything that linked her to him in any possible way. She had rid herself of all the objects they had bought together, all of his gifts to her and of any photos with him in them. But the one she was now holding in her hands had survived in the shadows. Hidden between the pages of a book, it had materialized in front of her like a time-bomb.

Feeling an attack of hysteria coming on, she jumped up and ran to the kitchen, a place she didn't usually go to. At first, her maid looked at her puzzled and when she saw Lisa switching on the stove and putting something on the fire, the maid exclaimed, worried: "But, madam, what...?"

Lisa hissed at her with a violent look. The woman withdrew, intimidated, while Lisa stood there watching the image slowly being consumed by the flames.

***

For more than half an hour after burning the photo, Lisa hadn't been able to appease the sense of anguish that she was feeling. Finding herself incapable of ridding the memory from her mind, she began looking at the locked drinks cabinet, and what temptations it held for her; if a bottle had been within reach, she would have drunk a few drops without hesitation.

Fortunately, her mobile phone started to ring, distracting her from the lure of alcohol. Yearning for peace and quiet, she impatiently waited for the device to stop ringing, but the person calling seemed unwilling to give up. Without any desire to answer she forced herself to pick it up, wanting to silence the unpleasant noise. The insistence of the caller, however, had stirred her curiosity and so, before switching the phone off, she looked at the display.

She immediately regretted this because she couldn't really say no to this caller. "Hi Luca," she said, trying to affect composure.

"Can you talk or is Vincenzo there?" the voice on the other side said.

"No, don't worry. What's the matter?"

"I need to see you."

"I'll be seeing you in a couple of days."

"No. I can't wait."

"Actually I…"

"Please. I need to see you."

It was a few minutes before six and she was almost sure that Vincenzo wouldn't be home before nine.

"Ok, honey," she said. "See you in one hour at the same place."

"Ok. See you soon."

Lisa would have preferred to stay at home but thought a drive out may help her to relax, and she couldn't ignore Luca. Without lingering further, she put her mobile phone in her bag and grabbed her car keys. As she turned to leave, Lisa jumped with fright as she saw Sabrina standing in front of her.

"Oh my!" she exclaimed, bringing her hand to her chest.

"When did you get here?"

"Just now".

Lisa looked at her carefully, doubting Sabrina's honesty for a moment. She saw her maid returning to the back of the house; she had let Sabrina in at the door and the fact that she was still there confirmed her sister's words. Lisa sighed, feeling relieved that she hadn't been discovered. "Why are you here?" she asked, after gesturing for her to sit down.

"What? I can't come to see you? This used to be my home too."

"And it always will be. But now you just come when you need something."

"It's true. You're right."

"What is true? What I say or that you need something?"

"I need to talk to you about the company."

"What?"

"What Vincenzo is doing is unacceptable."

Lisa didn't answer immediately. Her thoughts were somewhere else. If Luca had called back at that moment, she wouldn't know what to do. She took her mobile phone out of her bag to silence it. Putting it away, she realized time was passing and that she should be on the road by now.

"You know I'm not directly involved in the business." she said.

"But you should be," Sabrina replied, irritated. "After all, you're the major shareholder of the company."

Vincenzo Della Torre managed the capital and, even though he did have a lot of power, nothing actually belonged to him. Lisa had inherited her block of shares from her father, as well as real estate and other fortunes that her husband had nothing to do with. His commanding position was sanctioned by Lisa and could be removed from him at her will.

"I've never cared about these things," she repeated. "I fully trust Vincenzo and what he does. After all, he has always cared about my interests."

"This is what you believe. The only interests he cares about are his own. Anyway, that's not the point. Our father's projects have disappeared into thin air because your husband has destroyed everything. We are now at the end of the game and if you don't do something, it will be too late."

The clock was ticking and Lisa was becoming agitated. She should be on her way to Luca and the last thing she needed was being held up with a lecture from her sister.

"So, what do you want me to do? I'll talk to Vincenzo, if that makes you feel better. Okay?"

"No. That isn't enough. Don't you understand? The only way to change things is for you to take over the reins. I only need your vote. Not Vincenzo's. Plus, he will never listen to you."

The debate between the two women continued. Sabrina persevered in trying to convince her sister to help, while Lisa continued with her refusal to intervene. Lisa glanced at her watch and saw it was almost seven. She had lost all track of time. An hour had passed without her even realizing it.

"I'm sorry, I have to go out," she said, abruptly. "I have an appointment and I can't postpone it any longer. We'll talk about this another day."

She took her bag and headed towards the door.

"Sure! You carry on with your eyes closed," Sabrina screamed.

But Lisa had already exited the room, not bothering to respond to Sabrina's outburst.

CHAPTER 12

The day had been hectic. Franco had mail on his desk that he had received that morning. Urgent matters had kept him busy all day and so the remaining mail had stayed there, waiting to be read. After he read the senders' names, he picked up the SerT envelope, took his *Globusmen Solingen* and let the blade slide inside.

As he expected, it contained the file he had been waiting for. It communicated in detail what he had already read in the email, but he wanted to read it again, carefully, to be sure that he hadn't missed any important information.

He was examining the file contents when the telephone rang. Raising the receiver, he checked the number and saw that it belonged to his ex-wife. "Hi Tiziana. I was just thinking about calling you," he said.

"Oh, sure! I don't doubt it," she replied sarcastically.

More than one year had passed since the day they had separated, but little Diego would unite them forever. Thinking about his son, Franco smiled. He remembered it would be his birthday at the end of the month. He felt sure that this was the reason for Tiziana's call.

"So," he said. "What's up?"

"What do you think?" she screamed, embittered.

"Hey, what's wrong? Calm down."

"Calm down? Do you know what day it is today?"

"Yes, don't worry. I haven't forgotten about Diego's party."

"The party doesn't come into it. Apart from the fact you're not invited, I called you to remind you that it's now three months in a row, including this one."

"What do you mean, I'm not invited?" Franco asked, not understanding her words. "And what do you mean, it's three months...?"

Quickly realizing what Tiziana was referring to, he stopped talking and looked at the calendar on his desk. Wednesday of the previous week was marked with an X. He was meant to have paid the alimony and he had forgotten all about it.

"You're right. I had completely forgotten about it."

"I'm tired of your forgetfulness and apologies."

"I'm sorry, but you know how my situation is right now."

"That's your problem. It's been three months and I've not had any money from you. What reasons are you going to come up with this time?"

"You know they are not excuses."

For some time now, Franco had been very badly off. His finances were in crisis. Buying a house had been a real mistake. All of his savings had disappeared and his salary barely allowed him to live and pay the monthly loan. He had been forced to sell his sports car and to fall back on an old second hand beetle, colored a gruesome green.

"Give me some more time," he implored. "I've explained to you how things are."

"You should have thought about it before buying a house."

"I have to live somewhere. Isn't it enough for you that you took my son away from me?"

"What do you mean? It's him who doesn't want to see you."

"And of course you do everything you can, not to change his mind."

"Stop it," she yelled. "You're just being paranoid. I have told you what I needed to tell you. I'll give you another week. Then, I'll call my lawyer."

Tiziana hung up before Franco could reply, which was probably for the best. He knew her threats were real and he had nothing to offer that would change her mind. He had to find a solution as soon as possible, or he would face serious consequences.

The only way to escape the situation was to sell the apartment. But that would require time and time wasn't on his side as Tiziana wasn't allowing him enough of it. It was impossible to sell a property in a few days without losing a lot of money.

While pondering on a solution to his situation his gaze fell on to little Diego's photo, next to the one of Rosa. It portrayed his son at two years old. Remembering that phase of his life, and his happiness at being a father, Franco became quite melancholic. He felt that his desk housed all the failures of his life. His relationship with Rosa. His son issues. And even that old *Globusmen Solingen*. So many dreams and hopes that had been broken over time.

He loved his son like nobody else in the world. He couldn't accept that Diego didn't want to see him. But the judge had put a restriction to his visitation rights and he couldn't do anything about it. Overwhelmed with a sense of impotence, he sat there, staring at the photo, wondering if things would ever go back to how they used to be.

CHAPTER 13

Her working day had seemed longer than usual. Holding back her emotions had been an effort for Giada and, having had a sleepless night, she had come to the conclusion that her revenge could and must wait. She could barely tolerate her own image, so much was her hate for her sister. But surprisingly, Rosa had inadvertently revealed herself to be the goose that lays the golden egg and Giada felt that she would have to take advantage of the opportunity.

Feeling both rancor and happiness in equal measure, she took from her pocket a newspaper article in which Della Torre was pictured with his wife. According to the information provided, Della Torre was extremely rich. An extramarital relationship would damage his public image for sure and, no doubt, his marriage. Giada began pondering on a plan to blackmail him. Sure, she'd like to do more, but this way, she would add a great personal advantage to her revenge.

She contemplated the idea all the afternoon and now, she was feeling excited. Certain that some fresh air would help her to relax, she hastened to the changing room. As she hung up her working clothes, she was about to close her cabinet when the newspaper article came into her mind once again. She decided to attach it inside the shutter and, with an evil smile, she stared at the man's image.

"I hold you in my power," she said, satisfied. "You, and that fucking bitch."

***

Giada didn't have her car with her. A demonstration that was expected to cause a lot of chaos had been scheduled for earlier that morning, and so to avoid the chaotic traffic she decided to use public transport to go to and from work.

The metro stop was quite a distance, but she didn't mind, a relaxing walk was what she needed.

The spring breeze helped to improve her mind-set, clarifying her thoughts. Step after step, her tension began to decrease and she started concentrating on what she needed to do. Until that moment, everything had been in her imagination. She now realized that to obtain a concrete result she needed evidence, physical proof to present under Della Torre's nose. But obtaining this wouldn't be easy. What had happened the previous night had been a chance event that would hardly happen again, she thought. Unless the two of them were completely ingenuous, catching them together would be a serious issue.

Giada began to recall everything from the previous night, looking for any useful aspects that would remove any obstacle that separated her from her victory. Nothing came to mind. Thinking she had failed before starting, she felt crushed and despondent.

She was about to give up on her plan, when a van passing by gave her an idea. On its door, was the sign of a restoration company. She remembered the building under construction opposite Rosa's house. From what she had seen, Rosa's bedroom overlooked that structure; it would be the perfect place from where to take photos. Almost certainly, Della Torre would come back to his love nest and when that happened, Giada would be ready to take advantage of it.

But this time, she couldn't leave anything to chance. She would never forgive herself if anything went wrong. She needed to study every detail, beginning with the necessary tools required for the task. The old camera she had at home wasn't suitable for taking pictures from a distance, or at night, and she didn't want to miss her targets when they were going to be within her reach.

Giada had almost arrived at the metro stop when she saw a shop that would serve her purpose. She went in and started looking around, searching for something that would suit her needs. There were a lot of goods on the shelves, but since she wasn't an expert she decided to ask a sales assistant.

"May I help you?" one of them asked.

"I am looking for a camera that can take pictures in the distance and that has a good nocturnal visual," she answered.

The guy showed her some models that met her demands, suggesting to her the use of a telephoto lens, which would ensure perfect shots from afar. But the cost of the equipment was out of Giada's reach. Realizing Giada's lack of knowledge regarding cameras, the assistant proposed that she choose a digital video camera. This type would allow her to get everything she had requested for both night and day shots. Giada accepted his advice and said she would take the camera.

Not having enough money with her, she checked out and paid with her credit card. While entering her security code, she felt her heart sinking. Her bank account was almost empty and this expense was completely unplanned. If things didn't go as she hoped, she would have paid out unnecessarily. But, she had to play the game she had started. She couldn't avoid it. She knew if she gave up, she would regret it for the rest of her life.

CHAPTER 14

It was half past seven and Lisa hadn't showed up yet. Luca called her many times, but the irritating automated voice was the only response.

Impatiently, he remained on the sofa, checking his watch obsessively. He had the impression that time had stopped. This waiting was driving him crazy.

It didn't help that the heat of the afternoon had made everything feel oppressive and uncomfortable. Parched with thirst, Luca stood up, took a beer out of the 'fridge and began to drink. As he did so he felt a pleasant sense of rejuvenation spreading throughout his body. Pleased that the beer had softened both his thirst and nervousness, he sighed and went to the window, hoping to see Lisa's car. He squinted outside, but the road was completely deserted. Letting the curtain go he sat down again, miserable.

Looking around the apartment he thought back to when he and Lisa had first rented it. She had chosen this place because it was far away from everybody and everything. The area wasn't very traffic-congested and people living here seemed to mind their own business' rather than nosing into the lives of others'.

Five years had passed since the day of their first meeting. Time had flown by. Luca knew that his existence had been empty and meaningless before Lisa had begun to be a part of it. He would never confess it to her, but his need to have her next to him had increased considerably. He couldn't accept seeing her briefly once a week, or that it happened secretly and with lies. He wanted the entire world to know about his love; he wished he could blab the truth to everybody, finally ending this awful situation. Revealing the truth to Vincenzo would be enough and everything would be fine. Sharing her with him was now unacceptable. And this time, he would make her understand it. He would compel her to choose on which side to stay. His side or her husband's.

***

Lisa proceeded fast until she encountered a long line of cars that impeded her way. Because of men working on the road, only one lane was open and a long queue slowed the traffic movement until it stopped completely. She was now stuck in a queue and she felt agitated. She was already half an hour late and it would take quite a while to get out of this gridlock.

The fact that Luca was looking for her on a Tuesday heralded nothing good. Their day was a Thursday. They had agreed on it. Calls between them were pretty rare. Now that he had contacted her she knew that it would be for something urgent and she pondered on what bad news may be awaiting her.

These thoughts increased her agitation even more. She was miles from home and, until that moment, had been distracted by driving, but now the short stop had been enough to rekindle her concerns.

She tormented herself, recalling that damned picture again and again. She couldn't get it out of her mind. And now, having to meet Luca made everything even more difficult. Luca, the main unwilling actor in this tragic scenario; the final piece of the story.

***

It was eight o'clock when Luca, out of patience, looked at his watch yet again. Agitation was consuming him. Anxious, he went to the window again and bent as far forward as he could. Looking for Lisa, he desperately tried to expand his view beyond the street's horizon, but the only thing he was able to see was the incoming night. Picking up his mobile phone he once again redialed the last number. But, as before, he heard that little automated voice that he now hated so much. He didn't know what to think. Maybe Lisa had changed her mind. Or, who knows…? Opening the door, she had found Vincenzo returned home from work. That's it! That was what happened. Because otherwise, she would have called him back.

He was struggling to find other possible reasons to justify Lisa's delay, but nothing convinced him. Another more sinister thought had now started to relay itself in his mind. In his imagination he saw the image of two crashed cars after a head-on collision. And in one of them, in a heap of car-wreck and glass splinters, he could see Lisa's face, covered in blood. The thought only lasted a moment, it couldn't happen for real. Not now. She was the person he had waited for his entire life. And now, after he had finally met her, he couldn't lose her again.

***

Lisa didn't have the apartment keys with her. She kept them at home, in the drawer of a cabinet but tonight, in her haste to get away, she had forgotten to pick them up. Just as she was about to speak into the intercom the lock sprang and the main door opened. Evidently, Luca had seen her from the window. Instinctively, she looked up. Not seeing anybody, she made for the stairs.

Her stride was lazy and uncertain and she seemed to slow down the further she ascended the stairs. She felt that she was trying to postpone as much as possible the inevitable end. An agonizing sensation suggested to her to go back, to escape from there, far from Luca, but her love for him was stronger. Ignoring these fears she went up the last steps and once on his floor, she saw him moving towards her. He threw himself at her like he had never done before and flung his arms out to hug her. But Lisa sent him away with a resolute gesture. Pushing him away with strength, she thrust him inside the house, entered and closed the door behind her.

"Are you crazy?" She asked him once inside. "Have you forgotten the reason why we took this place? Do you want somebody to see us together?"

Without talking, Luca squeezed her. And he did it with such energy that he hurt her. "Hey, you hurt me," she said.

Completely indifferent to her words, he didn't let her go, nor loosen his hold.

"You're hurting me," she repeated, trying to wriggle free.

When Luca finally let her go, she looked at him as if to reproach him. But seeing the expression of terror outlining his face, she remembered his call and his request to see her that night.

"What's the matter? Why are you looking at me like that?" she immediately asked, worried.

For a few seconds, he stared at her, silent, with the exact same look of their first meeting. Finally, and full of anger, he yelled: "I've been waiting for you for two hours! Where the hell have you been?"

"I'm sorry, I've had a few problems. First, Sabrina showed up at home without letting me know. Then the traffic. I wasn't able to arrive sooner..."

"And why didn't you answer your phone?" he interrupted her.

"What?"

"I called you many times. Couldn't you have called me to let me know that you were going to be late?"

"Oh," she said, quickly looking at her bag. "It slipped my mind. I put it on silent when Sabrina arrived and I forgot to activate it again."

"Don't ever do this to me again. I didn't know what to think. I thought you'd been involved in an accident."

65

"I'm sorry, honey," Lisa said, passing a hand through his hair.

He was about to open his mouth to say something but, clearly overwhelmed with emotion, he stopped words that were probably unnecessary.

"Why did you call me?" she asked "What was so urgent?"

"I can't go on like this," he answered. "You have to tell him. It's time for you to tell Vincenzo the truth."

"We've already talked about this. You know what I think. The discussion ends here."

Tossing her bag on the sofa, Lisa raised her head and took a deep breath. It was an effort for her to remain calm, her stress levels were at an all-time high. Keeping her distance from Luca hadn't been easy. Then earlier, that 'photo landing in her lap, Sabrina's demands and now Luca's face, here, staring at her. She felt that all these events were conspiring against her.

In an effort to organize her thoughts she got up from the sofa and approached the window and looked out. As she did so, a bird landed on the windowsill and seemed to look in at Lisa. She remained still, observing it, until it opened his wings and resumed its flight. Lisa would have liked to do the same, to soar into the sky and be free from the turmoil that besieged her.

She turned back to Luca and saw his face no longer showed any anger.

"Yes, sure! I know perfectly what you think," he said. "But you...? Do you know what I think? Have you ever wondered? You can't even imagine how you would feel in my shoes."

Incapable of looking into his face, Lisa bent her head, staring at the ground. She knew it wasn't her fault. It wasn't his fault either. Despite this, she felt responsible. But the terror of her past and a feeling of incredible shame, prevented her from doing the right thing.

"I can't," she said in a low voice. "Do you understand? I just can't do it."

"Listen Mother," Luca poured out. "It's time to choose. It's him or me."

At that ultimatum, Lisa didn't know how to react. Feeling

overwhelmed with anguish, she was staring at her son without speaking. As so often happened, she saw his father's features in his face and felt a sense of repulsion. A constant reminder of their dysfunctional relationship. To love somebody so much, somebody who brought back memories of immeasurable sufferance wasn't easy at all, but her love was that of a mother and she couldn't avoid it.

"You can't do this to me," she said, in a pleading tone.

"But how is it not possible? Why can't you understand? It's been five years and I can no longer accept that I have to wait for a weekly visit to see my mother and to hide myself inside a miserable apartment like I'm doing something bad. So now, either you tell him, or I tell him."

***

Lisa was driving flat out along the streets, both windows completely open, letting the wind hit her face. She could feel tears darting off her cheeks, swept along by impetuous gusts. But this wasn't enough to remove the weight she felt in her stomach. Continuing to cry desperately, she couldn't help but think about her son's words. He had asked her to recognize him many times, but this time his request could no longer be ignored.

Feeling as if her back was against the wall, she thought about her life so far and how circumstances had led to this dilemma.

Lisa had just turned nineteen when Enrico raped her, making her pregnant. Love had turned into sincere and deep hatred resulting in her hating the son she was expecting too. Or at least, this was what she thought. But when she had been about to abort, she had changed her mind, realizing she wasn't hating that little life at all; it wasn't its fault that it had been conceived in violence, it was just an innocent little being. She had decided to keep the baby, against her family's will. But, unfortunately for Lisa, the experience had resulted in her losing her self-confidence and personal security. As a consequence of this when her father forced her to put her child up for adoption, she hadn't been able to oppose him.

Her father had taken care of everything. Keeping the press away from what had happened, he had left a life-time allowance to his grandson and, by appointing a guardian, he had washed his hands of him. Unlike Lisa, who had reached rock-bottom with losing her son and had started drinking.

Vincenzo was completely in the dark about what had happened. Everything had occurred years before their first meeting and she had always avoided telling him. She had asked both her sister and Elena to respect her silence, to keep the secret, and they had done so. The rest of the family had maintained a strict silence about it as well, and finally that secret had become something impossible to confess, a prison impossible to escape from.

But regardless of every trace being hidden, Luca had been able to find her. She remembered perfectly the first time he had appeared in front of her. Just seeing him had been enough to recognize something familiar in him. On that occasion, she had run away, panicking. And even though five years later she had learned to love and accept him, she had never been able to forget and ignore what he represented.

Despite this, he was still her son and she couldn't lose him again after having found him. The moment to confess had come. Vincenzo had to know the truth.

CHAPTER 15

The jockeys' red silks shimmered in the morning sunlight. Sitting astride their horses inside the starting pen, they emanated an urgency, waiting impatiently to dart out of the gates. The same appeared to be true of their pure-blooded horses fretting and feverishly pawing the ground, kicking and jerking their heads, eager to get going. Clasping the reins, the jockeys tried to hold back their enthusiasm. The anticipation of what was to come was felt by the spectators too; all were waiting excitedly for the start signal.

When the starter finally got the race under way, the classic metallic sound of the gates opening was the cue for the animals to sprint forward, dashing out to the roar of the cheering spectators. Clumps of earth were kicked out of the ground by the horses, leaving a dusty cloud in their wake.

Riccardo Monti was among the crowd and, like many others, felt the adrenaline rush at the start of the race. His heart felt like it was slowing down and he needed to catch his breath. Then, as the race got underway his heart began beating faster, caught up in the excitement of the chase. He loved the rush of the race and despite only going to the racecourse occasionally he was well known in the gambling houses, betting in astronomical figures. He hadn't been to the races for some time and had decided that today was going to be his day of pleasure, his racing fix.

He was fascinated with horse racing and loved to follow a race live, soaking up the atmosphere and to feel the adrenaline coursing through his body. His love for horse-racing had begun as a child when his father would take him to the hippodrome on Sunday mornings. To visit there now that he was older brought back happy childhood memories. Like his father, Ricardo loved horses; he had always loved them, they both enjoyed the thrill of the race and its competitiveness. But, unlike his father, Riccardo was addicted to gambling. He adored the feeling of bringing himself into play, the adrenaline he felt while betting on the uncertainty of something out of his control and his desire to win. He had always tried to make the master stroke, but what really caught him out were the short moments at the starting signal, during which he could dream, hope, believe that he would hit the trifecta. A very short time during which he could tell himself: "Come on, come on! This time I'll get it." Most of the time, his attempts had been failures, but occasionally he had won, and these times were enough to keep his dreams alive.

Riccardo had been moving in these circles for years now, and he knew a lot of people. For some time, he had been quite close with a man working in the stalls. More than once, the man had given him good tips and that morning the tip had been to bet on the number four for the third race. According to him it was a safe horse and so Riccardo had picked him as the winner. Plus he didn't like to bet on places. Sure, that made winning easier, since the placed horse had only to come within the top three. It didn't matter if the horse arrived first, second or third. But diminishing the risk was what killed the spirit of gambling for Riccardo, and he loved the risk.

The horses had already run half of the racetrack. Number four, a grey five-year-old Andalusian, was third. Well known as Tango, it had had a good number of wins. Before him were Mona Lisa and Capitano, outdistancing him by three and four lengths, respectively. They were two of the horses Riccardo had chosen for his trifecta, positioning Tango as the winner. Winning was within reach. A little more effort would be enough to realize a dream. But now Tango was starting to lose ground and with it, Riccardo's hope. Further along the track, his dream became even more remote, crumbling little by little. But then the jockey vibrated his riding whip in the air. He hit Tango vigorously and, shocked into action, the horse found a new energy, increasing his speed until he caught up with the other two. They were only one length ahead, but Capitano and Mona Lisa were paired and the little space between them didn't allow for overtaking. Riccardo, his veins pulsing and sweat pouring off his forehead, felt his heart jumping in his throat.

"Go, Tango! Go!" he said in a low voice. Then, tightening his hand around his betting slip, he addressed the jockey and added: "Go! Whip him! Make him fly!"

As if he had heard his words, the jockey hit the animal again, and with an incredible spring, it started to overtake its rivals from the outside. They were almost on the home straight and the three horses were side by side. It was impossible to see who was first. A few inches separated them. Ricardo held his breath until the three competitors crossed the finishing line. Only then, he rejoiced, letting out an incredible joyful yell.

"Yes! Yes!" he started screaming. "I made it! I won!" He raised his arms in the air and started jumping, happily. But his euphoria was short-lived. He heard the voice coming from the bullhorn. The Judge had decided to use the camera to determine the order of arrival. This didn't make any sense to Riccardo. Tango had arrived first. He was absolutely sure of it. But what of the other horses in the race? Clearly, Capitano and Mona Lisa were fighting for second and third place. Whatever the result would be, he had won. He was sure he had. And he continued believing it, until the voice from the bullhorn proclaimed the order. First was Capitano, Tango was second and Mona Lisa was third.

Remaining still, unable to understand what had just happened, Ricardo tried to convince himself that it was just a nightmare. But finally, when he saw the names on the scoreboard, he was forced to accept this result; his umpteenth loss.

CHAPTER 16

A cup of cold coffee in front of him, Ivano was sitting comfortably at the bar, well sheltered by a patio umbrella. He had a date with Giada at eleven thirty at a little place downtown, but it was now twelve and she still hadn't shown up. When he had arrived she had called him to say that she was running ten minutes late. But time had passed and ten minutes had become twenty and then thirty. He decided to not wait any longer. He had to start work at one-thirty, and he didn't want to be late because of her. So he asked for the bill and paid. He was about to stand up when he saw Giada coming from the other side of the square. Grumbling to himself, he sat down again. He was really pissed off, so when he saw her raising her arm in the air, he just made a gesture with his mug. He waited until she was a few paces away, before removing his glasses and giving her a dirty look to show his irritation.

"I'm sorry," she said, immediately getting his message. "I had a few issues."

"Okay, okay!" He said in a tone of surrender. "Anyway, what did you want to speak to me about? I hope it's not the same as before. I kept quiet, just as you asked me to."

"Yes, it is. It's a unique opportunity and I need your help."

"Huh?"

Puzzled by her words, Ivano studied her, worried. He remembered the last time she had asked for his help. She'd had the same expression on her face then as she did now. That had been eight years ago, when they were still together. On that occasion she had come to him desperate, imploring him to help her to get rid of her father once and for all. He hadn't backed off and together they had planned every detail to murder him. At the time, Ivano didn't have anything to lose. He was afraid she would leave him and so he hadn't hesitated to give her his support. But now, everything was different. He had quit drugs and, thanks to his new job, his life had finally changed.

"I don't like that look," he said.

"What look?" Giada replied.

"The one on your face."

"What are you talking about?"

"You had the same expression eight years ago. Do you remember? I certainly haven't forgotten it."

It was as if she had erased that memory from her mind. She sat there looking puzzled, staring at Ivano. Or maybe she had just realized that he wasn't the same person anymore, ready to accept everything she said without hesitation.

"What? Are you scared?" she said, trying to provoke him.

"Exactly so."

"Well, you don't have to be. This has nothing to do with it. It's a completely different scenario. And it can gain us a lot of money."

"Money?"

"Yeah. A lot!"

"What do you want to do this time? Do you want to get into trouble again?"

"No. I just want to blackmail my sister. Or to be more precise... The guy she's having fun with."

***

The rest of Ivano's day felt quite surreal to him. Thinking back over Giada's words, he spent the afternoon wondering if he had made a mistake in accepting her proposal.

The painting class had just finished and everyone was leaving the room. When he was alone, Ivano began the task of checking the room to collect the used brushes. Holding them tip up, he put them all into a large container and, having first rinsed them with water, he took them to the workbench where all the painting products were. He put on his latex gloves and poured some oil of turpentine into a small bowl. He immersed the first brush and, twirling the bristles, he cleaned it carefully.

The paintbrushes were essential tools. It was necessary to take care of them to maintain them for as long as possible. But it would be the cleaning itself that would consume them over time, wearing them out, a few bristles at a time. A paradox in which Ivano could see himself mirrored perfectly. In fact, in his dream to start a new life, he had included Giada. He had hoped to share his existence with her once more. But her reappearance was upsetting everything he had fought for over the last few years.

Earlier she had informed him about the relationship between Rosa and Della Torre and how she wanted to blackmail them. She had explained in detail her intentions and how she wanted to act. She had asked him to keep his eyes open inside the center, to share any useful details with her. In fact, while searching the Internet, she had discovered that Della Torre was married to the *VitaNuova*'s director, and so Ivano would be a perfect accomplice. He could freely move around the building and nobody would become suspicious if he asked questions.

At first, Ivano had thought it was a good proposal. After all, simply observing and reporting back didn't expose him to any risks. But something had begun to niggle at him, a niggle that suggested his becoming an accomplice was a mistake. This annoying sensation accompanied him for the rest of the day.

Mulling over his dilemma he concentrated on what he was doing and realized that the paint had already dissolved. He noticed that the oil of turpentine, which had been clear and colorless, was now full of color traces and, in the same way, he tried to imagine himself like a brush immersed in the solvent, transforming his uneasy thoughts into simple color traces for him to wash away.

The mundane task of cleaning the brushes had helped to clear his mind and, feeling relieved from as if from a heavy burden, he began to observe the artistic works that had been created that day, searching for their secret meaning.

Each work transmitted a personal message. Consciously or not, the creator had put it there to scream happiness or sadness to the world, pain or despair, or a will to live and fight. On canvas, it was possible to speak in silence. Ivano had the final task of extrapolating words from the images and putting them on paper. Something that wasn't easy at all.

After writing a meticulous report for each composition, he offered his opinions about the various subjects highlighting their positive and negative aspects. More than just artistic creations, his judgments were about the people who made them and what they were trying to express.

As soon as he finished his reports, he put them in a file and left the room to go to Rosa's office. He had to submit the reports to her.

The building was a real labyrinth. After turning right and left a few times he finally reached the corridor where the administration area was. Rosa's office was open and nobody was inside. Ivano looked around and decided to leave the file on her desk. To be certain that she would see it, he placed it in front of her chair. He exited the room, leaving the door open as he had found it, and made for the painting room. But after a few steps, he heard Rosa's voice coming from another office further back. Hearing her animatedly arguing with somebody he thought back to his agreement with Giada. He had to keep his eyes and ears open. He turned around and carefully approached the room from where the voices were coming from.

***

"...I didn't come here to argue. We said what we had to and there's nothing else to talk about."

"Oh, sure! What else could there be? Us, our relationship... Everything that matters?"

Rosa had been in Franco Mezzana's office for more than half an hour. She had gone there to discuss an issue relating to a patient but he had detained her, giving her the folder he had received from the SerT, delaying her departure. Then, as always, their conversation had switched to personal matters, things she didn't want to discuss.

"There is no relationship anymore," she said, replying to Franco's words. "Get it into your head once and for all."

"May I remind you, you have come to me? I wasn't looking for you."

"I came to talk about work, stop mixing work with private life. You need to behave in a professional way."

"Oh, sure! I'm useful for work but you never miss the chance to push me away."

"I already told you more than once. Work is one thing..."

"Bullshit!" he interrupted her, jumping up from his chair. "It's because of you that my son doesn't want to see me anymore. Do you know that? And now, you'd like to get rid of me just like that? You've really got it wrong."

"Stop it! I'm tired..."

Before Rosa was able to finish her sentence, Franco picked up the *Globusmen Solingen* from his desk and pointed it at her throat.

"I should kill you right now," he yelled, enraged. "You know I could do it."

Rosa immediately froze, but it was a controlled fear. She knew Franco well. This was his temper. They had argued many times and this wasn't the first time she had found herself in such a situation. She knew perfectly how to behave. She had only to let him calm down and everything would be fine.

"The day I let you go is the day you'll die," he started again.

Rosa didn't answer and, making little of those words, she moved his hand away from her neck and left the office. Crossing the threshold in haste, she couldn't avoid bumping into Ivano in the corridor.

"You!" she said.

"Oh, I'm sorry, Doctor Fogliani," he answered.

Rosa looked at him, wondering how long he had been there and what he had heard.

"I came to bring you my report but you weren't in the office, so I've left it on your desk."

"Oh, that's fine, thank you. I'll give it a look later."

"Perfect. Have a good night," Ivano said, heading towards the painting room.

Rosa stared at him, curious. She thought that her doubts about him were probably caused by her natural distrust of newcomers. But Franco's office was quite a distance from hers, when coming from that direction so why, she wondered, was Ivano Terravalle outside Franco's door.

CHAPTER 17

Sabrina had gone to the *VitaNuova* center to continue her conversation with her sister. She had arrived at lunch time and the building appeared to be deserted. Even Stefania was absent from her desk; the secretariat was left to its own devices it would seem. She knocked at Lisa's door and, without waiting for a reply, she opened the door a little. She put her head inside and asked: "Am I disturbing you?"

"Oh, Sabrina! No, don't worry, come in. I'm not busy."

"Good. So today you won't run away."

"You didn't come here to persist with that matter, did you?"

"I did. And this time you have to listen to me."

"I've already told you what I think."

Lisa's face seemed sad and lost and Sabrina couldn't help but notice it.

"What have you done?" she asked her.

"Huh?"

"What's the matter? Why do you look so sad?"

"Oh, nothing to worry about. I'm just tired."

Sabrina stared at her sister, skeptical, for a few moments. She didn't believe her, but she decided to let it go. After all, she had gone there with a specific task and she wouldn't force Lisa to share her thoughts if she didn't want to.

"I don't know what problems you have and I don't want to know," she said. "But I assure you it's nothing compared to the ones I'm dealing with."

"It's you who is creating them," Lisa replied, absently. "Nobody forces you to do what you do."

"Oh, sure! Who would take care of it if I didn't? Maybe you, you who doesn't even have the courage to contradict her husband?"

Sabrina wanted to provoke her sister, to force her to face a situation that she stubbornly ignored, but she remained imperturbable. Without speaking, she continued to sit there with a dark expression on her face, as if she was elsewhere. "What the hell is wrong with you? Are you even listening to me?"

"Yes, yes. I just have other issues on my mind at the moment."

"Lisa, I know it's hard for you to move forward," she said, knowing her sister's past well. "But you know… If there's something wrong, you can talk with me. What's wrong? Old ghosts have come back?"

"No, no. Why would you think that? But, you're right about one thing, I don't want to make any trouble with Vincenzo. This is not a good time and so it's useless for you to insist that I intervene."

"Why isn't is a good time? What's this about? Could it be the mysterious date you had the other night?"

At those words, Lisa reacted immediately. She turned suddenly and gave her sister a hostile gaze. Brusquely she replied, "Keep out of it. You got that? This is none of your business."

Sabrina's speculation became an absolute certainty. There had to be a very serious issue tormenting her sister. Uncertain whether to respect her feelings or to continue with her mission, she stayed silent for a few seconds, hesitating. She observed Lisa cautiously, trying to decipher what was going on in her mind. Then, dithering a little, she decided to try for the last time. Indirectly changing the topic, she said: "I was able to convince a pair of shareholders to support me. They are open to helping me. But the number of votes is ludicrous. I need your help. Do you understand? I can't do it alone."

"Can you explain to me why you keep doing all of this?"

"What?"

"This! You just fight against my husband. Is it possible that after all these years you're not tired of it? There must be a good reason. I sometimes wonder what it is."

"It's true. There is a reason and it's a very good one."

"What is it?"

"Dad asked me to."

Lisa turned, curious, giving her an interrogative look.

"Exactly," Sabrina started again. "Our father opened his eyes too late. Once he realized who Vincenzo really was, he wanted to give me his place. But he had already assigned Vincenzo the chairmanship, and he was already too old and ill to start fighting again. He told me this on his death-bed."

"What the hell are you talking about?"

"It's the truth. Your husband has always been a social climber. And he has fully achieved his goal. First, he got your trust and then our father's trust. You can ignore what I say but one day you'll regret it, because it will be too late when you realize the truth. Exactly as it was for daddy."

"You're just jealous. That's the truth! You hate Vincenzo because he succeeded when you failed. He represents everything you have never had. Or it could be you're jealous of me? Maybe because there isn't any man at your side."

"I already have too many responsibilities to think about men. And if somebody is responsible for that, that's you, you have never pulled your weight. Anyway, there is one thing I know. Our father died regretting something. He died regretting having chosen Vincenzo."

"You're a liar. I don't believe you."

"And I don't ask you to. You wanted to know what the reason was for my actions. Good. Now you know."

For a short moment, Sabrina derived a feeling of satisfaction and liberation. Finally, she had been able to tell her sister how things actually were. A truth she had hidden for years had now come out of the closet. But that pleasant feeling of triumph didn't last for long. It lasted the time it took to understand what an incredible mistake she had just made. Seeing Lisa look at her with contempt, like she was her worst enemy, Sabrina realized that even if she hadn't just ruined her relationship with her sister, she certainly had lost the chance to get her help, once and for all.

CHAPTER 18

The sun had set and the street lamps had been on for some time. But darkness was late in coming and across the clear sky, the last glints of sun glowed on the horizon.

Giada had been waiting impatiently on the top floor of the building under construction for more than an hour. Ivano had informed her that Della Torre would be going to Rosa's house that night. He had heard them speaking on the phone, setting a time for dinner at Rosa's later that evening. Mrs. Colasanti would be out of town for a conference and wouldn't be back for a couple of days. Thus Rosa and Della Torre were going to use the opportunity to be together. Giada thought that luck was working in her favor and hoped that the man would be staying all night, making her task easier.

Knowing that out of focus pictures weren't helpful and that she could leave nothing to chance, Giada had bought a lightweight tripod along with the video camera. While waiting for Della Torre to arrive, she carefully prepared her equipment, taking some test shots, pointing the lens at the bedroom opposite. The shop assistant hadn't lied. The device was perfect for distances. Good enough, at least for her purposes. From the end of the building, she was even able to film the living room, even though from down the street the framing seemed impossible.

After half an hour Della Torre still hadn't arrived and Giada was becoming anxious. Maybe some unexpected event had forced the two of them to change their plans. His wife may have changed her plans and he had been forced to stay home, with no good excuse to escape.

Minute after minute, her thoughts wandered and imagined what the hold-up could be. But as the gray of the night filled the air, the lights of a vehicle appeared on the street, coming to a halt at Rosa's house. Giada immediately recognized the car. It was the same one she had seen the night before. A moment later she saw the door opening and Della Torre stepped out. Thanks to his silvery hair, she was able to recognize him even from her position above. She switched on the video camera and filmed him as he headed towards the entrance to her sister's building. Obviously, she wanted pictures of a different kind but anything could be useful. If she wasn't able to film something more explicit, she would have to play the game in a softer and more allusive way. But, it was useless. The man walked away from the car without raising his face. From Giada's viewing point, it could have been anybody.

When the door opened and he disappeared inside, Giada anxiously waited for the bedroom light to be switched on. After a long wait, she realized she had made a big mistake. She should have positioned her equipment on the side where she could view the living room. After all, Ivano had been clear, he'd said they'd be having dinner. The two of them were in the living room, but in her impatience Giada had concentrated on the final moment, forgetting about everything that went beforehand.

Leaving her equipment where it was, she ran around to the other side and looked across to the window. Next to the table the couple were hugging and kissing passionately. Giada rushed back to get her video camera, raising the tripod and returning to observe the living room. Unfortunately, the two lovers had already separated and were now eating at the table like two friends, relaxed in each others' company.

Giada began cursing herself and her stupidity. She had lost a golden moment.

"Stupid! Stupid!" she repeated. And without stopping, she began to film what was happening in the apartment.

The dinner continued and, without sharing a single caress, the two just talked, almost as if they knew they were being spied upon. Giada knew it was impossible but she couldn't push the thought away. Her hate against her twin increased as what was happening couldn't be by chance, she believed.

A couple of times Rosa disappeared into the kitchen to re-appear swiftly with the next course. It was the same when the wine was finished and she went to get another bottle. But nothing of what Giada wanted to see occurred. Fired up with anger, she thought that if she couldn't blackmail her sister, she would have to take her revenge in a different way.

But then, finally, the two of them stood up.

Dinner was now over.

She started to zoom in when Rosa disappeared from view. Thinking she had zoomed in too much, Giada reduced it to the initial dimensions, but Rosa's image still wasn't there. She looked across at the apartment and realized her sister wasn't in the room.

Instead, Della Torre had remained in the living room, looking around. She then saw that a light had been switched on in the bedroom. Giada realized the final moment had probably arrived. Without wasting time, she rushed to her previous viewing point, prepared the equipment and waited anxiously. A few moments later, Della Torre entered the bedroom. Using a three-quarter frame, Giada zoomed in on him, filming him clearly. She then framed the whole scene: Rosa, who had started undressing, Della Torre taking off his tie. He was about to take off his shirt when Giada saw him turning unexpectedly to the window. Feeling exposed by his gaze, she jumped back a little and swiftly took her eye away from the viewfinder. For a moment, she had the impression his eyes could span the darkness to reach her on the other side of the street. But his only intention was to close the world out. Approaching the curtains, he released the ties holding them apart and let them fall.

Giada was suddenly in darkness. The video camera continued to run but it was impossible to see anything inside the apartment. It didn't matter though. Della Torre had been a little too late. She had already snapped a photo of him, his face to the window, and Rosa, half naked at his back.

CHAPTER 19

Franco had gone to Tiziana's house hoping to find a solution to his problems. Since their last conversation, it had been clear that if there was any chance of convincing her, it wasn't going to be by telephone. So he had gone there to confront her face to face. But now, standing in front of the main door, reality dawned on him. He would have to implore her to give him some more time to find the money; he had to be ready to prostrate himself before her.

Today was her day off. Almost certainly she'd be at home, Diego would be at school. He knew that she wouldn't have allowed him to enter if his son was at home. He had showed up more than once asking to see his son, but she had always refused him. Despite his repentance being genuine (he didn't have a hidden agenda), Tiziana always remained impassive. She was no longer the sweet and sensitive girl he had married. After their separation, she had become hard and intractable. It was as if her soul had lost the joy of living and there was no trace of her previous altruism.

A little afraid, Franco pressed the intercom and after a few seconds, he heard the crackle of a woman's voice.

"Who is it?" she asked.

"It's Franco."

"What do you want?"

"Can I come up a moment? I'd like to talk to you."

"Hum, ok. Come up," she said, buzzing the door open.

He pushed the main door and entered.

He had lived here for eight years but visiting now made him feel like a stranger; it was no longer home. The house was still his, at least on paper, but after the divorce the judge had assigned it to Tiziana as the custodian in charge of Diego. At the time, Franco hadn't had a problem with this situation, after all, his son's wellbeing was of paramount importance. But since Diego had begun refusing to see him, the idea of not being able to enter his own house had become unbearable.

When he reached the apartment, he found the door half-open. Entering, he didn't see anybody.

"Tiziana?" he said, in a whisper.

"Wait a moment," she answered, from the kitchen. "I'm coming."

He thought that she was preparing lunch; he could hear sounds of cooking. Franco stood there, waiting for her.

"So...?" she asked, finally appearing.

Puzzled by her harsh tone, Franco couldn't find the strength to speak. One look at her was enough to understand he had made a mistake. He needed time, but she would deny it.

"So, what do you want?"

"No, nothing..." he hesitated. "It's about what we said the other day on the phone."

"Did you bring the money?"

"No. On the contrary, I'm here to talk about this. I don't have the money now, but I can assure you that if you give me a few months I'll fix everything."

"So, I wasn't clear then," she said. "I'm not waiting any longer. I've been too patient with you as it is."

"I know, Tiziana. But you can't even imagine..."

"Stop it!" she silenced him. "I don't want to know about your messy life. I don't care about your problems. I have my own. I told you! Find the money or you'll face my lawyer."

Franco felt his anger grow inside him.

Sure, they had broken up, but he was still the father of their son. She treated him as if he was a nobody, or worse. She wasn't sympathetic and seemed to derive some satisfaction with his current financial state. He'd like to violently take her, to beat her but, knowing it would make things so much worse, he contained himself. "Why do you behave like this?" he asked.

"Is that a real question? After all you did to me, you have the courage to ask me that?"

Franco thought back about how his relationship with Tiziana had gotten worse over time. After all, she wasn't totally wrong. He wasn't the same anymore either. The difficulties he had faced had changed him. And, unfortunately, not for the better. Until that moment, he had blamed her for everything, but now he didn't know what to think. Understanding how much he had contributed to creating the person who stood in front of him, he felt overwhelmed with guilt.

"Ok," he said, recovering his strength. "But this was about the two of us. Diego wasn't involved. Why did you turn him against me?"

"Me? You did everything all by yourself."

Franco's question had been rhetorical. He hadn't been looking for an answer, he just wanted to change the direction of their conversation. So when Tiziana answered him, he wasn't able to contain himself.

"You're a damned liar!" he exclaimed. "A child doesn't change his mind in a moment. Admit it! It was you. What the hell have you told him about me?"

"Ask yourself what *you* didn't tell him, instead. Not a single word about why you left. And then… When you started dating your girlfriend? You didn't spare him a thought then either. You could have found an excuse. But no! You thought it was normal for him to see his father with another woman. Your son is just a child, but you've been more childish than him. So don't blame me. Blame yourself."

"Ok, ok! Yes, you're right," he admitted, knowing he was in the wrong. "So give me the chance to correct this situation. Let me talk to him."

She looked at him a moment, doubtful.

"I don't know." She said. "I'll have to think about it."

"Allow me to come to the party. You'll see, I can fix this."

"No! I don't want you to ruin that day too. We'll talk about it after his birthday."

"Ok. After his birthday."

"Mind you! I just said I'll think about it. I didn't promise you anything."

The visit hadn't been completely useless. The money issue was still there, but Franco had at least been able to break down some of Tiziana's determination and, he had avoided an argument. If there was any chance of a reconciliation with his son, Franco didn't want to ruin it.

"And now leave. Diego will be on his way back from school," she concluded, opening the door.

"Ok. I'll wait for your call."

Franco left, a big smile on his face.

As he was leaving the building, and was walking towards his car he remembered Tiziana's last words. Diego was about to return and Franco was desperate to see him.

It had been five months since he last saw the boy. That had been the day he had introduced Rosa to him. On that occasion, he had clearly seen disapproval in his son's innocent eyes, but he had chosen to ignore it. Because of his selfishness Franco had been a source of pain for his son; he'd assumed that Diego would be happy for his father. And now, Franco couldn't forgive himself.

He wanted to run away, away from his life mistakes, but then he saw Diego walking along the road. Franco crouched down next to a car and watched him. Since Tiziana had started working, her neighbor took Diego to and from school. Their sons went to the same school and one child or two didn't make any difference.

Franco felt comforted at seeing his son playful and cheerful. Maybe he had overestimated the problem. If Diego was still able to run and jump and smile, he couldn't have made such a big mistake, he thought. Sure, he had put his freedom before his son's needs, but he hoped that one day, Diego would understand.

CHAPTER 20

The *Santa Caterina* clinic was close to a pine forest. Every day at the same time the sun's rays filtered across the miniscule splits created by the mass of green pine needles. Riccardo Monti was in his office, checking some patients' files, when a nurse came in, traumatized.

"Come, Professor! Hurry up!" the woman yelled.

"What's happened?" he asked, calmly.

"There's a man in the ward who wants to kill himself."

The nurse's words froze him to the chair for a few seconds. And then, in the time it took him to process their meaning, he left the papers, jumped up without speaking and ran out of the office behind her.

A young patient was out on the parapet, threatening to jump. Admitted a week before, he was supposed to be having surgery later that day. A simple hernia operation that didn't involve any risks. But the guy suffered from a psychological disorder and he was convinced that the doctor wanted to kill him instead of treat him.

On the day of his admission, Monti hadn't been concerned about his patient's fears. Nor had he earlier that morning when he had been on his ward rounds with his team of doctors. But now everything was different. The guy was there, in front of him, ready to let himself drop into the void. "Did you alert the rescue squad?" he anxiously asked a nurse.

"Yes, doctor. Of course!"

The first thing that crossed Riccardo's mind was the clinic's reputation. Such a death would leave a mark for a very long time.

"Stay away!" The guy continued to scream at everyone. "Stay away or I'll throw myself over."

"Stay calm," Riccardo said, taking a step forward.

"I said stay back!"

"Yes, yes. Don't be afraid. I won't move."

The other patients had been quickly evacuated from the room, while various members of staff had arrived to assist Riccardo. After he had considered the mind-set of the patient, Riccardo turned and said: "Please, everybody step out. Everybody. Leave and close the door."

"But, Professor…" one of the nurses said.

The others also looked disapproving. But Riccardo repeated, determined, "I said, everybody out."

No one had the courage to contradict him and in a few moments, the room was empty. He remained alone with his patient. He knew he was facing an immense risk by acting in this way, but right now his mind wasn't as clear as usual. His head was in turmoil. Just as it was when he was at the races. After all, that situation wasn't so different from the position he found himself in now. He was there, ready to bet on himself winning. A game he couldn't lose. He had to avoid that guy committing such a foolish act at all costs. At least not here, at his clinic.

"So…" he said calmly. "How can I help you?"

"I don't want your help. I just want you to leave me in peace. I know what you want to do."

"Could you explain it to me?"

"No! You're one of them. I know you want to get rid of me."

The young man's words contradicted his actions. If he was afraid for his safety, it was impossible that he was trying to die.

Understanding what he was facing, Riccardo said, "You're right to be afraid. I would be too. You can't play with such illnesses. Maybe it's better if you throw yourself down."

"What are you talking about?" the guy asked, worried. Riccardo's little lie was enough to take the guy's mind off what he was doing. Riccardo quickly jumped forward and took hold of the young man by his belt. But the belt was loose and the guy let himself go over the edge. Hanging in the space below, he was holding on with his arms, kicking crazily.

"Come here!" Riccardo screamed. "Help me! Hurry up!"

Nurses ran into the room, rushing to help him. Some of them grabbed the guy by his bathrobe. Somebody else grabbed his arms. Finally, they started to pull him up, bringing his body back onto the parapet.

When the situation returned to normal, Riccardo ordered them to transfer the patient to a single room and to guard him. After a round of hand shaking, many compliments on a job well done, he returned to his office. Now the worst was over, Riccardo felt exhausted. Believing he had done what he had needed to do, he decided his work for that day was over. He advised his secretary to cancel his appointments for the rest of the day, before going to the elevator and down to the underground parking lot.

When the doors opened, he took his car keys and pushed the car alarm button. Feeling his fingertip sliding on it, he realized his hands were sweating; it must be from the excitement of the past hour he thought to himself. He put the keys into his pocket and continued walking, trying to calm down. After a few steps, somebody called to him from behind and so he turned to see who it was. With his face transforming into a mask of fear, Riccardo's eyes opened wide in horror as he stared at the two men walking towards him.

One was heavily built, with an untidy, dishevelled look about him. The other, slimmer and smartly dressed, hid his eyes behind a pair of sunglasses. Riccardo knew them both well. They were *Sbieco's* men. A loan shark who had gained the nickname thanks to his intimidating behavior. He couldn't speak to someone face to face and look them in the eye at the same time. It was quite a daunting experience for those who had the misfortune to be in his presence.

Riccardo owed him a large amount of money and on the few occasions he had had to see him he had felt a palpable sense of terror. He had since regretted asking *Sbieco* for money, but his gambling obsession and his endless need for funds, had put in him into debt and *Sbieco* was the only lifeline he could find, to help him out of his financial difficulties. Without Elena's knowledge, he had lost his life savings. His bank account was almost empty. But *Sbieco* had continued to give him credit; he knew that Riccardo owned many properties, and that sooner or later his loans would be called in, complete with interest.

Elena was unaware of her husband's situation. He had never admitted to her that he had a problem. Their bank accounts were separate, but their property portfolio was held in joint names; Riccardo couldn't touch them without her knowing about it.

"So, Monti," the man with the sunglasses said. "What do you have for us?"

"Wait. Calm down, ok?" he said, scared.

"*Sbieco* is tired of waiting. It's time to pay."

"Yes, I know. But you don't think I have all the money on me now, do you?"

"Of course not," the other guy said, amused. "If it depended on me, I would give you the time to go and get it. But I'm not the boss."

"Fine. So let me talk with him. I'll find the money. I'll find it."

"You said that last time. We just came to give you a message."

"Please. I..."

Riccardo couldn't finish the sentence. The heavy man punched him violently in the stomach. Then, taking him by the shoulder, he started hitting him repeatedly, until Riccardo started to spit blood and saliva. The underground parking lot didn't have a security camera. Nobody would come to help him. He wanted to scream. Escape. Maybe defend himself. But he was overwhelmed. The two men hurled him to the ground and began kicking him. Pulling his legs close to his body, Riccardo brought his arms to his head, curling up to protect himself as best he could. When the two men finally stopped, he remained on the ground, unable to move a single muscle.

The guy with the sunglasses told the other one to take the car keys. He loomed over Riccardo and began checking his pockets, until he found what he wanted. Throwing the keys in the air, he smirked a little and said: "This will do as a deposit, eh?"

"This is just a taste," the other guy said. "Hurry up and pay off the debt. Or next time you won't live to tell your story."

The two men walked away, satisfied, leaving Riccardo in a heap on the ground. One got into the car they had arrived in whilst the other drove away in Riccardo's.

CHAPTER 21

Rosa didn't feel like going out. Feeling out of sorts, she was lying on the sofa, not wanting to do anything. It was a little past four pm when somebody rang the doorbell. Looking towards the door, she wondered who it could be. She wasn't expecting anybody and for sure, she didn't want to see anybody. She remained still for a few moments, ignoring the ringing sound. Then, forcing herself to stand up, feeling as if she was dragging a weight on her shoulders, she headed over to answer it.

"Who is it?" she asked. Nobody answered. "Who is it?" she repeated. Again, no answer.

She waited a few moments, uncertain whether to open the door or not. On television, they advised you to pay attention to anything out of the ordinary. She had heard a lot of scare stories; a knock at the door, an excuse to enter, and in the end somebody got killed. However, her curiosity was stronger than her caution, so she decided to open the door.

A woman was standing there, with her back turned. Rosa silently waited for her to turn around, but she seemed to be reluctant to do so, she said: "May I help you?"

"How long," the other replied without moving.

"Who are you?"

"I'm you," the woman answered, finally turning and showing her face.

Caught off guard, Rosa jumped backed. Her eyes opened wide as she brought a hand to her mouth and emitted an exclamation of fear. The woman was her exact copy. Her face. Her behavior. Her haircut. Even the clothes were similar to the ones Rosa had been wearing the night before. Stunned into silence, she stood there, immobile. Perhaps the stranger wanted to imitate her, she wondered, maybe using plastic surgery, and now she was here to carry out who knows what absurd plan. Rosa realized that she had watched too many movies and her mind was racing to find an explanation, but she couldn't explain the resemblance. Her astonishment at seeing this woman had overwhelmed her.

"What's up?" Giada asked. "You don't recognize your little sister?"

Rosa didn't react immediately. She needed a few moments to process what she had just heard. When she did, her eyebrows raised even more and her eyes felt ready to pop out of her head.

"Giada?" she asked, incredulous.

"Ah! At least you remember my name."

"Giada," she repeated, unable to create a sentence.

"I'm pleased to see I surprised you."

"But how…"

Rosa was speechless. She was stunned into a mix of emotions; wonder, happiness, fear, melancholy, love. Instinctively, she raised her arms to hug her sister, but Giada stopped her with a curt and harsh gesture.

"Do you think I've come for a courtesy visit?"

"What?" Rosa asked, completely disoriented.

"Do you really think after so many years I would have come without a precise reason?"

Without asking for permission, Giada made her way inside the house. Rosa closed the door, still shocked. She didn't understand. Everything was happening too fast and it was an unreal situation. Since the divorce, her mother had always refused to talk about her sister, effectively erasing her from her life. But now, after twenty years, she had unexpectedly materialized from the past.

"Take this! It's a little gift for you," Giada said harshly, handing Rose a little folder. "I hope you like it."

"Oh, thanks," she replied, smiling slightly.

"Open it, before thanking me."

Rosa looked at her sister suspiciously. She saw she was smiling a sinister, ominous smile, and she began to feel uneasy. When she opened the folder, she saw a picture of herself in her bedroom, half-naked, with a close-up of Vincenzo next to the window. "What the hell…"

Taking hold of the picture, she saw there were other photos inside the folder. All from the previous night.

"What is this stuff? What does it mean?" she asked furiously, starting to rip them up, letting them fall to the floor.

"Don't waste your time. They're just copies."

"So what? What the hell do you want from me?"

"You haven't got it yet? I want money."

"What are you talking about? I don't have any money to give to you."

"You don't. But he does," Giada said, pointing at the pictures.

"You're crazy," Rosa replied.

"Maybe. But if you don't want the photos to be published, it will cost you one hundred thousand euros per month."

"What?"

"Take it," Giada said, throwing a piece of paper on the table. "I'll give you two days to make the payment."

"You can't do this to me."

"Two days. Not one more," Giada interrupted her. "You have until one p.m. the day after tomorrow." And, on saying those words, she headed towards the door, leaving hastily.

***

Rosa couldn't believe what was happening. She stared at the prints scattered over the floor, imagining what people would think of her if they became public. Worried about Vincenzo's reaction, she wondered what the consequences would be on their relationship. Without waiting any longer, she grabbed the telephone and selected his number. She had to speak to him urgently.

As she started punching in the numbers, she felt a sense of disgust and nausea. Her chest clenched a couple of times, and her throat felt closed, as if in a vice. She ran for the bathroom but before she could take a step, she felt her body lurching forward, her mouth opening and vomit spewing out.

While waiting to recover, Rosa remained in that position for a few seconds. Then, overwhelmed by anxiety, she wiped her mouth with her hand and, without cleaning up the mess, she made the call.

"Come immediately," she said, as soon as she heard Vincenzo's voice. "Leave what you're doing and come here. I'm home. It's really urgent. Come immediately."

"Rosa? Is it you?" he asked, puzzled.

"Yes. Don't waste time! Hurry up."

"Hey, calm down. What's happened?"

"That... No, no. I can't explain it you on the phone? You need to come here! Hurry up!"

"I have a very important meeting now. I can't miss it. I'll call you back when it's over."

"No! You don't get it. You have to come here. Now, I need to talk to you now."

"What's wrong? Tell me what's going on?"

"Damn it! Listen to me. If you want to keep your job and you don't want your wife to know about us, then do as I say."

On the other side, silence. But Vincenzo was still there. Rosa could still hear the background noise that accompanied the call.

"Hurry up," she said once more. "I'll be waiting for you."

***

Rosa's request was inconvenient but Vincenzo knew that she

wouldn't demand his presence unless it was really necessary. He felt a mix of anger and frustration on his journey to Rosa's house; she was obviously distressed but by what, he wondered. He hoped that it wouldn't take too long to sort out. Sabrina and the other shareholders had asked to schedule an extraordinary Board meeting. In order to realize his projects, his attendance was essential. Angrily, he called his secretary to advise that he had left the building and that he may be slightly late for the meeting.

He arrived at Rosa's and, having pressed the intercom several times she let him in. He raced up the stairs two at a time, and then he saw her. Clearly upset and in a state of agitation he screamed, "Do you want to ruin me?"

She turned and walked into her living room. Puzzled by her behavior he followed her, waiting for an answer, but as soon as he entered the room, his confusion grew even more. The floor was covered with vomit and torn paper.

"What the hell has happened here?" he asked.

But Rosa remained silent. She bent to pick up the photos from the table and then, holding them to her chest, raised her head to face him.

"Damn it! Tell me what's going on?"

"Take them. Look for yourself," she said, handing him the pictures.

A few had survived her earlier angry explosion, but in each of them, both her and Vincenzo appeared as a couple, a very intimate couple.

Vincenzo didn't understand. He became agitated and asked, "What are these? Do you want to blackmail me?"

"What? Do you really think...?"

Rosa was crying. She let herself collapse onto the sofa, leaving her sentence unfinished.

"So, who is the bastard who has taken them?"

"My sister," she murmured. Then, with a sense of relief, she told him her life story.

Vincenzo let her speak without interruption, her agitation was palpable and realised that he needed to listen and understand the situation. But the more he listened, the more it seemed unreal. After all, she had never even talked about a sister, let alone a twin.

"You have to believe me," Rosa insisted. "It was like meeting someone for the first time. I don't have any idea of what a kind of person she is, nor what she could do."

Still uncertain whether to believe her or not, Vincenzo looked at her, doubtful. Guessing this, she stood up and went to the kitchen, shortly reappearing with a picture in her hands.

"This is the only evidence of her that I have," she said, handing it to him.

He saw immediately that the two girls were identical. He also thought Rosa wouldn't have any reason to lie to him. If she wanted something from him, she had only to ask.

"Ok. Calm down," he said. "I'll take care of it."

He moved his gaze to the paper with the bank account number and decided the only possible solution at that moment was to give in to the blackmail.

"What do you think you will do?"

"Pay. For the moment, it's the only solution. Then we'll see."

CHAPTER 22

That afternoon the headquarters of *Co.S.Mic* descended into complete confusion. Rumors transpired with the false news of a possible merger with a foreign company. Many employees feared they would lose their positions. The air was filled with tension and uncertainty. The area managers, who were in contact with those in power, weren't able to reassure their subordinates.

The tales had casually reached Sabrina's ear who, somehow, found it funny. It was odd noticing how events could change, if seen as a whole or from only a certain perspective. Inside the management offices, they were playing another game, one she knew perfectly well. A big company had offered to buy the *Co.S.Class*, the company her father had founded and from which the *Co.S.Mic's* empire had developed. As the company's balance had been overdrawn for the last two years, Vincenzo Della Torre had immediately proclaimed to be in favor of the conveyance. But Sabrina was totally reluctant. And not just for sentimental reasons.

The previous month, Vincenzo had proposed the matter to the Board of Directors, obtaining, as always, the majority of votes. But when the negotiations had finished and everything seemed to be set, Sabrina had been able to convince three of the main shareholders, thus giving her the majority vote by a few points. After accurate and careful research, she had then convened an extraordinary Board of Directors meeting to discuss the subject further.

Her renewal plan provided for the restoration of buildings, a modernization of the infrastructures and cuts to save what was left. Also, a marketing revival that, from what the experts said, would allow them to cover the investment and bring the company back to its former splendor within a couple of years.

Even though the cost of the project was large, it attracted the attention of the shareholders. After Silvestrini backed it (also the third majority shareholder), the Vice President De Paoli and, finally, Terenzi had agreed, with some reservations.

Thanks to their support, Sabrina had been able to convene the new assembly. Despite this, she was still uncertain about how things would go during the meeting. She felt perplexed about Terenzi's hesitation. She wondered if the man would have the courage to continue to go through with it.

Entering the meeting room, she saw that most of the board members were already there. They each had taken a seat and were waiting to start. Sabrina looked around and sat down too. As she did so she realized that Vincenzo was the only one absent; surely he would arrive soon, she thought.

Marinelli was concentrating on checking some documents. Sabrina looked at him for a second, with a sort of commiseration before regarding the other occupants at the table. Observing the vice president and the other two shareholders she tried to guess what their intentions were. For a moment, Silvestrini reciprocated her gaze, but she wasn't able to decipher it. She felt anxious, but when the secretary entered and announced that the president wouldn't be attending, any fears that she had disappeared like a soap bubble. She felt her heart stop for a moment, then immediately to beat, frantically. Without Vincenzo, who had a third of the block of shares, she would win, even if Terenzi abstained.

"Well! I think we can start," she said, satisfied.

She noticed Marinelli was observing her and their eyes met. Apparently, the news had taken him by surprise too, because she saw him steeple his fingers to his lips and was looking around, uncertain about what to do. All the people present were staring at him. He hesitated a little longer but then, having no alternative, he started the meeting.

Sabrina began to present her modernization project, giving them each a copy of her report and went on to explain, in detail, the recovery plan. She showed them the statistics on potential growth in the long term, underlining the various positive aspects. She was also trying to strengthen Terenzi's trust in her. His vote was now unnecessary, but a future ally would be useful.

"I have to agree that the project is well developed and almost too exhaustive," Marinelli said, after the presentation.

"If the calculations are correct, it would be a real occasion for the *Co.S.Mic*, however, we can't ignore that right now our shares are falling. Such reckless action could cost us a lot." The man's words diffused any uncertainty among those present and Sabrina felt it instantly. To avoid the damage becoming permanent, she proposed that they vote, immediately.

The members looked at each other, but nobody said anything.

The first votes were against it. These were shareholders who Sabrina had tried to convince in the past without succeeding. She didn't expect anything different from them this time. But when Terenzi followed them and voted against her she couldn't help but feel contempt for him. Yet the worst blow came when De Paoli also voted against it. It was clear that her brother-in-law had been working behind the scenes, maybe offering them bribes to ensure they change their minds.

Overcome with agitation, Sabrina stared down at Silvestrini, almost as if to threaten him. His vote was the only one missing and the final verdict depended on it because, without Vincenzo, it was enough to change the situation. Everyone was staring at him. He held the casting vote and everyone seemed impatient to discover how the game would end.

The man, clearly amused by the situation, remained silent for a few moments. Sabrina, like everybody else, kept her eyes on him. Then, meeting her gaze, he smiled lightly, and said: "I vote for it."

"Yes!" she exclaimed, euphoric. And, unable to contain herself, she raised her fist in the air.

Satisfied, she looked at Terenzi and De Paoli, both having again supported Vincenzo. It was clear that he had planned everything, but not his absence. Still half-incredulous, she thanked God for whatever inconvenience had stopped him from being at the meeting and, triumphant, she left the table.

CHAPTER 23

The luxury hotel's meeting room was hosting a seminar for six hundred attendees. The morning's business had been concluded with some speeches and had now stopped for lunch. In the lower floor dining room, guests found an enormous buffet waiting for them.

Lisa participated in the proceedings without enthusiasm. The previous day's events kept her in a state of permanent confusion and the conference was just a blur of voices. Nothing of what had been said moved her. It was only during lunch that her tension seemed to decrease when, forced to be sociable, she was able to distract her mind from her worries.

Earlier that morning she had run into Gilberti before the start of the conference. He now approached her, asking what she had thought about his speech. He found her completely indifferent. Having not listened to a single word of his discourse, Lisa sought an excuse. She tried to reply but an unfinished sentence remained in the air.

"Don't worry," he said. "You're not the only one who is skeptical about my methods. It always happens when something is new. It takes time for it to be accepted by everybody."

Gilberti had misinterpreted her hesitation. She smiled slightly, as if to agree and, afraid to make a gaffe, she didn't say a word. Gilberti resumed speaking.

"I've heard a lot about your center. Very good things, actually."

"Oh, really?" she asked. "I'm glad. Come visit us sometime. Who knows, we could start a collaboration between our clinics."

"I'd be happy to, but I don't think it will be easy. Time is always so limited. It's a miracle I was able to participate in the conference today. But, I'll think about it."

"I feel the same. Time and work don't get along well."

"Yeah! One life isn't enough," he said. "Now, excuse me. I've noticed a colleague I haven't seen for a long time. I'll take the chance to greet him."

With those words, Gilberti turned and disappeared into the mass of people filling the room.

In the meantime, Guido Bielli, General Director of *VitaNuova,* made his way over to approach her. Lisa didn't see him with a friendly eye. The affable behavior she adopted with him hid a false relationship. A truth they both were aware of, but ignored.

"Hi, Guido. How are you?" she said when he reached her.

"If I said well, I'd be lying," he answered, sipping a little wine. "You really surprised me. Or maybe, I should say 'disappointed' me."

"About what?"

"Threatening to resign to obtain the introduction of art therapy is something I would have never expected."

"Would you have listened to me if I hadn't? You pretend to not hear if it's not convenient for you."

"At least I hope you're now satisfied."

She just smiled slightly while Bielli, looking at her with rancor, added: "You know I want you in my team. But I warn you. Don't ever test my authority again."

Lisa's mind was filled with her own problems and the warning left her completely indifferent. Her only regret was that she hadn't answered him before he moved away into the crowd. She wasn't afraid to tell him to his face what she thought, but at that moment, she wasn't in the mood for confrontations. She felt sad and needed to be alone; if only I could walk away from here, she thought. Unfortunately, her position within the company meant that she would have to stay at the conference until the end. So, in an effort to detach herself from the throng of people she found an isolated corner where, hopefully, nobody would disturb her.

It worked, no one was taking any notice of her standing alone, their lunches were continuing without her contributing to any conversations. She realized that maybe her absence would go unnoticed. At least until the resumption of the conference after lunch. She decided to go outside for some air to forget about everything and everybody for a while.

Without hesitating, she made it all the way to the exit, when a man suddenly stopped in front of her, barring her way.

"Lisa!" he exclaimed. "I can't believe it. How are you?"

She looked at him surprised, wondering who he was. For a few moments, she tried to recognize something familiar in him, but his face was completely unknown to her.

"Do we know each other?"

"You're right. I'm stupid. After all this time… It's me! Carlo."

That name didn't mean anything to her in terms of the person standing in front of her, she frowned to show her confusion.

"Damn it!" he started again. "It's impossible I've changed that much. Is it possible you don't remember me? We were in a team at university."

Those words were a bolt from the blue to Lisa. Old memories were revealed on the face of the man and suddenly everything became clear and awfully tragic. The guy who stood in front of her had been Enrico's best friend back then. Seeing him, Lisa felt a sense of terror. He knew exactly what had happened at that time. The very thought that he may say something about her past made her tremble. But what agitated her the most was that her past had decided to come back into her life.

"My God!" she exclaimed, her eyes wide. "Carlo? What are you doing here?"

"What do you mean? You invited me."

"Me?"

At first shocked, she soon realized the misunderstanding. Stefania had sent the invitations with Lisa's name on them. She had just approved them. The list of names had been provided by headquarters and clearly Carlo's name was among them, after all, he attended the Faculty of Medicine and so there was nothing strange about him being invited.

"Oh, you're right. I forgot," she said, trying to cover her embarrassment.

"Honestly, I wasn't that interested in the conference. But when I saw it was you inviting me, I was happy to accept."

"Well, thanks."

"It's been a long time."

Suddenly affected with dizziness, Lisa brought a hand up to her head and closed her eyes, pained.

"Hey!" Carlo said. "What's wrong? Are you ok?"

"Just a migraine," she answered. "Please excuse me. I need to lay down for a while."

"Do you want me to come with you."

"No, thank you. Don't take it the wrong way, but I would prefer to be alone."

"As you prefer," he said. "But don't disappear, okay? Let's keep in contact."

"I promise," she concluded, rushing to leave the room.

***

Lisa was overwhelmed with an immense sense of discomfort. Crouching in a corner of the living room, her forehead leaning on her palms, she moved her head around continuously, stretching the muscles in her shoulder and neck trying to ease the knots of stress. Unable to cry, she wanted to scream, but her throat was so incredibly dry. Even talking would have been an effort at that moment. Her world was collapsing, and she had no idea how to deal with the events unfolding around her. Carlo's appearance affected her deeply. Filled with dread, she had run out of the hotel to her car. She had escaped, shocked, abandoning the conference and everything else. She had sped along the highway for three hours, wondering what kind of messed up joke fate was playing on her.

When she finally arrived home, she locked the door firmly, but a closed door wasn't enough to block the memories of her past. She needed to switch off her brain for a few moments. Too many things were happening all at once.

Her maid knew something was wrong. More than once she went into the living room, worried, and asked if Lisa needed anything.

The rest of the day passed by without Lisa being aware. In the turmoil of her mind, time had stopped. She thought that she had been crouched in the corner for a couple of minutes, but the sun had gone down some time earlier and the night had already arrived.

She came back to the present when she heard the door being unlocked and she raised her head with fear. She hadn't heard the car pull up and Vincenzo's arrival took her by surprise. Huddled on the floor, she stretched her neck like a vulture, waiting for the door to open. For hours, she had sought the right words to say to her husband, but it had been useless. When he appeared, she just stared at him, afraid, waiting for him to speak.

Vincenzo didn't notice her at first. But as he went to sit on the sofa he saw where she was and without showing much interest, he asked, "What are you doing there?"

Unable to stand his gaze, not knowing where to start, she lowered her eyes without saying a single word.

"So?" he insisted. "Why are you sitting on the floor?"

"I need to talk to you," she replied. "But before that I need to have a drink."

"What did you say?" Vincenzo asked, incredulous.

"You heard me. Don't make me repeat it."

Twelve years had passed since Lisa had touched a bottle and her words shocked him, as well as herself. They had been spoken without any conscious thought on her part. But once she had pronounced them, she realized that the need to be lost in alcoholic oblivion had returned. She couldn't help it. The moment she had feared for a long time had arrived and now, in her hour of despair, she didn't have the strength, nor the will, to oppose it.

"What have you done?" Vincenzo yelled at her.

"Give me a drink," she repeated.

"No chance," he reproached her. "Maybe you have forgotten what we went through?"

"No. I remember it perfectly. But now I need it."

"Well, resist and tell me what the hell has happened."

"I said I want to drink," she screamed, furious.

She had caught him off-guard. In fact, he had been about to speak, but he closed his mouth and stepped back as if he feared being assaulted. Lisa had never reacted in such a wild way, but something had seemingly snapped inside her and there was no way to stop it.

"As you wish," Vincenzo said, as if washing his hands of the situation. "If you want to ruin your life again, that's your business."

Without looking at her, he went to the bar and took a key from his pocket, signifying a line being drawn between the past and the present.

Lisa remained silent as she watched Vincenzo place the key in the lock. She heard it click one, two, three times. When finally she saw the doors opening, she knew that everything was about to change. She had seen her husband opening the cabinet many times to take something to drink for himself, but this time; the dynamics of his normal routine had been shifted to include Lisa's apparent needs.

Vincenzo took out a bottle of whiskey. He filled two glasses. Then, outraged, he handed one to her.

"So?" he said, sitting again. "What are we toasting?"

Without answering, Lisa took the glass and downed it in a gulp. She felt the liquor slipping down her throat and realized that she had reached a point of no return. After years of abstinence, she had once again fallen into the trap of an addict; she could only finish what she had started. Guessing that one glass wouldn't be enough to give her the courage she needed, she stood up and grabbed the bottle. She refilled her glass, drained it and filled it up again. Only then did she sit in front of her husband, who was glaring at her, shocked. To avoid his look, she kept her eyes on the glass she was turning in her hands. Finally, she took a deep breath, drank deeply and, before her courage disappeared, she said: "I have a son. His name is Luca."

Silence fell between them.

When Lisa raised her eyes, she saw Vincenzo observing her with detachment and curiosity. She realized her statement puzzled him.

"What are you talking about?" he asked. "You know you can't have children."

"Yes! But for a completely different reason than the one you know about. It wasn't always like this."

Clearly suspicious, he tried to talk, but Lisa anticipated him, rushing to speak again.

"Did you really think I had started drinking because of a heartbreak?" she asked, trying to sketch a smile.

Then, without waiting for an answer, she began to tell him every detail of her story. She told her husband how she had gotten pregnant when she was nineteen and about the violence she had suffered. She spoke about the son she believed she had lost, and how destiny had given him back to her. She told him about how her father had arranged to separate her son from her, and how much she had detested him at that time. She talked for half an hour, almost without breathing, spilling out all that she had hidden over the years.

"Why did you lie to me all this time? And why are you telling me now?" he asked, apparently calm and without showing any emotion. In his voice, there wasn't any disgust, pity, or bitterness, just curiosity.

"I thought I could forget everything. But I was wrong."

"What do you mean? Why have you suddenly changed your mind?"

Lisa looked at him, silent. She took the bottle in front of her and poured some more whiskey.

"I decided to recognize my son," she said, downing her glass again. "He will have my name and half of the block of shares."

"What?" Vincenzo started. "Are you crazy or what?"

"No. Actually I have recovered my sanity."

"And did you decide this, or did he ask for it?"

Lisa was about to answer, but Vincenzo added: "And tell me… Have you at least checked him out? How can you be sure he is who he says he is?"

"I know it. I don't need to check."

"Listen, honey…" he said, suddenly changing his behavior. "I know you've always wanted a son. But did you think about the fact he could be a liar who is trying to take advantage of you?"

Lisa looked at him severely to show him her determination. He exploded in all his anger.

"Fine!" he thundered, pounding his fists on the table. "Recognize him, if you wish. But you won't touch the shares."

"Ah, the shares! They are all you care about."

"No," he screamed. "You know that I have always taken care of your interests and I'm worried. You're not being reasonable."

"Oh, you're wrong. I've never been so clear-headed."

"Think very carefully about this, Lisa," Vincenzo concluded, filling her glass and putting the bottle on the table. "You could be making the biggest mistake of your life."

CHAPTER 24

Rosa had been suffering with nausea for days. She hadn't paid attention to her menstrual cycle being slightly late. It had always been irregular and she didn't think anything was wrong; it was normal for her. But that morning, she realized her breasts were tender and felt swollen, and it all made sense. She stood in front of her mirror, looking at her body, smiling pleasantly, caressing her belly. Until today, she had never thought of having a child, but now she couldn't avoid seeing herself as a mother. Feeling incredibly happy, she let her fantasy run wild, imagining her life with Vincenzo and thinking about what a child would mean for them.

She went to work thinking about the idea of a happy family. Not even the unbearable stress caused by the traffic was able to affect her happiness. It was the first time for her and nobody could kill her buzz. Along the way, she stopped at a drugstore, bought a pregnancy test and, keen to reach her destination, sped in her car to the *VitaNuova* center.

As soon as she arrived at her office, she threw everything on her desk. Excited, Rosa ran to the bathroom, closed the door, took out the instructions and started reading meticulously. She knew perfectly well what to do. It wasn't anything complicated. But her fear of a negative result, of her dream disappearing, prevented her from carrying out the test immediately. To postpone the result she wasted time reading the instructions again. Then, out of time for excuses to delay the inevitable any further, she took a deep breath, crossed her fingers and decided to proceed. She urinated inside a little plastic glass, took out the indicator and immersed it in the liquid, then discarded the box and returned to her office.

Swamped with anxiety, she remained standing willing the waiting time to pass quickly. Eventually, with a mix of trepidation and hope, she brought a hand to her eyes and peeped between her fingers. A little rose line indicated a positive result and she was filled with joy. A new life was growing inside her. Never in her life had she felt such happiness. Nothing could be compared to that moment. As if to have further confirmation, she brought her hand to her belly, smiling to herself, to life, to love, to the being she would give life to.

Rosa was still in the center of the room when a voice behind her said, "Am I disturbing you?"

Startled, she turned fearfully to be faced with Franco standing in front of her. Instinctively, she brought her hand behind her back to hide the test.

In her state of excitement she had forgotten to lock her office door and Franco had arrived in the room without warning. She cursed herself for her carelessness, and turned her anger at Franco. "Didn't they teach you to knock before entering?" she said, furious.

"I did," he said calmly. "I knocked three or four times but you didn't answer. I thought you weren't here."

"So, why did you come in then?"

"I wanted to leave this on your desk," he answered, irritated.

"What is it?"

"Your new patient documents. Soon there will be the first interviews and, if I'm not wrong, that involves you." Franco brusquely threw the papers on the desk and added, "Do what you want. I brought them to you. So don't complain if…"

Without reason, he left the sentence hanging in the air, and looked at Rosa strangely.

"So? What?"

"What are you hiding there?" he said, moving his head forward.

"Nothing!" she rushed to answer, pulling her arm further back. "Nothing that concerns you. Now leave."

"Hey! Calm down."

"You said you came to give me that," she said pointing at the folders. "You've done it. So now go and leave me in peace."

As she spoke, she realized she had given herself away. When she had pointed at the folders, she had revealed her arm. And with it, the test she was holding in her hand. Her eyes filled with anger and fear, as she watched Franco, in the hope he hadn't noticed it. There was an unbearable silence in the room and Franco stood staring at her, puzzled. Rosa could tell just by looking at him that he had understood what he had seen in her hand.

"You're pregnant!" he exulted, with a big smile on his face. "You're pregnant, aren't you?"

Taking a deep breath of resignation, Rosa closed her eyes for a moment. Thinking about her stupidity, she grimaced, biting her lip. Her mind tried to find an excuse to fix her mistake, but it was too late. There was nothing she could do or say to change things.

"I don't have to explain anything to you, it's none of your business" she railed at him. "I want you to leave. Now. This is my office and you're not welcome."

"You can forget that," he answered. "Not now that I know what's going on. To have a child you need a man. And if that child is mine, I have rights."

"You don't know anything. What makes you think you're the father?"

"What do you mean?" he asked, his face darkening.

Rosa felt a new energy empowering her. She thought she had found the perfect weapon with which to rid Franco from her life.

She smiled, as if amused, a mocking smile aimed at Franco.

"What? Why are you grinning in that way?" he asked.

"What do you want me to say? You're right. I am expecting a baby. The funny thing is that you're not the father."

"Oh, sure. Maybe it fell from the sky."

"God forbid! As you said, to have a baby you need a man."

Franco's face, which had been darkened to excess, now paled. Suddenly, his flushed face became waxen and Rosa realized he had gotten the hint.

"Do you think you're the only man on earth?"

"What are you saying?"

"You haven't figured it out yet? A man like you can't guess such a simple thing? I am in a relationship. Another man. Is that clear enough for you?"

"What the hell are you talking about? Only a few weeks ago you were with me? Home, work, home. How could you be in a relationship? Maybe in another life, perhaps."

"How credulous you are. I don't know if I should feel pity or boredom. Did you really believe I was visiting my mother every week? I went there the first few times but after she passed away... Did you never wonder where I was going on the weekends? It was enough to tell you I needed some time to recover, to be alone and you fell for it. You're a real idiot."

Franco looked ready to explode and his face displayed all of his animal fury.

"And how long has this been going on?"

"Is it important? I don't think it changes anything."

"It's important to me."

"Well, if you really want to know, I'll tell you. We met in the clinic when I went to visit my mother and I found a man. A true one. Not like you."

Rosa wanted to hurt him in the worst of ways. She had chosen these cruel words as an attack to his masculinity. She preferred his contempt than his love. She wanted Franco's feelings for her to become pure hate. At least, that way he would finally leave her in peace, she hoped.

"I asked you, how long?" he thundered.

"I told you. Since my mother fell ill. Can't you count? It's been five months."

Franco turned without speaking. Keeping his head down, he crossed his arms and stood there thinking about what Rosa had said. Rosa just stared at him silently, wondering whether to rub salt into the wound. But in the end, and sure she had gotten rid of him once and for all, she thought it would be superfluous to add anything else. Satisfied about how things had gone, she looked at her pregnancy test that was on the desk. She thought that an unexpected baby was really a gift to embrace and, even before it was born, it had already given her more than she could ever have hoped for.

"Fine!" Franco said, looking at her again. His voice was unwavering and firm and his gaze extremely serious. "I will try to stay calm. I don't want to make more difficulties. But, you'll have to take a test to confirm whose child it is. After all, your squalid relationship doesn't mean anything. You can't exclude that I may be the father."

"Forget it!" Rosa exclaimed, realizing that what she had said had actually made the situation worse.

Without realizing it, she had unconsciously, avoided considering that option; she didn't want the baby to be Franco's. Seeking happiness, her mind had carefully eclipsed Franco's figure, leaving space only for Vincenzo, as the one and only father of her unborn baby. Understanding that Franco's words were not meaningless, she felt the ground crumbling underneath her feet.

"No!" she said again, sitting down in her chair. "I won't do any tests. Nothing."

A statement that was more for herself than for him. But now the idea had been voiced she couldn't avoid wondering who the father of her child really was.

"Now you've really annoyed me," Franco said, overcome with anger.

Taking Rosa brutally by her arm, he pulled her from the armchair and started pulling her towards the door.

"Let me go, you're hurting me!" she yelled. "Let me go!" Ignoring her pleas and like a man possessed, he dragged her along the corridor until they reached his office. Once inside, he grabbed her by the hair. In a violent move, he shoved her head down onto his desk. Holding her in that position, he took his son's picture and shoved it in front of her face.

"Do you remember Diego? Yes!" he said. "Do you remember him? My son doesn't want to talk to me or see me. Do you know why? Answer me. Do you know why?"

Rosa couldn't answer, even if she wanted to. Her mouth was crushed between the desk and Franco's hand. Besides, terror prevented her from moving a single muscle. She couldn't even cry. Sure, he was an irascible man, but he had never had such a violent reaction before and she feared for her life. With her eyes wide open, she stared at the picture, hoping everything would soon be over and he would release her from his grip.

"What? Suddenly you've lost your voice?" he started again. "It's your fault my son refuses to talk to me. Yes. You took him away from me. And now you want to take this one away too? Forget it! I'll kill you with my own hands rather than humor you. Understood? I'll crush you like an insect. You know me. You know that if I have to, I will do anything. So listen to me. You'll do that damn test. And if the child you are expecting is mine, you'll stop pissing me off and you'll let me be the father I am supposed to be. Okay! Understood?"

Rosa stayed silent. She tried to open her mouth but Franco's pressure was too much. Moaning, she tried to move her head to nod, to say that she had understood.

Franco loosened his hold a little, finally allowing her to breathe.

"Yes. I've got it," she said. "I understand."

"Good! Better for you that you do. And don't play any games or you'll pay for it dearly," he concluded, releasing her completely.

Rosa stood up and looked at him in the eye and realized he wasn't making empty threats. She'd like to beat him, step on him, or at least scream, spill out all the poison she felt, but in that moment, she wasn't able to move. Feeling tears streaming down her face, she couldn't do anything except run away.

CHAPTER 25

The grandfather clock in the corridor indicated ten past nine. Giada was supposed to be at work, but that morning she had called in sick. She was perfectly healthy but her overriding thought was the ultimatum she had given to her sister. The deadline for the funds she had demanded was about to expire and she had begun to worry that things wouldn't go as she had planned. Checking her bank account the night before, she had found that nothing had changed; her financial state remained dire. In the hope that the situation had changed overnight, she went to her computer to check.

But just as she was about to start, something strange happened. Her hand hesitated over the keyboard and an involuntary tremble had set in stopping her from touching the keys. She raised her other hand to the keyboard and the same thing occurred. Shocked, she stared at her hands wondering what was happening to her. Realizing she was breathing quickly she recognized these symptoms were classic signs of stress. She had put all of her expectations into this operation and now she desperately needed it to have worked. Whether it had or not, from this day forward, everything will have changed. She already knew how she would react if the money hadn't been deposited and the thought of having to admit to another failure sent a shiver down her spine. But these negative thoughts lasted just a few minutes. The fear of failure diminished when she thought about her sister. An intense feeling of hate developed with all its ferocity. Suddenly her hands were released from their trembling and her breathing returned to normal, leaving her with a deep need for revenge.

Now the money seemed less important. All the money in the world wouldn't be enough to satisfy her hunger for justice. Giada wanted her sister to pay for a lifetime of misery. She grieved for the life that they had torn from her. But no matter how things went with her plan to extort money from Rosa, she would have achieved her goal. Now she knew what she wanted. The hate that she felt was immeasurable and would only be quelled by destroying her sister.

However, greed has its limitations. Life had forced many sacrifices upon her but she knew that no amount of money would ever give her the peace she was looking for.

Quitting her musings and not wanting to waste anymore time, Giada returned her attention to the computer to check her account. Once on the bank website, she pressed a couple of buttons to insert the access codes and open the page she needed.

Not one euro had been deposited. Her balance was the same as the previous night. Giving an indolent look at the corner of the screen, she saw the clock marking twenty past ten. There was still time. Her ultimatum ended at one. To occupy herself until then she closed down her bank account and opened the folder containing the photos.

On the night she had collected her evidence she had saved everything onto her computer. But she wasn't so good at technology. Not knowing how to use the *cloud*, she had duplicated the pictures onto four CDs. One had been given to Ivano. Another was in her work locker and the third one in a secret drawer, in the old grandfather clock. The last one was there, on her desk, already in an envelope and ready to be mailed.

When she opened the first picture, she saw Rosa's satisfied face. The images gave her a feeling of envy. She couldn't help but look at them one more time. Deep inside her, she almost hoped that they wouldn't make the deposit on time; she would happily mail the photos, at least then they would know she was serious in her quest.

Filled with conflicting emotions, she remained in front of the screen until the appointed hour came. One o' clock was now a few minutes away. The money had to be in the account by now, she thought. She checked her bank account once again and found that, on the contrary to what she had hoped, her account had not been credited with any funds. She became agitated and asked herself where she had miscalculated her actions. The fact that the money wasn't there could only mean one thing. She had played her cards wrong.

Unable to fully decipher the emotions she was feeling, she took the envelope containing the disk. She wrote the *VitaNuova* address on it, for the attention of Mrs. Colasanti, then she stood up and headed to the exit.

The post office wasn't far from her house. A few minutes were enough to reach it. Sure, the package would take a couple of days to arrive, but in the meantime she would feel satisfaction that her plan was underway.

Before leaving she thought she should just check her account once more. The computer was still on. The page of the account balance was still open and so she pushed the page refresh button and waited a few moments for the result. A few seconds in and the six-figure amount appeared in front of her eyes; she stared, incredulous at the sum, laughing quietly to herself.

"Yes, yes!" she screamed, throwing herself onto the sofa.

After years of abstinence, her lucky star had finally decided to shine again. Although she was unable to forget her deepest thoughts of revenge against her sister today she would forget everything. She may even go out to party all night long. The following day, however, the game would start again.

"Don't think it's over, dear sister," she said to herself. "It's only the beginning."

CHAPTER 26

It had just turned eight o'clock when Gianni Spada, in his cabriolet – a black Boxster S Black Edition Porsche – was making his third round around the block where Giada Rubini's house was situated. The girl had gone out ten minutes earlier, but he continued to check the area carefully, proceeding slowly. Studying every detail of the street, he observed each main door, shutter, window and building, looking for any sign of life. He noticed the shops were not yet open and the area was quite deserted. Just an old man out walking with his dog. Spada drove another couple of rounds to be certain that the way was clear; he wasn't taking any risks. To avoid becoming the attention of any curious people, he parked the car a few blocks away and walked back in the opposite direction.

The sun hadn't risen yet, but he wore his sunglasses anyway, protecting him from prying eyes. Indifferent about the sobriety his job required of him, he wore a branded suit. On his wrist, a Rolex in steel and gold, with a white pearl dial. He really loved extreme luxury. And if he had to get his hands dirty in order to afford it, then he was ready to do just that.

He and Della Torre had known each other for years. He had

worked for him in the past. Each time to resolve shady affairs. When Della Torre had called him a couple of days ago, he had asked him to check out his wife's past and the alleged existence of an illegitimate son. But before that, he had given him the task of taking care of the girl, informing him about the delicate situation and underlining the urgency of the matter. Once he reached the building's entrance, Gianni started reading the names on the intercom list. He saw that Rubini's was flat number one and, realizing it was the basement, felt relieved. With nobody around, he didn't have to worry about who was going up and down. After having checked around once again, he rang an apartment on the last floor. He could have forced the lock, but the idea of doing that from the outside, in view of any curious eyes, wasn't the ideal way in which to proceed, he thought. He waited patiently for a few seconds and, not receiving a response, he pushed another button and then another, until the intercom started to croak. "Who is it?" somebody asked on the other side. "Mail," he answered, having brought with him fliers and magazines for that reason.

He had taken them from a mailbox nearby. Noticing the leaflets protruding from under a door, he thought they would divert attention away from suspicious neighbors. Should somebody look out of the window, they wouldn't be alarmed at seeing him there. Sure, his smart clothes may betray him, but he hoped the distance from window to door would help.

In the end, his precautionary measures were not needed. Apparently anxious to get rid of him, the man on the other side opened the main door without asking any questions and Gianni rushed to enter, closing the door behind him. He threw the mass of papers on the ground and walked through the little entrance hall and down a flight of stairs. As he had thought, Rubini's apartment was in the basement.

There wasn't any noise coming from the two neighboring apartments; the owners were, hopefully, not home, Gianni thought. The girl's apartment doorway was hidden in a corner that was impossible to see from the main entrance. The door had a simple cylinder lock and Gianni smiled; lady luck was shining down on him.

Gianni took a little leather case containing a set of picklocks from a pocket in his jacket. After he had examined the keyhole, he chose the most suitable pick, put the rods inside the split and started to tinker. The technique left no signs of breaking and entering, so, until the girl's return, nobody would notice it. But his manual dexterity skills with the equipment weren't great. He would need some time to open the door, but he really didn't care, given the circumstances.

Gianni Spada was a former agent, expelled from the police because of an illicit misappropriation of funds. After the trial, which had concluded with a plea bargain, the disciplinary measure hadn't been late in coming and Spada found himself out of work. He knew he had transferable skills and began working autonomously, offering his services to anybody that asked for them. His contacts inside the police department had been useful on more than one occasion. Bribing officers here and there, it was easy to obtain information. For this task, he had asked Taurini to find out about the girl but from the police's databank, no significant data had been revealed. There was just an identification photo and information regarding the death of her father, with whom she had lived until the day he had been killed. Realizing that her address was still the same, he felt a sort of admiration for the young woman. To remain in that apartment showed she had guts.

When the door finally opened, he realized it had only taken him a couple of minutes. He smiled, satisfied. He had beaten his last record.

Once inside, the first thing he couldn't avoid noticing was the grandfather clock positioned in a corner of the hallway. It seemed like a decent collector's item, despite it being quite shabby. He entered the living room and saw that the walls were completely empty with rectangular clean spaces clearly showing where paintings had once hung. He felt almost disgusted by the poverty of the house, but then, he wasn't there to enjoy the view. He went to the computer and after switching it on, he checked the chronology of the most recent files. The search result contained various documents, but he was only interested in those from last week. A file soon got his attention. The one labeled with Fogliani's name. Inside, there were a lot of image files portraying Della Torre with his lover.

It was while looking at a few of the photos, that he noticed an envelope next to the computer. It was addressed to Mrs. Colasanti; this wasn't a good sign. Picking it up, he saw it contained something rigid. Finding a disk inside, he inserted it into the compact disk player to check its contents. As he supposed, it hosted the same pictures he had found on the PC. Given what the girl was doing to Della Torre she was likely to be cautious and Gianni thought that more copies could exist.

He started to look around, wondering where the best place in the apartment would be to hide something. He quickly toured the house, checking every possible corner, then returned to the living room and started to search through the collection of books. He found romance and recipe books, but nothing resembling a CD or USB or any sort of external memory. Failing to find anything in the living room, he moved on to the bedroom. He rummaged in the drawers, under the bed, inside the mattress, searching for over half an hour before something of interest appeared.

It was an old photo album. In almost all the images, Ms. Rubini appeared alone, apart from three or four shots where she was with a man. Curious, he took them out and put them on the table to examine them more carefully. He noticed that, unlike the others, these had been dated. All of them had been taken eight years earlier. Also, one had a dedication from a certain Ivano. Looking again at this guy, Gianni realized it had been him grabbing his attention. He was sure he knew him. He had seen that face before, but he didn't know from where. Trying to remember, he began to study Ivano's features, but it was useless, he couldn't place him. But he was more than certain that their paths had already crossed.

For some minutes, his memory failed him, and then finally, he remembered that face and where he had seen him. If he hadn't recognized him immediately, it was because of elapsed time. The picture had been taken eight years ago but Gianni had seen the guy only a couple of days ago, at the *VitaNuova* center. He had gone there to look for information, the same day he had been hired for this job. He was convinced it had been a fool's errand; he hadn't gleaned any useful information. But now, he had to admit that the visit had been more favorable than he'd first thought. This guy has known Ms. Rubini for years, he realized. Plus, the fact that he works at the rehab center couldn't be pure chance surely. This knowledge could be very useful indeed, Gianni thought.

It was time for Spada to leave. He realized that he'd exhausted all the options in his search so gathered together the PC, the disk and the picture and put them in a bag he'd found. Already thinking about his next step in these events, he left the apartment.

CHAPTER 27

Vincenzo was in his office, busy examining the Board meeting minutes. Concentrating on the papers was impossible though. He couldn't stop thinking about his current problems; he felt as if his ordered life was spiralling out of control. Too many dilemmas had landed on him all at once. He had no idea how to escape from these and so he read the minutes hoping they would divert his mind for a while. He knew, already, that the proposal to transfer the *Co.S.Class* had been rejected, but reading these documents, where every detail was written down in black and white, he felt his anger burning up inside. Sabrina had done more damage than he could have imagined. The hundred thousand euros he'd paid for the blackmail sting was nothing compared to the millions that would be lost. His absence at the Board meeting had been a real catastrophe but at this moment in time, feeling overwhelmed by personal issues, he was in no condition to fight. He thought that, for the time being, Sabrina had won. He would limit himself to observing the development of events, and leave things alone.

That last thought was interrupted by the telephone. The call was coming in from his private line. Having asked Spada for a daily report, he instinctively thought about him and lifted the receiver. He hoped to receive good news or at least some updates on the development of the investigation.

"Hi, Vincenzo," the voice on the phone said. "Can we meet?"

"Ah, it's you," he replied with disappointment when he recognized it was Rosa.

"I need to talk to you. It's about something serious."

"Don't worry. Your sister is not a threat. I told you. She wants money. We have time to make a plan. I already paid what she asked for. So, relax."

He knew he was lying both to himself and to Rosa. He was panicking and he had pronounced those words in an effort to reassure himself, and for Rosa's sake.

"It's not about that. There is something else we need to talk about."

"Tell me."

"No. Not on the phone."

"What's up? It's not more problems, is it?"

"No. I have good news to tell you, but I want to tell you in person."

Vincenzo looked at the clock on his desk and saw it was ten past twelve; almost lunchtime. He realized he had no desire to work.

"Fine," he said. "I'll be at the center in half an hour."

"No, no! You'll find me at home," she answered. He was about to ask her why she hadn't gone to work but, fearing the answer, he preferred to stay quiet.

"Okay! See you soon," he simply said.

Closing the file he was reading, he stood up, preparing to leave when the interphone started to ring. He sat down again and answered the secretary.

"Yes?" he said.

"Professor Monti is here. He asked to see you."

"Not now, Gilda. I'm leaving," he answered, interrupting the communication.

Again, he stood up, again the device rang.

"What now?" he asked brusquely.

"I'm sorry, Mr. President. But the professor insists. He says it's very urgent."

"Fine!" he replied. "Let him enter."

A few seconds later, somebody knocked at the door and he saw Riccardo walking into the room.

"Hi, Vincenzo," he said. "I'm sorry to insist, but I really need your help. I don't know who else to ask."

"What the hell happened to you?" Vincenzo asked, noticing a series of bruises and cuts on Riccardo's face.

"Huh? Ah, you mean this," he replied, indicating his face with his hand. "This is nothing compared to what could happen to me. That is why I came here."

"Okay! Sit down and tell me everything. But hurry up because I have an appointment and I should have left here already."

"Yes, don't worry. It won't take too long."

Monti sat, crossed his legs, leaned his elbows on the chair arm-rests and, desperate, let his head fall between his hands. "I don't know where to begin," he said.

"Start from where you want. But speak."

"I need money, Vincenzo," Monti said, without lifting his eyes. "I came to ask you for a loan."

Vincenzo was puzzled by the request. Riccardo was quite a rich man. He was paid well for his job. And like him, his wife was too. He really couldn't understand how they could have financial problems; he didn't really have the time to take care of this crisis at the moment.

"Come another day," he rushed to say. "I don't have time right now to sort this for you."

Standing up, he was about to set out, but Monti unexpectedly jumped from the chair. Kneeling on the floor, he grabbed Vincenzo's leg and desperately started to say: "No, Vincenzo, you don't understand. I can't wait. I need money now."

"What the hell are you doing? Let me go!" he replied, feeling assaulted.

Taking Riccardo by his jacket collar, Vincenzo tried to free himself, but despite the fact he was of a strong build he felt the man's arms squeezing his leg, hurting him.

"I have my back against the wall from the usurers. And if I don't pay as soon as possible, they will kill me. Please! Help me!"

"Okay. I'll see what I can do. But now let me go," he said, wanting to be free of that grip.

As soon as Riccardo's hands loosened a little, Vincenzo took him by his shirt, lifted him from the ground and pushed him against the wall.

"Don't you dare touch me again," he screamed. "Next time, I'll kill you."

At this, Riccardo started crying like a baby, realizing his friend had no intention of helping him. Vincenzo stared at him for a few seconds before letting him go. He let him fall to the floor, turned and, without saying a word, left the office.

"Gilda, I'll be out for the rest of the day," he said to his secretary. "Take messages and forward only urgent calls to my mobile."

"Sure, don't worry," the woman replied.

At the elevator, Vincenzo pushed the button and waited patiently for it to arrive. As he did so an idea began to formulate in his mind. Riccardo could be an unexpected resource, he thought. Maybe he could be the solution to his current problem. Impulsively, he turned to go back to his office then, stopped. He realised that he would have to confide in Riccardo, at least a little. It was possible that he would not agree to the plan that Vincenzo had just devised; after all, he had treated his friend in the worst of ways just now.

Riccardo had spoken about usurers and being afraid to die. He didn't know how Riccardo had ended up in such trouble and he didn't really care. What mattered was that Riccardo needed money urgently and would, hopefully, do anything to ensure he got it. So, confident that the man would have to accept Vincenzo's proposal, he headed back to his office.

When he entered the room, Riccardo was still on the ground, sniveling. Vincenzo closed the door and, approaching him, gave him a handkerchief.

"Take it, dry your eyes," he said calmly. "Forgive me, my friend, but I'm going through a bad period also. You can't imagine the situation I'm in. But don't worry. You can count on me."

Riccardo stopped sobbing and, raising his head, he rose to his knees.

"Are you being serious?" he asked, incredulous.

"Sure. You know I never joke about money. I have decided to help you, but..."

"Thank you, Vincenzo! Thank you!" Riccardo interrupted him, while a mix of happiness and relief revived the color in his face. "I'll be grateful to you for the rest of my life."

"Don't thank me yet," he retorted. "I'll help you, but you'll have to do something for me. I ask only for a small task in return."

"Tell me. What do you want me to do? Ask me for anything."

Vincenzo looked at his friend without speaking, unsure whether to trust him or not. He knew that confiding in Riccardo was hazardous. His wife was Lisa's best friend. Should he refuse, he could blab everything to her. It was a risk to ask him to carry out the task that he had in mind, but the seriousness of his situation had forced his hand.

"So? Tell me. What do I have to do?" Riccardo asked again.

Without giving him too many details, and without revealing to him why, Vincenzo told him about his wife, about how she had become an inconvenience to him. And, mentioning the recent relapse, he finally said: "I'll make sure that she returns to alcoholism, so at the right moment, I'll have her admitted into your clinic. And you'll find a way for her to never get out of it."

Riccardo opened his eyes wide in amazement. Without speaking, he stared at his friend, shocked. Seeing the perplexity in his eyes, Vincenzo started to fear for the worst. He decided to push Riccardo's current Achilles' heel; money.

"How much did you say you need?" he asked shamelessly. "Oh, right! You didn't tell me."

Riccardo's expression changed radically. Still hesitant, he persisted in his long silence, but it was clear those words had hit him.

The silence was suddenly broken by the untimely ringing of the telephone. Vincenzo rushed to switch off the device and, to avoid any further distractions, he went to his desk picked up a pen and said, "Well, let me do this... I'll write an amount here. You tell me if it's okay or not. Okay?"

When Riccardo didn't answer, Vincenzo began to write, indifferently, and then approached him, shoving the paper under his nose. He saw Riccardo's eyes open wide and realized he had hit the mark.

"So?" he said. "Are you with me?"

Riccardo waited for a few moments, still unsure whether to accept or not.

"It's fine," he said finally. "But I need the money now. I can't wait for your wife..."

"Don't worry," Vincenzo interrupted him. "The money will be in your bank account by tonight."

The two men shook hands to seal the agreement. However, Riccardo's behavior still showed some hesitation. "Don't worry. Everything will go smoothly," Vincenzo said to encourage him. "Now forgive me, but I really have to go."

Feeling relieved, he left his office. His troubles weren't over yet, but at least he could see some light on the horizon.

***

The click of the door lock sounded in Vincenzo's head like a warning. A warning to proceed with caution. The fact that Rosa wanted to talk to him face to face again didn't suggest anything good. Especially after recent events.

He was still on the stairs when he saw her coming out of the apartment. Apprehensively, he stopped, but she rushed to reach him and wrapped her arms around him.

"I've been waiting for you for over an hour," she said happily.

"What's up with you?" Vincenzo replied, once they were inside. "You've always complained about your gossipy neighbors and now you make an exhibition of yourself on the stairs?"

"Today I don't care about anybody," she answered. "Why did it take you so long? And why didn't you answer the phone?"

"Oh, it was you! Nothing. I was busy. A small issue."

As soon as they reached the living room, Rosa took his hands. "Sit down," she said. "I have wonderful news for you."

Sighing, he let himself sit, liberated from her grasp. Up until then, he had continued to fear that some other problem had arisen. Despite Rosa reassuring him on the phone that everything was good, seeing the serenity in her face calmed his fears completely.

"So?" he then said. "What's the good news?"

Holding back her smile, she looked at him strangely. Maybe trying to generate suspense, she seemed to dampen her happiness to prolong the moment. "I'm pregnant!" she finally exclaimed, starting to laugh and gesture frenetically.

"What?" he said.

"Yes! We're expecting a baby."

That statement took him by surprise. Caught wrong-footed, he stared at Rosa, unable to speak. Immediately, he thought about what a problem this would be for him. Things between them both were already complicated enough because of her sister turning up, but this made the situation unbearable.

"I wanted to tell you immediately," she said, not caring about his silence. "I found out a couple of days ago."

"What?" he said, his head somewhere else.

"Yes, I did the test a few days ago."

He raised his gaze and, just to say something, he asked, uninterested, "And why the delay? Why are you telling me about it now?"

Rosa's face darkened for an instant, but immediately reverted to her happy state again.

"Oh, nothing," she answered. "I had a little problem and I dealt with it."

"A problem? Does it regard your sister?"

"No, I told you. From now on, I don't want to think about any of it. Don't let other issues ruin this moment."

Actually, Vincenzo wasn't looking for answers. He wasn't interested in what had stopped her. He wanted to keep talking, he needed to gain some time before trying to find a way to tell Rosa what he thought. And what he thought was, he didn't want a child.

"So!" she said. "You don't have anything to say? I know you're surprised. I wasn't expecting it either. But, gosh! Say something."

"Are you sure I'm the father?"

"Of course. What kind of question is that?"

"Well… After all, it's not been long since you broke up with your ex. The child could be his."

"Absolutely not," she said, resentful. "It had been over with him for a long time. We were sharing a bed only to sleep."

Vincenzo observed her carefully. He had plenty of problems already and he didn't need to add anymore to his life.

"I'm sorry," he said without niceties. "But we can't keep it."

"What the hell are you talking about?"

"You know my situation. A child is something I can't afford. Should it become public, it would have catastrophic consequences."

"Oh, so this is the only thing you care about. I should have known it. For you, money always comes first."

"Come on! Don't be like that," he said, trying to calm her. "You know you're important to me."

"So tell me you're as happy as I am, and that we'll have this child together."

"I'm sorry, Rosa."

"Okay, I'll do this alone," she said, irritated. "I don't need you."

"I see you don't want to understand," he raised his voice, taking her by her arms. "I'm saying you can't have the baby. You have to stop the pregnancy."

"Let me go, you're hurting me."

Realizing he was being insensitive, Vincenzo released her.

"I'm sorry. I'm not thinking clearly," he said. "It's just that I'm stressed. You'll think I'm stupid, but so many things are happening, and too quickly." Brushing her face to break the chill between them, he added, "I don't feel like talking about this now. Can we postpone to another time?"

Rosa remained silent, pissed off by what had happened. She made an expression as if to agree.

"Thanks, my love," he said. "And please, forgive me."

Overwhelmed with unease and unable to say anything else, he let his silence speak for him. He went to touch her face again, but she brusquely moved away.

Anxiously he made his way to the corridor without saying goodbye. His thoughts were in chaos as he sought a way out of this damned situation.

CHAPTER 28

Spada contacted the *VitaNuova's* administration department. Thanks to his own simple strategy and charm, he got Ivano's name, address and work shifts from the secretary. The woman told him that Terravalle had been working at the center for only a few days; that piqued his curiosity even more. He didn't like coincidences.

Ivano's house was in the southeast area of the city, in a suburb that Spada knew well. In fact, it was where he had grown up and he knew that the people living there were of a certain kind; fly-by-nighters, thieves, drug addicts, mobsters and prostitutes. Without scruple, he parked his car in front of the main entrance. He knew he could work in peace there. People in that neighborhood focused on their own business. Nobody wanted to get involved with the police. Sure, a few people had noticed his Porsche, but nobody would talk.

Before getting out of his car, he called Taurini to obtain some information about Terravalle. "Can you talk or are you with somebody?" he asked his friend, as soon as he answered.

"Don't worry, I'm alone. What do you need?"

"I want to know what you have on a guy called Ivano

Terravalle," he said, giving him the man's address.

"Ok. Let's see," the officer said. "Oh, yes. Here we go. He has a record for drug pushing and he's been in prison a couple of times, but nothing serious. Anyway, it was a long time ago. He's probably settled down now."

"Or maybe he became smarter."

"If you're following him, I doubt it. He must have done something big."

"I'm not sure yet. But I'll let you know," Spada concluded. "And be sure I'll return the favor."

With those words, he got out of the car and made his way to the main entrance. It was unlocked. He entered without a problem and sought out Ivano's apartment. All was quiet. No noise came from within but, before forcing the door, he knocked a couple times to be certain that the property was definitely empty.

The unbearable air inside the apartment forced him to bring his hand to his face to cover his nose. Some kind of substance seemed to have impregnated the walls and everything inside. He rushed to open the windows in the kitchen and, when he went to the living room to do the same, he realized that that was where the smell was coming from. The room was filled with paintings. A pair of easels held half-finished canvases, while a mass of brushes, pencils, colors and chemical products rested on a little table.

When the air finally became breathable, he started his search. He explored the living room and the bedroom, but these yielded nothing of interest. He turned his attention to the bathroom and found in the toilet tank, a carefully sealed plastic bag containing a compact disk. It was probably a copy of Della Torre's pictures he supposed, but he would check it later.

After checking that the bathroom held no further pickings, he began searching the entrance area of the apartment. He went to the cabinet but found it was storing mainly, to his eyes, useless items. But on rifling further into its depths he found an old diary. He opened the first page and saw it had been signed by Giada

Rubini. He returned to the living room with the book and started to leaf through it. Realizing it was a journal, he skimmed through it, quickly. The dates were from around eight years earlier. He flipped the pages to the last one, and noticed that one sheet had been ripped out. He could see some deep indentations on the page in front of him, where the writer had pressed hard on the torn out sheet. Taking one of the many pencils nearby he started to slide it over the page. The strokes were very deep and enabled Spada's pencil to restore the entire text, title included.

FINALLY FREE

Oh, yes! It's finally over. Now I can breathe. I got rid of that bastard, my father, and today everything is really over because I got away with it from the police too. And I need to talk about this story with somebody. Doing it with Ivano would be useless. He doesn't understand me like he used to. So, dear diary, I write to you, because I can tell you everything.

I killed my father, closing that bad chapter once and for all and now I don't know whether to laugh or cry with happiness. He humiliated me for my entire life, but he paid for it dearly. I took it away, that shitty life of his.

But I have to tell you the story from the very beginning.

Ivano gave me the idea without meaning to. It happened the last time they caught him. He told me: "Nowadays, you need an alibi even to go to the bathroom, or you're fucked."

And I didn't stop to think about it until I found an alibi. A perfect alibi! I asked him to cover my back and he did it. So one day, I gave him my mobile and I returned home, making sure nobody saw me. Then, at night, when that pig of my father was sitting quietly at the table, I hit him over the back of his head with that enormous ashtray that he liked so much. And even though I smashed his head, he didn't die immediately. He kept staring at me almost for a minute, incredulous, while blood continued to pour out of his head. He seemed to not believe it.

I didn't even care about the stains. I live here so it's normal that they are all over the place. But the brilliant idea came later. I took the telephone and I called Ivano at home. After ten minutes, I phoned him again, while he was calling the taxi company with my mobile, following my instructions. He turned on the speakerphone and put the mobile near the telephone receiver. So I reserved a taxi, while I was still here at home. When the police checked the call records to see where the call had been made from, they discovered it came from Ivano's area and I couldn't be in two places at the same time. When they came to interrogate me, I started crying like a child. "Yes, dad called me at my boyfriend's house and reproached me because I was late," I told them, with my eyes full of tears. "He told me I had to come home immediately. To be as fast as possible, I called a cab, because at that time public transport doesn't pass often."

Ivano covered my back from the beginning, confirming that I had spent the whole day with him. Also, the taxi operator recognized my voice. Luckily, those stupid cops didn't verify the cab ride. I hadn't really thought about it, but thank God they didn't either. Everything went smoothly. When they didn't find any sign of breaking and entering in my house, they immediately suspected it had been me, but I fooled them all. In fact, today they informed me that the case was being dropped due to a lack of evidence. They said it was a murder by means of persons unknown. Unknown only to them though, because I knew how things had gone down. And now, you know it too. This is a goodbye, my dear diary. From this moment on, I can do it by myself.
Giada

Spada read the text straight through.

His eyes felt heavy; the writing was quite dense and he'd had some difficulty in deciphering parts of it. He looked at Giada's testimony once again, the testimony in which she was admitting to murder. He knew that this evidence would be enough to get rid of her once and for all. He smiled, satisfied, knowing that he had earned his pay, and more besides.

CHAPTER 29

Days passed and drifted into summer and, after a series of hot days, today was the worst one for sure. Giada couldn't breathe. She waved a piece of cardboard in front of her face, trying to relax. But it was impossible. She had the feeling that everything was slipping out of her hands. The day set for the second payment had elapsed, and no further funds had been deposited.

Unsure what action to take, she had continued to wait and hope. She had considered mailing the pictures to Lisa, but then thought better of it; Della Torre had clearly orchestrated the breaking into her and Ivano's apartments. And as she didn't know how he was going to play the game, she preferred to let him call the shots before she did anything.

She'd put one of the remaining disks in a safety-deposit box, while the other she left in the relative safety of the grandfather clock. But the fact that they had been able to trace Ivano was her biggest worry. Since the day of the robbery, he had become tiresome. More than once he had asked her to drop her plot against her sister. She refused to do so. Giada feared that the intrusions into their homes masked more dangerous threats and so a more subtle approach was needed.

It was time to show her cards and face Rosa openly.

***

The *VitaNuova* corridors were full of people and it took Giada a few minutes to reach her sister's office. When she got there, she opened the door without knocking and entered.

"What game are you playing?" she asked, before her sister could even raise her eyes.

Taken by surprise, Rosa jumped up from her chair.

"No game," she said, amazed.

"So where is the money?"

"You seem nervous. Maybe you should take a seat."

"Stop joking. Why didn't you pay?"

"Because the party is over, my dear sister."

Giada felt overwhelmed with uncertainty. Her anger had been the one thing that had driven her to this course of action against her sister but now she could see her plans disintegrating.

"I was waiting for you," Rosa continued. "I was wondering when you would show up."

"What do you mean?"

"Take this! Look for yourself."

Giada took the folder her sister was giving her, worried. When she opened it, she found a piece paper that, on the face of it, meant nothing to her. It was a graying page that had white inscriptions on it, brought into relief by the chiaroscuro contrast.

"What is this?" she asked, puzzled.

"You tell me. It's you who wrote it."

Giada started examining the text more carefully. Reading the title was enough to understand it all though. With an incredulous look, she read a few lines to be sure that she wasn't dreaming. A page of her old diary was in front of her eyes. When she had written it she hadn't worried about destroying it and she had eventually given it to Ivano for him to get rid of for her. The diary should no longer exist.

"When I read it, I almost couldn't believe it," Rosa said. "But

I can understand your motive at that time. Despite having a vague memory of our father, I do remember what a bastard he was. Who knows, maybe I would have done the same in your shoes?"

"So, what will you do?" Giada asked, fearful.

"Nothing, if you keep quiet. But be sure that if those pictures come out, you'll go to prison."

Giada stared at her sister with contempt. She regretted she hadn't carried out her homicidal plans. She would cheerfully have done it this minute, but common sense prevailed, she didn't want to make any reckless moves that would land her in more trouble. She felt that a strategic withdrawal was the only reasonable thing to do.

***

Since the day somebody had entered his house, Ivano hadn't been able to find a moment of peace. What Giada had defined as a simple and risk-free job had turned out to be something different. From the beginning, from the moment she told him about her plan, he had felt things would become complicated, but he had continued to ignore that little voice in his mind, warning him to back away.

These worries were ruining him daily and wearing him down. Needing some fresh air, he left his painting room and went outside.

He immediately noticed a woman coming out from the building. He thought it was Rosa, but then he realized it was Giada. Seeing her at the center, he realized the situation was worse than he supposed; the thought chilled him.

"What's happened? What are you doing here?" he asked when he reached her.

"Son of a bitch. You're a piece of shit," she screamed, as soon as she saw him. And, mad with anger, she started hitting him. "You were meant to get rid of it. Why didn't you get rid of it?"

He raised his arms, trying to stop the punches. But she wouldn't stop. He grabbed hold of her and blocked her in a firm grip. "What the hell happened?"

"The diary," she replied, continuing to struggle. "Why didn't you destroy it? Damn! What have you done with it?"

"What diary? What are you talking about?" he asked, not understanding.

"*My* diary. Idiot! What do you think I'm talking about?"

Suddenly, a sequence of flashbacks crossed Ivano's mind. A rush of thoughts took him back to the day of the robbery. Not even the *surplus cabinet* had survived the looting and, thinking about it, among the objects that had remained there was no trace of the old notebook.

Feeling uncomfortable, he let her go. Clearly, Giada felt betrayed. But he couldn't understand what the diary had to do with her current temper.

"Do you want to know what happened? Here! Look!" she said, giving him the paper she was holding.

"What's this?"

"What language am I speaking?" Giada replied, still screaming. "It's a page of my diary. The *last* page. Now, do you get it?"

"Impossible," he replied. "It's true, I kept the diary. But I tore out that page."

"Oh! What a good job! And so how do you explain this?"

"What do you want me to say? I don't know! But what has this got to do with…"

"Don't you see it yet? You've put us both in a vulnerable position. Now they know everything about us and about how things went down eight years ago. They have enough to send us to prison."

Giada informed him about her sister's threats. Then, without waiting for his reply, she began to walk away from him, still fuming with anger. Ivano followed her with his gaze, until she disappeared from view. Ivano felt the fear rising up inside him and, not knowing what he should do to ease the situation, he turned and went back into the building.

CHAPTER 30

Luca had become a real obsession for Lisa. As a victim of her own indecisions, she didn't go to work for a week. She spent the days introspectively trying to understand her real needs and desires. Luca was her son and she loved him. Despite this, he represented the emblem of a difficult and suffered past. Recognizing him meant that she could finally close a traumatic chapter of her life once and for all. But Vincenzo's reluctance to offer his support made the situation difficult. Since the day she had opened up to him and told him the truth about Luca's existence, he hadn't been the same towards her. He had left her alone in their bedroom at night. Moving to one of the guest rooms, and with all the coldness he could muster, he had continued to show his opposition to her plans. Without giving any explanation, he had halted their relationship, waiting for her to make a decision. Lisa had tried to speak with him many times, but he had always avoided her with absolute determination. But that morning, it was harder than usual. She had made her choice, knowing that it would completely ruin her relationship with her husband.

Vincenzo had been the pillar of her life, but Luca was part of her. Drawn by that awareness, she looked for her lawyer's number in the address book. She had decided to put everything down in writing. After punching a few buttons on the phone, she saw her fingers hesitate. She felt her courage lacking and realized that she needed a drink. Lisa knew that having a couple of drinks so early in the morning was a habit that she couldn't stop and, pushing that thought aside, she filled her glass and sat down again. Placing the bottle next to her, she sipped some more liquor, aware that she had given in to her addiction once again.

Since that night when the hidden truths had been spoken, Vincenzo had stopped reproaching her for taking up drink again. Evidently, he understood her frame of mind and every time one bottle was emptied, it was replaced with a full one. He was letting her do what she wanted. He seemed to recognize her need, even if he tried to deny it, and even if he was upset by her behavior. But despite her failings he had stayed with her, albeit in silence.

Having convinced herself that Vincenzo was, perhaps, not going to go against her, she thought that acting behind her husband's back was wrong. He had the right to know about her decision. But first she needed to contact the lawyer and began dialing the number again. She needed to take advantage of the fortified courage that came from the glass of whiskey, she knew that once its affects had worn off her nerve to make the call would disappear.

After she had scheduled the appointment, she felt relieved and took another sip to relax. She then called Vincenzo, who she assumed would be at his office. But the telephone rang hollow. She made another two attempts, but still he didn't answer. Eventually she left him a short message to update him on what she had done. Then, feeling a mix of relief and melancholy, she began drinking again in the hope that it would help alleviate her self-pity.

***

Vincenzo avoided answering his wife's call. Thinking she was calling to ask him to change his mind, he let the device ring until the sound finally ceased. However, like the annoying buzz of a fly, the irritating trill sounded two more times. He was about to turn off the ringtone when his mobile phone went off again. A few moments later, the device emitted a little beep and, seeing Lisa had resigned herself to leaving a message, he opened his voicemail.

Discovering that his wife had set an appointment with the lawyer for the following week, he realized he had underestimated her.

He had been sure that in her alcoholic state she wouldn't have been able to do anything positive regarding her plans for Luca. He had concentrated on assisting her to become dependent on alcohol again. But it seemed this strategy hadn't worked. He thought for a moment; what should he do next? He concluded that the only solution was to set his plan into action. He called Lisa, hoping that his plot to admit her into the clinic would still work. He couldn't force her to enter it. But he knew that the only way to convince her to go voluntarily was to use her son as reason for her to get better.

Her mobile continued to ring hollow and he thought that maybe she wanted to pay him back for not answering her calls earlier. He was about to hang up when he heard his wife's voice on the other end.

"Vincenzo, I had to do it," she said, as soon as she answered. "He's my son."

He remained silent, looking for the best words to use. From her tone, it was clear that she was tipsy and maybe convincing her would be easier than he had thought.

"Tell me you don't want to us to separate," she started again. "I need you."

"I don't want us to part either, I'm not going to leave you but you have to do something to help our relationship work again."

"Don't ask me to give up on him."

"I'm not talking about him, but you."

"Tell me what I have to do and I will."

"I'm asking you to postpone the lawyer's appointment for a few weeks. I want you to go to the clinic. What will you tell your son otherwise? Do you think he'll be happy to have an alcoholic mother? Once you get out, you can do what you want. I won't fight you. But before that, you have to get treated."

"And you'll stay with me?"

"Of course, I told you I would."

"Then it's fine. I'll do what you want."

The phone call finished and, smiling to himself, Vincenzo thought that everything had finally worked in his favour for once.

Without wasting any more time, he called Riccardo to inform him.

"Get ready," he said abruptly, when he answered. "It's time for you to pay your debt."

After a few silent moments, the hesitating voice of the man spoke.

"Listen, Vincenzo... I have thought about it a lot," he said. "I don't think I can..."

"No excuses. You can't refuse," Vincenzo shouted as he slammed the phone down, ending the call.

He couldn't allow anything to ruin his plan, including Riccardo's self-doubts. He needed to be in control again and he needed Lisa out of the way. He thought that if everything went as it was supposed to, soon all of his problems would be solved, including Rosa's pregnancy.

CHAPTER 31

Still unable to believe what was happening, Ivano returned to the painting room. Waiting for the students to finish their class and still shocked by what Giada had told him, he remained silent. Isolated in his memories, he thought about how everything he had fought for during the last few years was slipping through his hands. He had been in prison and didn't want to go back. Not now that his life had become something precious. He remembered his efforts to get out of the filth of prison. He recalled his sufferings to get away from a life that disgusted him and that even death had refused to take away from him. The thought of returning to living an almost forgotten past once again filled him with horror.

When the class finished and, almost as if he knew that there wouldn't be another one, he observed the individuals as they left. Without speaking, he followed each of them with his gaze, as if he was saying goodbye to a loved one. He stood there, staring into space, a multitude of thoughts all cramming for attention.

Ten minutes passed before one of the class returned to the room and broke Ivano's trance, startling him. "I'm sorry, I forgot my glasses," the young man said.

"Don't worry," Ivano replied, catching his breath. "I was lost in my thoughts."

"I can see that! See you."

"I hope so," Ivano whispered.

Resigned to feeling defeated, he started to do what, for him, was a pleasurable ritual. He put on his protective gloves then collected the used brushes with devotion and care. He filled a container with oil of turpentine and started immersing the brushes in it. In the past, this task had always eased his negative thoughts. Hoping that the same magic would happen again, he stared at the residue of the paint as it dissolved in the solvent, but it didn't help. Fear anchored him to his new reality and to a past that was stronger than anything else he had experienced.

Feeling he needed to do something, he left everything on the table and made his way to Rosa's office. He didn't know what he could say or do, but a force stronger than him projected him towards her door. Maybe, he would ask for leniency. Maybe he would tell her that he hadn't wanted to be involved in the ordeal. Maybe he would betray Giada to save himself. Or, who knows? Maybe he would simply look into her eyes and realize it had all been a bad nightmare, one from which he would soon wake up.

He continued walking hesitantly, wondering what destiny had in store for him. He pondered if there was to be a tomorrow in his life, or if it would all end today. He was a few meters from Rosa's office when he heard voices coming from within. He recognized Franco Mezzana's voice and, despite the door being half-closed, he could clearly hear words breaking out forcefully. The two of them were fighting again. Ivano pressed his shoulder against the wall and listened in. This time, he didn't do it for Giada, nor for the feelings that compelled him to follow her, but for himself. He was listening in the hope that the argument would be endless. He was worried at the thought of meeting Rosa face to face. Worried about what he needed to say to her and her reaction.

When the shouting calmed and silence fell, he feared that his moment had come, but, after a few moments, he heard Mezzana begin talking again.

"Do you understood what I have told you or not?" he heard Franco saying.

"I'm not deaf."

"So, what is your answer?"

"I already told you what I think."

"I don't give a damn about what you think. You're already at the third month. You can have the paternity test. And you'll do it. Whether you want to or not."

Ivano leaned forward, curious to see what was happening.

"This child is not yours," she said. "I've told you and I am telling you again."

"How do you know?"

"I know it, that's all. I feel it."

"Bullshit!" Franco replied, advancing a few steps.

"Don't move," she said immediately. "Touch me and I swear this time I'll report you."

Finally realizing what provoked their anger, Ivano shook his head. He remembered the previous argument he had overheard. He recalled how both of them had insulted each other and how Franco had threatened to kill Rosa. He visualized the image of the blade at her neck and thought that Franco Mezzana would be the perfect scapegoat.

Suddenly, Ivano felt breathless and his heart started beating crazily in a mix of fear, hesitation and anxiety. He was about to bring his hand to his forehead, when he noticed that in his haste he had forgotten to take off his gloves. But he couldn't worry about that at the moment. He dried the sweat from his face and took another look inside Rosa's room. He saw that the two of them were still fighting. Without wasting any more time, Ivano ran towards Franco's office.

The door was open. Ivano stopped for a moment on the threshold to check that the corridor was empty, he then took a deep breath and entered. Once inside, he closed the door behind him and ran to the desk. He had seen the object of his search the last time he was in here. He lifted the various folders from the table, paying attention not to miss anything. He would have liked to throw everything in the air, to turn the room upside down, in an effort to speed up his hunt but he couldn't afford to do this as if somebody was to hear him, his new plan would fail. He tried to control his nerves while being careful to put each object back in the same position he had found it. He concentrated on not leaving any trace of him being there. He started on the drawers and, after a few minutes, he managed to flush out the longed-for-tool. Only when it was in his hand, did he realize that it was an old razor. Without waiting a moment longer, he put it in his pocket, put the drawer's contents in order and, before his luck abandoned him, rushed out.

CHAPTER 32

Ivano had sneaked inside the deserted administration area to sift through the personnel archives looking for Rosa's address. He hadn't asked Giada for it and for sure, he didn't want to do so now. When he finally found it, he quickly copied the address on a piece of paper and put everything back in order. He passed the rest of the day as he would normally do, remaining at the center until the end of his shift. When he eventually got home Ivano let himself fall into the armchair to unwind; he needed to think about what to do. He knew very well what the 'what' was; the 'how' was the problem. He had thought about how to execute his plan during the afternoon but he hadn't come up with an ideal strategy. His imagination continued to wander over hypothetical solutions to his problem, but nothing seemed suitable. Besides, despite his feelings towards the police he had never gone as far as he may do now. He had never killed anybody.

He spent a full hour imagining the scene, visualizing everything in real time. Once he had mentally worked his way through the scenario that he had in mind and when all of the details had fallen into place after his original vague idea, he stood up, ready to act.

Ivano arrived at Rosa's apartment and parked his car where nobody could see it. In the darkness of the night, he positioned himself behind a car not far from the main entrance. There he remained, keeping watch on the doorway.

Afraid somebody may see him from above, he hunkered down behind the car, but soon realized he couldn't withstand too long in that uncomfortable position. Five minutes had passed, and his discomfort became too much for him. As he made to move and stand up he saw a figure on the inside of the darkened glass of the entrance door. A shadowy form moving towards the exit that eventually became a man leaving the building.

Ivano moved with all the agility he could muster, and before the door could close, he rushed inside. He now needed to find where Rosa lived. He illuminated his mobile phone and went to the mail boxes to check Rosa's apartment number. He saw her surname next to Mezzana's; he felt that luck was with him. It would become a clue that would send the police investigation in Mezzana's direction, he thought.

Before going up, Ivano put on the latex gloves that he had remembered to bring with him; he didn't want to leave any traces of him being there. He was about to ring the bell to Rosa's apartment when he heard steps coming up from below. Agitated, he moved away from the door. His intention was to go up a few floors, but he didn't have time to reach the stairs. He saw the figure of a man coming closer, so he crept into the shadows and was thankful of the dim lighting on the landing.

A column was jutting away from a wall that was big enough to hide Ivano's presence and he snaked behind it, waiting for the man to come past. But the man stopped, turned and made his way to Rosa's door. Ivano saw him take some steps and then turn again. From his cramped position, Ivano was experiencing pain in his feet to such a degree that he began to unconsciously stamp the ground. The other man must have heard him, he was standing still, with his face turned toward Ivano, looking into the darkness. Ivano recognized the man, even in that deep shadow; it was Franco. Ivano's anxiousness went in to overdrive. Seeing him there produced a fear that threatened to overwhelm him and, certain that he had been discovered, Ivano decided to attack him. He took the razor out of his pocket and opened it, ready to jump out to take Mezzana by surprise. But Mezzana lowered his gaze and, without further hesitation, went to Rosa's door.

Ivano flattened against the wall, trying to calm his breathing. He felt clammy and his heart seemed to be beating out of his chest. Taking deep breaths, he passed a hand over his forehead, feeling the latex of his gloves and an unexpected sensation of coldness. It took him a few seconds to realize that the sharp blade was across his forehead. Alarmed at his stupidity he moved his hand away and remained hiding in the shadow of the wall until it was time for him to make his move.

Mezzana began violently hitting Rosa's door. Furiously screaming, he was threatening Rosa and telling her to open up.

A soft light appeared from the upper floor. Ivano saw the head of a woman who, moving forward cautiously leaned over to see what was happening. Immediately, Ivano became one with the wall. He was safe from Mezzana's sight, but from his position he couldn't escape the woman's gaze. He could see her clearly and assumed that she could see him but he soon realized that the dim light was his ally; if he could see her, it was only because of the pale light behind her. Happy with that realization Ivano shifted his attention back to what was happening at Rosa's apartment.

He had been distracted and hadn't noticed Rosa opening her door. She and Mezzana were face to face and Ivano just had the time to see them disappearing into her apartment.

This plan of his was going to take longer than he had expected, but he was there now and he would wait, no matter how long it took.

***

Ten minutes had passed since Mezzana had entered Rosa's apartment. Waiting for him to leave, Ivano hadn't moved from his position. Moving his feet occasionally, he tried to alleviate the atrocious pain he was feeling. He wanted to take his shoes off for a few moments, but he had to be ready. He had already made the mistake of not considering contingencies and it had been a minor miracle that had saved him. To hope that lady-luck would continue to assist him was too much to ask.

Still hiding in that dark corner, he began to reflect on the incidents of the day. Then, thinking about how everything had started, he went back to the series of events that had rendered him temporarily frenzied and were about to transform him into a killer. He was living moments of pure madness and would, probably next day, be unable to look at himself in the mirror.

After a few more minutes, Mezzana left the apartment. He came out bursting with anger, with Rosa screaming at him. She slammed the door in his face, and he started going down the stairs, cursing out loud. In a few seconds Mezzana disappeared completely. But to be certain that the man had left the building Ivano waited for the metallic crash of the main door before he made his move. Only then did he approach the door and, keeping the razor in his hand, he knocked. From the inside of the apartment, he heard words he couldn't decipher. After waiting in vain for a few moments, he decided to ring the bell. He rang two more times before hearing steps coming to the door.

When Rosa opened it, he could barely see her face. The hall was as dark as the stairs. But now, his eyes were accustomed to the obscurity and the little light coming from the living room was sufficient. In a sharp and strong movement, he turned his arm diagonally and, in the deep darkness separating them, he cut her throat neatly. The woman brought her hands to her neck and fell onto the floor, a puzzled look on her face. Ivano was sure everything was over but, hearing her groaning in pain, he realized she was still alive. Now laying there, her body contorting with almost invisible movements, she continued to fight for her life. The life he had just torn from her.

The scene lasted a few more seconds, until Rosa, exhaling one last breath, stopped struggling.

PART TWO

CHAPTER 33

It was just past nine in the morning when Inspector Nardi arrived at the victim's house. Besides a crowd of curious onlookers, an ambulance and a few police cars obstructed the driveway, so he parked a little way back and proceeded on foot. Walking among the throng of people, he reached the main entrance. There were a couple of policemen checking anyone who wished to enter the building. One of them lifted a hand, making a sign for Nardi to stop but, noticing his badge, he greeted him and let him pass.

If it wasn't for his unfriendly, curious and inquiring gaze that always seemed watchful and a little irritated, Massimo Nardi could undoubtedly be mistaken for a man older than sixty, despite the fact that he was in his early fifties. After his wife's death, he had lost all interest in his life. He had let himself go and had become a shabby and constantly dissatisfied man. His job continued to give him a reason to wake up in the morning and gave him purpose. The thought that one day his work would come to an end rendered him incapable of enjoying his successes.

Along the stairs, the forensic team was already hard at work. Some of them were looking for traces of evidence inside and outside the apartment. Having completed their preliminary checks they signaled that it was ok for the inspector to pass.

A little further on from the door, a woman was lying on the floor in a pool of blood, her hands closed around her neck. Her eyes were wide open, icy, and seemed to be staring outwards, even in death. But what struck Nardi was the reddish hue that framed that lovely female face, it was almost unnatural. The woman's hair color seemed to have become one with the blood surrounding her. It was difficult to determine where the solid red of her hair separated from the semi-liquid red of the coagulated blood.

He had seen a lot of dead people, but there was something curious about this set-up, he thought. Expressionless, he scrutinized the body and its position on the floor but couldn't identify where his unease concerning the scene came from.

"Oh, Inspector! You're here," a voice at his back said.

Turning, he saw his sergeant, Ettore Lanzi, coming towards him and, nodding, he said, "So, what do we have this time?"

"The victim is Rosa Fogliani. At first examination, she was killed by a cut to her throat. The housecleaning woman found her this morning when she arrived for work. We've put her in the in the apartment next door for now; she's very shocked."

Without replying, Nardi bent over the woman's body and stared for a few seconds at the clear incision going from one side of her neck to the other. A numbered label marking the murder weapon was set next to the corpse. The hand razor was half open, and the blade was covered in blood.

"It doesn't look like an attempted robbery," Lanzi said. "They didn't touch any money or precious objects. Whoever did this had a precise reason and probably knew the victim. There isn't any sign of breaking and entering. The living room is completely trashed. It looks like there had been a violent scuffle beforehand."

"What do we know about the woman?"

"Twenty-eight years old. Psychologist. She worked in a rehab center for drug addicts. According to her neighbors, until a while back she lived with such..."

"Good morning, gentlemen," somebody at the door said. "Forgive me for being late."

Nardi and Lanzi turned at the same time. The medical examiner was behind them and, breathless, he crossed the threshold into the room.

"Good morning, doctor. What happened to you?" Lanzi asked.

"Eh! My boy… I'm not your age anymore, you know? With this hot temperature, even two floors feel like a real hike."

Nardi and Lanzi knew Doctor Padovani well, and they were bound by mutual respect. They never crossed a line, always keeping their relationship at a professional level.

"So, Doctor," Nardi said. "What can you tell us?"

With difficulty, the man knelt on the floor to check the body's temperature and its rigidity. Once he had finished his examination, he took off his glasses and passed his handkerchief over his face, he had been sweating profusely.

"Well…" he said, showing hesitation. "From the rigor mortis, I'd say she died at least ten hours ago. That's not conclusive, however. There is no trace of hypostatic haemorrhages on the corpse, so you'll have to wait for the autopsy to have more precise information."

"Is it normal?" Nardi asked.

"What?"

"The lack of hypostatic haemorrhages."

"Oh, yes!" Padovani said. "It's because of the excessive loss of blood. The quantity of haemoglobin in the vascular system is insufficient and doesn't allow for the appearance of the *livor mortis*. It's useful in determining if a body has been moved from its initial position in death."

Just then, Prosecutor Mellis, the Assistant District Attorney who coordinated the preliminary investigations, arrived. She greeted the three men, who she knew well, and asked about the case.

Nardi smiled at her arrival. He had always liked Ms. Mellis. She was always very cooperative at every crime scene they attended, holding him in high regard and trusting his ability to get results. Because of this she had allowed him unlimited scope during his inquiries. Even the times when he had gone too far, (he had a fiery temper), she had turned a blind eye. And this meant a lot to him.

"Have you already informed her family?" Prosecutor Mellis asked.

"We're taking care of it," Nardi answered. And, after sharing a few more words, he left her with Lanzi and Padovani, both of whom updated her on the current situation.

Nardi began his initial exploration around the apartment. He was looking for anything that could appear as extraneous to the crime scene. But he didn't find anything. As Lanzi had said, the only interesting thing was that the living room was a complete mess. It was almost impossible to determine what was in its rightful place with furnishing fragments scattered over the floor. The other rooms, however, were all as they should be with nothing out of the ordinary; nothing that grabbed his attention. He thought it was probably best to leave the forensic team to do their job. If there was something important, they would find it.

Nardi returned to Rosa's doorway where he saw that Padovani was preparing to leave. He said his goodbyes then, accompanied by Prosecutor Mellis and Lanzi, Nardi left the apartment and went next door to talk to the woman who had found the body.

The officer who was with her was trying to calm her down. Nardi asked her a couple of questions, but she was still in a state of shock and could only mutter incoherently to him. He realized that he wouldn't get any significant information from her while in this state. Knowing that she needed to be removed from the scene he ordered the officer to take her to police headquarters; she could give her statement there.

Looking for a line of investigation, he knew he needed to explore the movements of the residents of the building. Usually he left that task to others, but since he hadn't got much to go on from the crime scene, he decided to spend his time doing something productive.

In the meantime there was nothing further that Prosecutor Mellis could do and so she said her goodbyes to the two men before leaving for her office.

Beckoning Lanzi to follow him Nardi was approached by an officer who had arrived to report a possible witness. An old man living three floors above had apparently seen someone behaving suspiciously.

"Good morning," Nardi said, when standing in front of the man. "I'm Inspector Nardi. Can you tell me exactly what you saw?"

"I already told this guy," the old man answered, indicating the officer in a sullen manner.

"Sure, but I'd be grateful, if you could repeat it to me."

"So…" the man started, snorting, "It was half past ten and I was going out to have my usual walk…"

"Morning or night?"

"What?"

"Half past ten in the morning or night?"

"What is this? Are you pretending to not understand? I already told your colleague. I'm talking about last night."

"Perfect. Please, continue," Nardi said, realizing he was in front of an odd type of character.

"Good," the old man continued. "Like I was saying, I was going out for my usual walk, when I heard a man at the main door, shouting. I think he wanted to enter but he couldn't. He'd jumped out of a car and ran to the door. And, when he couldn't reach it in time, he started shouting."

"Did you know him?" Nardi asked.

"Who?"

"The man. Had you seen him before?"

"No. I don't think so."

"And seeing a stranger trying to gain entry in that way and at that time of the night, you didn't think about calling somebody?"

"I didn't say he was a stranger."

"What do you mean? You said you didn't know him."

"I don't, but maybe someone else did. As far as I know, he

could be somebody who had forgotten his keys."

"Well… I guess you would have recognized one of your neighbors," Lanzi intervened.

"Why? Do you think I know everybody here? I haven't lived here for long and I only know a couple of people in the building. I mind my own business."

"I have to say you are not helping us much," Nardi said. "Can you at least describe the car?"

"No, I didn't notice what it looked like."

"But do you think you would recognize the man, should you see him again?"

Nardi was beginning to lose his patience.

"Maybe. I don't know. It was dark and…"

"Ok, ok. That's enough," Nardi said. "We'll need you to come to the police station to sign a statement and… If you can… help us reconstruct the features of the man."

"What? I don't want to go out."

Nardi didn't answer. He didn't have any intention of wasting any more time with the man. He gave the officer the task of taking care of him and he began his descent down the stairs with Lanzi.

When they arrived at the second floor, another police officer approached Nardi.

"Inspector, we have spoken to all the residents," the officer said. "Apart from four people who have already left for work and a fifth, Rita Visentini. It seems she left this morning to visit her family. Her neighbor says she should be back in a couple of days."

"Fine. Keep me informed," Nardi replied, continuing down the stairs. "I want all the details ready as soon as possible. And try to locate the Visentini woman."

The two of them were now in the hallway and as Nardi saw the mailboxes he decided to check whether the victim's mailbox contained anything of interest. Mail could tell a lot about a person, he knew.

Unfortunately, the box was empty, but the inspector noticed the name written next to Fogliani's.

"Who is Franco Mezzana?" he asked Lanzi.

"Oh, right. With the Doctor Padovani's arrival I forgot to mention it. It seems the woman had lived with this man until a few months ago. Unfortunately, I can't tell you more than that. Apparently, the other residents didn't know him very well. Even though from what I understand, he'd lived here for a year."

"Let's find everything we can about him then," Nardi said.

"Ok," Lanzi replied.

Despite the fact that a couple of hours had passed when they left the building, the crowd outside hadn't dispersed. On the contrary. It had almost doubled. A scene Nardi was more than accustomed to. However, each time it happened he couldn't help but ask himself the same question: why do people find other peoples' tragedies interesting. Sure, death was always fascinating but only for the survivors, for those who could still talk about it. But, in his line of work he had become detached from both the dead and the living, not allowing his emotions to get in the way of an investigation.

Leaving Lanzi on the threshold, Nardi said his goodbyes and, giving one last look at the chaotic mass of people he turned, took his sunglasses from his jacket pocket, put them on and proceeded to his car.

CHAPTER 34

Once back at the station, Nardi went immediately to his office where he signalled the deputy to come to him. Nardi was just about to sit down when he heard the man knocking at the door. "Did you want to see me, Inspector?"

"Yes, Cataldo, come in. Look into this Rosa Fogliani," he answered, giving him a piece of paper. "And also this Mezzana. It seems he had lived with the woman for the last year. Here are their full names and the address."

"I'll start now."

"Update me as soon as you have some news."

The man left the office and Nardi flopped back onto his chair to think about what he had seen so far that day. The act of mulling over the crime scene and reliving the morning's inspections allowed him to evaluate details that may appear meaningless, but were often useful for the investigation. Even though he valued his forensic colleagues, he didn't love technology. He had always trusted his instinct; the amazing machine that was the human mind.

He thought back to the messy living room and the bloody razor next to the victim, and concluded that it hadn't been a crime of passion. Sure, a violent argument could bring about an impulsive, irrational action, but the cutting weapon wasn't where it should be. The corpse was on the threshold, and its position clearly indicated that the woman was facing the door when she had been attacked. The proper place for a razor was the bathroom, he mused. If her killer's homicidal impulse had exploded inside the house, the murder would have occurred differently; in the living room perhaps, or the bathroom or even in the corridor, where they had found the body. But if that had been the case the victim would have been looking at her aggressor, with her face to the inside of the apartment.

Nardi was assuming that if the crime scene hadn't been altered, it had to be a premeditated murder. In this case, the razor, left there, led him to think it was an attempt to throw the inquiry off the track. But for the moment, this was just speculation on his part. Unfortunately, the medical examiner couldn't say if the body had been moved; there was nothing he could do but wait for the lab report to confirm his assumptions.

Nardi was so engrossed in his thoughts that he jumped when somebody knocked at the door. "Yes?" he murmured, still lost in his hypotheses.

"Inspector, the statements from the old man and the woman have been recorded," Sergeant Lanzi said. "This is what we were able to reconstruct based on the man's indications," he added, giving Nardi a piece of paper. "But I don't think it's that useful."

The print showed the hint of a face that could represent a million different people. "And this is meant to be an identikit?" Nardi queried.

"Unfortunately, the old man is a little out of it. I don't know how much we can trust his statement. But, according to what he says, the man he saw should be between one meter seventy and one meter eighty tall."

"Slim, overweight...?"

"He couldn't say."

"So we don't have anything," Nardi said, bored.

"We'll need to wait for the crime lab report before we can

come up with any firm theories as to the sequence of events."

"Yeah"

The deputy returned to Nardi's office and entering said, "Here's the information you wanted regarding the man, Mezzana. This is his current address." He put his results on Nardi's desk and turned to leave.

"Ah! Cataldo..." Nardi called him back.

"Yes?"

"Please, make sure that the victim's family has been informed."

"Of course."

When Cataldo had left, Nardi and Lanzi began reading the information regarding the victim and her ex-partner.

"Here he is," Lanzi said.

"Who?"

"Mezzana."

The sergeant handed Nardi the picture. He frowned and put it next to the identikit picture to compare them. Unfortunately, the description given by the old man was so vague that making any comparison was useless, he gave up and went back to examining the information.

"Here's something interesting," Nardi said, a little while later.

"What?" Lanzi asked.

"They both worked at the same place."

"You're right," Lanzi said, who in the meantime had started reading the other report. "He still works there."

"At last, we have a starting point. I suggest we go there to... What's the name?" Nardi looked again at the documents. "Oh, yes, here it is. *VitaNuova*. Maybe we'll discover something useful there."

"Do you think the woman's job could have something to do with it?"

"I don't know, Ettore. We'll find out when we get there, I think. In the meantime, let's go talk to this Mezzana and see what he can tell us."

Seeing a smile appearing on Lanzi's face, Nardi looked at him, curious. He was about to ask him the reason for his odd expression, when he realized that he had called him by his first name. It wasn't the first time. Ettore Lanzi had been transferred to the headquarters a few years ago. Nardi had never become comfortable in maintaining formal behavior between himself and his team. Sometimes he forgot that the relationships were merely professional. But with Lanzi it was different because he reminded Nardi of the son he could have had. The boy had died when he was born, and would now have been the same age as Lanzi. Nardi liked to consider their relationship as more than a simple bond between officer and subordinate; his paternal feelings becoming more evident.

To cover his embarrassment he said, indifferently "It's funny."

"What is?" Lanzi asked.

"The center's name. *VitaNuova*. A little comical I would say, since we are investigating a murder... That old man, is he still here?"

"Yes. Why?"

"Show him Mezzana's picture. Who knows, maybe he can recognize him from that?"

"Ok. But it won't help much. That guy's mind doesn't work as it's supposed to," Lanzi concluded, leaving the office.

Nardi gave Cataldo a further task of researching the rehab center and its employees. He then waited at the station's doorway for Sergeant Lanzi to return. After a while, he arrived and, from his dark look, Nardi realized that the attempt of facial recognition from the old man had been futile.

***

Now at the *VitaNuova* center they parked and got out of the car. Nardi and Lanzi made their way to the center's entrance where Nardi noticed the architectural beauty of the place and the stunning flower-beds that surrounded the entire building. Since he had never been in a rehab community, he wondered if the environment was part of the therapy. After all, overcoming a problem like drug addiction was no joke. And maybe the visual counted in the recovery process.

Three men were smoking at the entrance to the building, but none of them turned to look at the visitors. Wearing plainclothes, the two policemen looked like regular people. As soon as they entered, they saw a board showing a plan of the building. It also gave the directions to reach the various departments. Lanzi immediately began to study it.

"It's right there," he said, pointing with his finger.

Seeing the reception area Nardi saw a woman behind a desk and, approaching her, he said, "Good morning. We need to talk with the director."

Before they could introduce themselves, the woman shook her head and said: "I'm sorry, sir. But unfortuna…"

"I'm Inspector Nardi," he interrupted her, showing her his badge. "It's important that I talk to the director."

The woman frowned, looking at the two of them with a puzzled expression. Then she said again, "I'm sorry, but the director isn't here. I don't know what to tell you. Usually, she isn't absent. But she hasn't been here all week."

"There must be a substitute. A person we can talk to."

"What's happening?" somebody asked at that moment.

Nardi turned around and saw that a man had appeared in the hall.

"These are police officers," the secretary said.

"I'm sorry, who are you?" Nardi asked.

"I'm Giampaolo Bernini, the HR manager."

"Oh, good! Then maybe we can talk to you."

"Yes, but about what?"

Nardi was about to answer, but then realized that the woman would hear and stopped. He looked at Bernini for assistance.

"Come," Bernini said. "Let's go to the director's office."

"But Mr. Bernini…" the secretary said.

"Don't worry, Stefania. The Doctor won't mind," he reassured her. "My office is at the end of the corridor and I think these gentlemen are in a hurry."

They entered the director's room and, once the door was closed, Bernini invited them to sit; he sat on Mrs. Colasanti's chair.

"So, gentlemen. How can I help?"

Nardi stared at the man for a couple of seconds. He briefly looked at his sergeant, unsure whether to speak or not. "You see, Mr. Bernini..." he finally said. "We are here to investigate a murder that happened last night. We know the victim was one of your employees. Rosa Fogliani."

"Doctor Fogliani? Killed?" Bernini said, startled.

His brow crinkled and his eyes widened, the man was struck dumb, a confused expression on his face, shocked by what he had just heard.

"Can you tell us what her job was?" Nardi asked, after a short pause.

But the man didn't reply. Bewildered, he seemed to be wondering whether to believe what he had just been told.

"Mr. Bernini," Lanzi said.

"Eh? What?"

"Did you hear the inspector's question?"

"Oh, I'm sorry. You've shocked me with this news. What were you saying?"

"I was asking you what her job was here, at the center," Nardi repeated.

"She was the therapy coordinator. Mainly, she managed the center operators and was the mediator between them and the directorship. But she also supervised various patients' cases, and she collaborated during the preliminary meetings." Bernini explained.

"So, if I understand correctly, she had contact with everybody here. With the personnel, as well as the patients." Nardi said.

"Well yes, I would say so," Bernini agreed, baffled.

"And you don't know if somebody may have wanted to get rid of her for any reason?" Lanzi asked.

"I don't think so. On the contrary! Everyone loved the doctor. Maybe apart from..."

As if fearing he had made a gaffe, the man didn't complete his sentence but his expression had changed to one of distress.

"Apart from..." Nardi urged him.

"Well, you see... well... I don't think this would concern your case."

"Let us decide. What name were you about to say?"

"I mean, there has been some friction between Ms. Fogliani and Mrs. Colasanti for some time. Everybody knew it. But it was about stupid things. Nothing serious. Stupid arguments between women."

"And this person is...?"

"Oh, right. I'm sorry. Lisa Colasanti is the director."

Nardi turned his gaze to Lanzi, as if to ask for his opinion. He had immediately connected the woman's absence with a possible involvement and, from the thoughtful look of the sergeant, he realized he had arrived at the same conclusion.

For a moment, Nardi thought that the name reminded him of something, but he couldn't link it to anything or anybody that he could remember at the moment. Leaving those thoughts aside he asked, "What can you tell me about Franco Mezzana?"

"I don't understand. What's Mezzana got to do with this?" Bernini asked.

"Please, Mr. Bernini. Just answer my question."

"Well, what can I tell you? He is the medical-legal branch manager. But I assure you you're getting the wrong end of the stick. It's true that things didn't always go well between them, but he would have thrown himself from a rock, if Ms. Fogliani had asked him to."

"Can you ask someone to call him? I'd like to ask him some questions." Nardi said.

Without replying, Bernini lifted the receiver and asked the secretary to call Mezzana. She told Bernini that Mezzana had left before the end of his shift. A knowing glance went between the two policemen but then, the unexpected entrance of a woman into the office interrupted their thoughts.

"What's happening? What are you doing here?" she asked.

Noticing her irritation and her determined demeanour, Nardi thought that she must be the director.

"Oh, good morning," Bernini said, standing up and approaching her to shake her hand. "You can't imagine what has happened."

The woman looked at both the inspector and the sergeant, before turning her gaze to Bernini, seeking an explanation.

"Oh, right! I'm sorry," he rushed to say. "These are Inspector Nardi and Sergeant Lanzi." And, for the sake of the two officers, he gestured towards the woman and added, "Sabrina Colasanti. She is the director's sister."

"Inspector? Sergeant?" she said, shocked. "What's happening? Why are you here?"

"It's about Doctor Fogliani," Bernini answered. "Apparently, she's been killed."

A gasp of surprise came from outside the room. The door had remained open during this time and Bernini's words had reached the secretary. Bernini rushed to close the door, but it was too late. Doubtless the news would now spread quickly throughout the center.

Nardi didn't give too much importance to it and, turning to Sabrina, he asked: "Can I ask you something, Ma'am?"

"Sure. Go ahead."

"Do you know where to find your sister? We need to talk to her as soon as possible."

"Could I talk to you privately?" she said, making a sign to leave the room.

Nardi stood up and followed her into the corridor. Once alone, the woman briefly looked around her. In a soft tone, she said: "Inspector, my sister has just been admitted into the clinic. This is why I'm here. I came in person because I wish to keep this confidential. I'm sure you can understand that."

"Actually no. I don't see what there is to hide."

"Lisa is an ex-alcoholic and now it seems she has relapsed. Her story was a scandal once before and should the press discover it, they would embroider it. Sometimes, it's not easy to have our family name."

It was then that Nardi was able place the name. Lisa Colasanti was Della Torre's wife, a business bigwig. Nardi knew he had already heard the name. "I understand," he said. "You can count on my discretion."

"Thank you," she answered, smiling slightly.

"And where has your sister been admitted?"

"Why?"

"Because I need to talk to her."

"Forgive me, Inspector," the woman replied, frowning again. "You're not thinking what I imagine, aren't you?"

"What do you mean?"

"I hope you don't believe Lisa is somehow involved in this murder?"

Nardi didn't reply. Rephrasing his words, he asked again where he would find Lisa Colasanti. Sabrina's face darkened as she unwillingly gave him the information. She then abruptly turned and walked away, ending their conversation.

Inside the room, Lanzi was still talking with Bernini, asking him some more questions. Nardi waited for him outside the office until, finally, the sergeant shook Bernini's hand to thank him for his time, Bernini returned the gesture and together they left the office.

"What do you think, Inspector?" Lanzi said. "Should we visit this Mezzana?"

"Of course!" Nardi answered. "But before that, I suggest we eat something. It's lunch time and I can't think clearly when my stomach is empty."

CHAPTER 35

Ivano went to work as he usually did but he was somewhat reluctant today. In different circumstances, he wouldn't have minded taking a day off. But today he didn't want to risk it.

It was lunch time and his shift was over. But before leaving, he decided to go to the administration office to check what was happening there. He wanted to see whether somebody had noticed Rosa's absence.

As he walked down the corridor to the secretariat, he crossed paths with two men coming from the opposite direction. The oldest one turned his eyes slightly toward Ivano and looked at him in a strange way. Keeping his eyes straight ahead Ivano continued to walk, frowning, a feeling of dread coming over him. He ignored the man who had looked at him so piercingly and continued along the corridor.

Soon enough, the two men left the area. Ivano, no longer hearing the sound of their steps, looked back. For some reason, the image of the man had remained strongly imprinted on his mind.

He finally arrived in front of the administration office and, once inside, he found Stefania crying. Seeing her face wet with tears, he handed her a tissue. Trying to comfort her, he asked her what had happened, but she didn't answer. In a succession of sobs and moans, she continued to dry her eyes without being able to talk.

"Come on! Stop crying," he said, putting a hand on her shoulder.

She raised her face, her expression sad, and tried to talk. But she was unable to articulate a reply to Ivano. Stefania was distraught and Ivano was losing patience with her. He was about to say something when Stefania sighed: "Doct... Doctor Fogliani..."

Her hesitant words caught Ivano's attention immediately. His expression changed. With his eyes wide open, he stared at the woman with an intense and inquiring look. He wasn't going to allow his anxiety to overwhelm him, he needed to remain calm. Ivano stayed silent, waiting for Stefania to start speaking coherently. It was clear that she needed to talk to somebody. Soon she stopped crying, sighed two or three times, dried her eyes completely and began to speak.

"Doctor Fogliani has been killed," she said in a firmer tone.

"What?" Ivano said.

He tried to show extreme incredulity, with a mask of disbelief, as if the news had taken him by surprise. He didn't have to make much of an effort because he was truly surprised. The fact that they already knew about it at the center alarmed him. He knew it would happen. But he didn't think it would have been so soon.

"But who told you this?" he asked, a skeptical expression on his face.

"The policemen. They just left."

"And what did they say?"

"I don't know. They came to ask the Doctor some questions. They spoke with Mr. Bernini in the director's office. I don't know what they said. I've just heard Mr. Bernini informing the Doctor's sister about what had happened."

Ivano felt himself freeze.

"Which sister?" he asked, frantic.

Stefania looked at him puzzled, almost annoyed by his behavior.

"The director's sister," she answered.

"Ah!" he said, holding back a sigh.

For a moment, he thought Stefania was referring to Giada. But he wasn't thinking straight and knew it was illogical that they would have been talking to her.

"And what did they tell you? Didn't they ask you anything?" he asked.

"No. They wanted to talk with the director."

"What an awful thing to have happened," he said, wondering if he should try to talk with Bernini.

Bernini was the only one who knew the situation, and Ivano wanted to be sure that the police were there for Mezzana and not for him. That was the plan; misdirection. However, the thought that something may have gone wrong made him reluctant to seek out Bernini. He remembered the look from the guy in the corridor as well, the policeman, he felt that in just a short glance he had studied him from head to toe. Ivano was certain that he had left enough evidence to connect the murder to someone else, he just needed to know what, or who, the police were looking for.

He couldn't take any risks. The idea of asking Bernini for explanations was a gamble he preferred to avoid. After all, there were many signs connecting the crime to Mezzana. With the evidence he had left at the scene, he didn't think he needed to worry.

While trying to convince himself that everything was going the right way for him, he faked a sorry expression and said goodbye to Stefania, before leaving the secretariat.

***

Going home, Ivano remained stuck in the rush hour traffic. A moment of stalemate, during which his misgivings about the whole scenario returned.

He had tried to push his fears away in any way he could, and he would have liked, at that moment, to step on the gas, and speed away into oblivion. But the heavy traffic prohibited that course of action. The traffic lights changed from green to yellow and then to red and cars proceeded intermittently. Observing the slow stopping and starting, made of quick accelerations and sharp brakes, Ivano noticed the paradox of the line that moved with the red light, and how it stopped when the green light appeared. A discordant process that finished only when he approached the intersection, where everything returned to normal. There, the green and the red lights alternated in a regular way, in a timeframe that permitted the first cars to move forward, giving the others at the back the impression of proceeding slowly. He thought this to be an apparent contradiction in terms underlying, in its oddness, a hidden truth. The rhythmic movement of each car proceeding one after the other actually seemed to express how the whole world depended on a separate and distinct element, despite always being connected.

He knew that these were very profound thoughts running through his mind but they had cleared his consciousness enough for him to realise that his fear of being caught was overwhelming him. He also recognized that what had happened between him and Giada the previous day was part of the problem. After all, historically, their destinies had joined in a deep and indissoluble link, where the freedom of one depended on the freedom of the other. In that moment of lucidity, Ivano felt the abrupt need to see her, to explain, to find a solution that would bring them back to the starting point of their relationship. Now free of the traffic jam, he made a U-turn and headed to her house.

When he was about a kilometer from her house, he saw Giada from his car. Stopped at an intersection by traffic lights, he saw her entering a park, a place where she used to go to enjoy its serenity and peace. It was where he had first met her. Waiting for the lights to change he remembered their relationship and the way it had ended, and he realized that that part of his life had never completely closed. Ivano felt that destiny had given him a second chance, reuniting their paths, and he didn't want to throw this opportunity of a reconciliation to the wind. As soon as he was able to park the car, he ran out to look for Giada.

A metallic fence surrounded the entire park, interrupted by a high iron gate that allowed for access.

Once inside, Ivano scanned the area but there was no trace of Giada, just a tramp sitting quietly on a bench. The park was immense, with trees and bushes everywhere serving as potential places for an individual to hide. Along the narrow paths it would be possible to disappear with the utmost ease. Wondering if he would be able to find her, Ivano approached the man sitting on the bench, threw a few coins into the box at his feet, and asked him if he'd seen a woman pass by; he hadn't. He began to wander, hopelessly. His worries and concerns now morphing into frantic impatience.

At that time of the day, the park was practically deserted and had an almost unnatural silence about it. Giada seemed to have disappeared. Ivano was fast becoming anxious, where could she have gone?

He continued to walk around for a further twenty minutes or so until, finally, she was there, in front of him. Sat on a bench in the shadow of some trees. Ivano recognized her immediately, thanks to her mass of red hair blazing in front of the backdrop of trees.

Without hesitating, he made his way to her and when he was a few steps away from her, he pronounced her name in a whisper.

She turned, with her lazy, almost imperturbable temper simmering on the surface. As soon as she saw him, a shocked expression appeared on her face and, abruptly, she jumped up from the bench.

"What the hell are you doing here? What do you want now?" she screamed.

"Giada, please. We need to talk."

"I don't have anything to say to you," she replied. "We are over. You've let me down and I don't want to ever see you again."

"Giada, please…"

"I told you to leave. Leave me in peace!"

"You don't get it. Today the police came to the center," Ivano said. "Things are slipping out of our hands."

Curious about what he had said, Giada stopped shouting. She stared at him, willing him to speak. But Ivano, suddenly feeling as if he was being judged, couldn't find the courage to continue.

CHAPTER 36

Stressed with the weight of what was happening between Rosa and himself, Franco hadn't been able to complete his working day. He had gone home early, still shocked by the multitude of competing issues threatening his sanity. His head felt ready to explode with so many mixed emotions vying for his attention.

The dirty crockery from breakfast was still on the kitchen table but he wasn't going to worry about it at the moment, he really didn't want to do anything while contemplating his immediate problems. Plus, the untidy environment mirrored his mood perfectly. He wished he could leave his thoughts there too, together with the dishes scattered on the table. But he knew that he couldn't. To rid himself of his worries would not be as simple as clearing the table. Resigned, he went to the living room, hoping to find a bit of peace.

That morning, Rosa hadn't shown up for work and he thought that she was probably avoiding him. After all, it would be a normal reaction, following the awful argument they had had the night before. Realizing that he had crossed all acceptable lines, he understood that he could only blame himself if she didn't want to see him anymore. Up until recently, he had been certain that he could change. But he was weak and events that were out of his control inflamed his short temper, inevitably, and not sure if he could blame fate, his decisions when facing one dilemma after another, generally led him to choose the wrong path each time.

Lost in these thoughts, Franco was sprawled on his sofa evaluating his mistakes and wondering if there was any way to reverse them. His gaze turned to his son's picture, resting on a shelf. Franco felt that everything in his life had gone wrong, and he couldn't help but wallow in self-pity. He thought back to when, a week after Diego's birthday, he had gone to Tiziana on a mission to talk to his son. All hopes were dashed as he realized that his ex had no intention of surrendering to his requests. Meanly deceiving him, she had at first given him some hope of reconstructing the pieces of a ruined family, only to kill those expectations with an irrevocable refusal.

Tiziana had made it clear that her decision was non-negotiable. He had been forced to close this chapter of his life. After this final devastating blow he was certain that he would never experience the love from his son again. Franco had reluctantly said goodbye to Diego, leaving him in a negative, resentful environment.

Crushed with feelings of guilt, Franco had left Tiziana's house cursing himself. He realized that he had ignored the whole situation for too long and now that his life felt shattered he knew he couldn't blame anybody but himself.

This was why he couldn't humor Rosa.

Maybe, because of her lack of experience, she'd thought she could manipulate the lives of others. The experience of losing his son was one he didn't want to repeat. He couldn't allow it to be happen again. So certain was he that the child was his he decided that, now the dust had settled from last night, he would call her. Maybe talking to each other on the phone, and their not being able to touch each other, would assist them to have a civil and quiet conversation without their anger getting in the way.

He dialed the number and waited to hear her voice. But the telephone rang hollow. After a couple more tries, Franco hung up and let it go. Since he hadn't seen her at work, he was sure he would find her at home, but her not answering his call felt to him to be a bad omen somehow. Not wanting to deal with questions for which he didn't have an answer, he tried to convince himself that she had perhaps gone for a walk. To get some fresh air and collect her thoughts. But then Franco remembered that she had spoken about another man. Perhaps she was with him, in his arms. This notion was unbearable to Franco so he picked up the telephone again. As he did so somebody rang his doorbell.

Positive it was likely to be a salesperson, he didn't answer. He thought that, whoever it was would soon get tired of waiting and would leave. But the bell kept ringing insistently. The person on the other side didn't want to go away so, resigned, he stood up from the sofa and made his way to the door.

When he opened it there were two men standing there. One middle-aged and a younger one. Both were looking at Franco quizzically.

"May I help you?" Franco asked.

"Good morning Mr. Mezzana. I'm Inspector Nardi," the older man answered. "If you don't mind, we have some questions for you."

"The police? What do you want with me?" Franco replied, puzzled.

"Can we come in please?"

Curious and a little shocked, Franco led them into the living room and, as soon as they took their seats, he asked again, worried: "So… can I know why you're here?"

"We're investigating a murder and maybe you can give us some useful information."

"Murder? Who? And what does it have to do with me?"

The policeman who had introduced himself as Inspector Nardi was about to answer when something seemed to stop him. For a few seconds, he looked at Franco hesitantly and, then finally said: "It's Rosa Fogliani. She was found dead at her apartment earlier today."

"What?" Franco cried. "You're joking, aren't you?"

"Unfortunately no. The murder happened last night but wasn't reported until this morning."

"No, no! It's impossible. You're wrong."

Franco thought the two men had made a terrible mistake. They had identified the wrong person, hadn't they? But they didn't look like they were joking. They knew what they were saying was true. But, refusing to believe their words, Franco remained staring into space, unable to understand the turmoil of his emotions.

"We know that you and the doctor had been in a relationship," Nardi said.

Franco didn't react. It was as if the two men weren't in the room. He continued to sit with a vacant gaze on his face, not speaking or moving. When he eventually absorbed what Nardi had told him, he felt his emotions welling up inside of him in anguish. His features transformed into a mask of pain, of true despair. Leaning an elbow on the arm of the sofa, Franco raised a hand and sunk his forehead onto it. He tried to hold back his tears, but he couldn't stop them from falling.

"No. It's impossible," he started to repeat, almost as if to convince himself. "Tell me it's not true."

Nardi and Lanzi looked at each other puzzled and, giving Franco time to vent his emotions, they waited in silence. "But how did it happen? Who did it?" he asked, still trying to understand.

"She was assaulted in her house with a sharp weapon. Possibly by somebody she probably knew," Nardi answered. "But for the moment, we have no suspects. We are checking all possible lines of investigation."

Franco felt choked with a grief like a brutal pain searing through his emotions and, trying again to hold back tears, he brought a hand to his mouth.

"I'm sorry," he said. And, standing up, he tried to regain his composure. "Please, give me a second."

As soon as he was alone in the bathroom, he opened the tap to refresh himself. He let the water run cold before throwing it on his face. Feeling his legs give way, he leaned on the sink, until he felt the urge to vomit and instinctively brought a hand to his chest. He was about to vomit but the regurgitation cut short in his throat. He sipped some water to get rid of the taste in his mouth, composed himself and returned to the living room. "I'm really sorry," he said. "But the news you have given me..."

"So, Mr. Mezzana... Can you confirm your relationship with the victim?" Nardi asked again.

"Yes. Rosa and I were a couple until recently."

"Is there any particular reason why you broke up?"

"Well, I wouldn't say so," he answered, a little puzzled. "You know, people change over time."

"But working in the same place, you had to meet each other fairly regularly I would have thought. Did you have a good relationship?"

"Forgive me asking. But are you referring to something in particular?" Franco enquired, beginning to grasp the insinuations against him in these questions.

"Well, according to what people say, there was some kind of hostility between you two." Nardi replied.

"Yes, it's true. We hadn't been getting along lately. So what?"

"Could I know why?"

"I'm sorry, Inspector... Are you accusing me of something?"

"I am just trying to reconstruct the trail of events leading to her death. Where were you last night between ten and midnight?"

There was no doubt any more. The policeman was trying to trap him. To answer truthfully would mean serving his head up on a silver plate. That was exactly the time he had left Rosa's house and, by admitting it, he would become the prime suspect. He didn't have an alibi for this timeframe and so there was nothing he could do or say that would prove his innocence. Overwhelmed with fear, he decided that lying to the police was the best option.

"I was home," he said, avoiding the policeman's eyes.

"Can somebody confirm it?"

"No, nobody. I live alone now and I don't think anybody saw

me coming home."

"Ok," Nardi said, standing up. "Enough for the moment. But remain at our disposal. We may need you again to clarify your story."

"Of course," Franco replied, accompanying the two men to the door.

They shook hands on the threshold. But from their skeptical look, he realized that his answer hadn't been enough to convince them. He understood that lying to them had been a stupid decision. Soon, they would discover the truth. And, at that point, demonstrating his innocence would become even more difficult. But it was too late to fix it.

CHAPTER 37

The following morning, Nardi made a small deviation from his usual path into work. The *Santa Caterina* clinic was on his way and so, before going to the station, he decided to go there first to speak with Lisa Colasanti.

Leaving the parking area, he saw a black Porsche stop a little way ahead of him and a very elegant man stepping out of it. Looking around, Nardi noticed that there were many luxury cars parked. He realized that the place hosted some very wealthy people.

He had often seen Mrs. Colasanti in the newspapers and on TV and, even if on occasions he had heard negative reports about her, he would have never thought that she had an alcoholic past. Nothing was ever as it seemed. He knew that well. His job had taught him that reality and fiction were closely entwined.

Every day he faced some very good actors who almost perfectly hid their features, emotions and moods. People who could compete with some of the best actors but who, by choice or chance, had taken paths that crossed legal lines. For this reason, he didn't differentiate between criminals and witnesses. He just divided the guilty ones into two simple categories: aware and unaware.

Nardi's belief was that if the first ones lied (the criminals), to protect their freedom, the others (the witnesses) did it when, feeling involved, they feared being implicated in a crime. In both cases it was impossible not to change the course of events. Reasons changed but, soon or later, everybody lied. And that rule didn't exclude him; he continued to lie to himself day after day, thinking that incompetent doctors were responsible for his wife's death. An excuse that allowed him to live with the suffocating feeling of guilt that had accompanied him for years.

It was clear that the director had her own skeletons hidden in the closet. He wasn't interested in her alcoholism and what had driven her to become an alcoholic he just needed information from her that connected her to this case. Moving to the entrance door, he wondered if the lies she would come out with would be relevant or not.

As soon as he entered, he headed to the reception desk to ask the whereabouts of Lisa Colasanti's room. But before reaching it, he heard somebody calling him by name and, turning, he saw Sabrina Colasanti walking towards him.

"Oh, good morning," he said. "Have you come to visit your sister?"

"Why would I be here otherwise?" Sabrina replied, bluntly.

"Yeah! It was a stupid question. Well, it seems we both have the same idea."

"You're wasting your time, Inspector. I told you. My sister wouldn't be able to lace up her shoes without her husband. Let alone figure out how to kill somebody."

"That might be true. But I have to do my job." Nardi said.

"Well since you're already here, judge for yourself," she said, giving him a sign to proceed. "I'm sure once you've seen her it will resolve any doubts you may have about her."

"I hope so," Nardi replied.

The two of them walked through a small entranceway to reach the elevators. When the doors opened, a woman was coming up from the lower floor.

"What floor?" she asked.

"Fifth, thanks," Sabrina replied.

The doors closed and the elevator started its ascent.

***

Monti had just finished his daily tour around the building. As soon as he entered his studio, his mobile phone started ringing and when he answered, Della Torre's voice echoed on the other side.

"Oh, it's you," he said.

"I wanted to be sure everything was clear."

"Listen, Vincenzo…"

A trembling voice underlined his hesitation.

"Listen to me," Della Torre shut him up. "This must be done today. I hope everything will go as it's supposed to. There's no room for second thoughts. So do what you have to and don't make me regret having helped you. Or, I can assure you, you'll pay for it."

"Please, Vincenzo. I can't…"

Riccardo was about to add something else, when he realized the communication had been interrupted. With his mouth half open, he remained looking at the mobile phone. He was very reluctant about the idea of killing. The fact that they were talking about Lisa made everything even harder. With what courage was he to look his wife in the eye having killed her best friend?

Since the day he had accepted Vincenzo's proposal, he had begun to detest himself and his situation. At the thought of what he was being asked to do, there wasn't a part of his being that didn't fight against it. But he couldn't avoid it. He had taken the money, and he had already spent a lot of it. He had gotten rid of his debts, but was now stuck in an even bigger problem.

During the days following his meeting with Vincenzo he had continued looking for a solution to escape his horrific situation. But it was useless. Riccardo knew that, should he not carry out the task, that Vincenzo's "friends" would be more of a threat to him than those of *Sbieco's*. And to make the situation worse Vincenzo had threatened Riccardo's wife as well. Riccardo couldn't tolerate the thought that Elena may be at risk because of his actions. He wanted to retain his final piece of dignity and, taking courage, he made his way to fulfil his own death sentence. He had sold his soul to the devil and now he had come to collect.

Passing various wards, he arrived in front of the room where Lisa was staying. Ensuring that nobody was around, he knocked at the door and entered and, without attracting attention, blocked the lock before speaking.

"Hi, Lisa," he said. "How are you today?"

"Oh, Riccardo! Come. It's a pleasure to see you. I really needed to see a friendly face."

"I bet," he replied. "It must be difficult for you."

"It is. But I'm trying my best."

Not being able to meet her eyes, Riccardo bent his head to stare at the violet points pigmenting the floor, while Lisa's voice became a sound in the distance. He was sure she was talking, but he couldn't understand what she was saying. His mind was elsewhere, somewhere relaxed and peaceful; he wanted everything to remain that way. Nonetheless, he knew he had to do what he had come for. He went out onto the room's small balcony and, looking out, he nodded to Lisa to follow him.

That side of the building overlooked the pine forest, far away from prying eyes. His task was to throw her over in order to stage a suicide. After her admission, nobody would doubt it. She would appear like a depressed woman who had decided to end her own suffering.

"Come," he said. "Some fresh air will help you, it'll do you good. It's a glorious, sunny day."

"I'm sorry, Riccardo, but I don't feel like it," she answered.

"Come on! You need to move, you want to get better don't you?"

She looked outside, unsure whether to stand up or not.

"Come!" he repeated. "It's only a few steps."

"Okay," Lisa said, getting up from the bed. "You're right," she said once up. "It really is a lovely day."

"Lisa…"

Leaving the sentence unfinished and full of worry, Riccardo made a step back to reveal his anguish.

"What's up?"

"Forgive me. I don't want to. But I can't let Elena… He threatened to kill us both."

"What are you talk…"

At that moment, Riccardo bent forward and quickly lifted Lisa from the ground. Using all of his strength, he catapulted her over the balcony rail.

She instinctively caught hold of the railing, clinging on for her life. Feeling her body hanging in the void, she emitted a scream of terror. Riccardo looked into her shocked eyes, still incredulous.

"I'm sorry," he said. "But Elena's life is at stake."

And saying this, he caught those hands that, rebelling against death, refused to let go. Forcing them, he lifted one finger and then another and another, until the strength of one of her hands lost its hold. Lisa's body started to swing in the air and her screams became louder.

***

Nardi let Sabrina Colasanti lead him along a series of corridors. They were a short distance from the room, when they heard a scream coming from inside. Instinctively, the two looked at each other and ran to investigate. Nardi immediately tried to open the door, but it was locked.

"Lisa!" Sabrina screamed. "Lisa! What's happening? Open the door."

"Help! Help me!" they heard her screaming from the other side.

Nardi launched himself at the door, kicking frantically to get it to open. When the lock finally broke, he saw a guy on the balcony. The man was grappling with the body of a woman who was behind the railing and who continued to scream crazily, while swinging in the void.

Throwing himself inside, he caught her by one arm. Turning to the man, he said, "Don't just stand there. Help me."

But the man just looked at him, terrified. He then turned quickly and ran out of the room. Nardi suddenly realized what had been happening. At first, he had thought the man was there to help the poor woman, but clearly it was exactly the opposite. His intention had been to throw her down.

Sabrina, at first petrified by the scene, hurried to reach the inspector and help retrieve her sister from disaster. The two of them pulled at Lisa with all their strength until she was returned to the safety of the balcony.

"Are you ok?" Nardi asked.

She stared at him in terror and then realizing that she was safe, slumped to the ground. He left her in her sister's care and ran out to find the man who had fled the scene.

But the aggressor had disappeared.

"Where did he go?" he asked a couple of nurses.

"Who?" one responded.

"The man who came out of here. The guy wearing a white coat. Where did he go?"

"He turned right."

Nardi set off in pursuit.

For a fraction of a second, he saw the doctor in the distance, it looked like he was going into a ward. Nardi ran as fast as he could but the distance separating them was too great and he wasn't in good shape.

When he reached the point where the man had disappeared from view, Nardi realized he had lost him. Noticing the stairs' access a little way ahead, he went along to check if the doctor had escaped that way, he hadn't. Returning to the ward, Nardi came across the elegant man that he'd seen in the parking lot; visiting someone no doubt, Nardi quickly assumed.

"Did you see a man in a white coat pass here just now?"

Indicating a negative response the man just shook his head. Nardi let him go his own way and began to check all of the rooms.

The doctor had to be in one of them.

His search was suddenly halted, screams could be heard from outside. They came from down below and the inspector, curious, leaned out of the window. Even from this distance, he was able to see the man's body, surrounded by a pool of blood and a growing group of spectators.

Wondering what had made the guy carry out such a desperate act, Nardi remembered the shocked expression on the doctor's face before he fled Lisa's room. Finally, moving away from the window, he took his mobile phone from his pocket and called headquarters, he needed some back up, urgently.

CHAPTER 38

Rosa Fogliani's autopsy was scheduled for that morning at eleven. Nardi arrived at the morgue way past that time. Mrs Colasanti's attempted murder and her attacker's unexpected death had forced him to stay at the clinic longer than he had anticipated. Accidentally passing from the role of inspector to that of witness, he had stopped to update his colleagues. When he had finally managed to check the time, he'd remembered the autopsy.

As he entered the forensic science department, he felt overcome with a sense of claustrophobia. It happened every time he set foot in the place. He didn't like the environment at all. He understood that this was just one aspect of his job, he saw corpses all the time, but it was the one that he knew he would never get used to. He hated being there. He hated seeing bodies violated and being ransacked of everything that made them human. It was something that appalled him. Plus the few times he had attended autopsies, he had been nauseated by the terrible stench coming from inside the bodies.

Nardi stood in front of the autopsy room, and could detect that the atmosphere was clouded with a mixture of sweat and decay. The sickening air pervaded everything, from the walls to objects and clothes. It was an odor that seemed to cling to your body and stayed with you long after leaving the autopsy suite. He wondered if it was just him who was aware of the odors or did other outsiders sense it too. After all, those that worked there were probably immune to it, he thought.

Looking through the window of the metal door, he saw the victim's body on the autopsy table. In attendance was Doctor Padovani, his assistant and two other guys, probably senior medical students.

The autopsy was almost over. Both the external and internal examinations had been completed and Padovani was now stitching the body back to some semblance of a human being. Looking at those who were present and so full of interest, Nardi wondered what the attraction was, to want to undertake this type of work. Perhaps he was just envious; they had the courage to do something that he couldn't, something vital and important but still, he wouldn't have had the nerve, ever. In fact, at that moment he would have given anything to be somewhere else. But now he was here and he needed to know the outcome, so he waited patiently for Padovani to complete his task. Cutting tools of all sizes and shapes were placed on the steel counters. Knives and slicers, vibrating hacksaws, scissors and medical pliers, all the tools needed to section a body in the most intimate way. Various shelves housed labeled containers – small, medium, large – storing all types of organs in formalin; it looked like a small horror collection.

Luckily, he didn't have to witness the gruesome scene for much longer. He saw Padovani move away from the body, take off his protective garments and exit the room. He met Nardi waiting for him outside.

"Hello doctor. What can you tell me?"

The man passed a cloth over his face to wipe the sweat away. He toweled his neck and arms and then said: "The cause of death is confirmed as the laceration to the throat. There were some scratches at the base of the neck and a series of bruises on both arms. These wounds were inflicted before death. And we've found skin cells under the fingernails."

"So there was a fight?" Nardi asked.

"Yes. It seems that somebody grabbed her repeatedly and with significant intensity. The woman must have tried to struggle. But I can't tell if that's related to what happened afterwards." The doctor replied.

"Anything else?"

"From the wound's angulation I would say that the aggressor was around one meter eighty in height. Could be right-handed or ambidextrous."

"Is that all?"

"I think so, yes."

"Okay. Thank you for this. I'll not take up anymore of your time. Goodbye."

"See you soon, Inspector," Padovani replied.

Nardi was about to leave when the doctor slapped his forehead, and started to speak again.

"Oh! I almost forgot the most interesting thing," he said.

"What?" Nardi asked.

"The woman was pregnant."

"Pregnant?"

"Precisely. From the size of the fetus, I'd say she was just past her first trimester."

"Is it possible to find who the father was?"

"We'll soon have the DNA for possible comparisons. I have already taken a sample for the histological examination. But you'll have to wait a couple of days for the results."

"That's fine, doctor. Thank you." Nardi replied.

"For what? It's my job."

"Of course," Nardi said, feeling a little uncomfortable. Making a great effort to smile, he repeated: "It's your job."

As much as he considered pathologists' work to be gruesome and brutal, he deeply respected it. Padovani's role was essential for successful investigations into suspicious deaths.

Both men said their goodbyes and, before heading for the exit,

Nardi shot a last glance beyond the glass. He remembered that, as they had been unable to trace the victim's only relative, her sister, it had been suggested that a co-worker of the victim should be given the task of identifying the body.

He needed to contact the prosecutor, Ms. Mellis, to bring her up to speed on the events so far. He took his phone out of his pocket and called her. As always, Ms. Mellis had complete confidence in him. Without talking at length, she just asked that he keep her informed and to let her have the case files in a timely manner. It was a short call.

Leaving the building, Nardi felt liberated, as if he was leaving a prison, but one with the smell of death in place of bars. Feeling relieved, he took a couple of deep breaths, enough to fill his lungs. The air that day was anything but fresh but that simple and vital gesture revived him. His brain started to work again and, his energy restored, he thought again about the turn the investigation was taking. The fact that the woman was pregnant opened the door to new hypotheses and could represent the key to solving the mystery of her murder. It could be a dissenting father or, maybe a man who the woman had rejected and who had subsequently lost his temper. Someone like Mezzana, Nardi mused. Essentially, the relationship between the two of them supported the idea that he could be the baby's father.

However, Nardi knew that he must wait for the autopsy and DNA test results before getting that information. And, if the results confirmed his theories, he would still need to find out if the man had known about the pregnancy.

Nardi left the area feeling more confused than when he had arrived. He had so many questions but very few answers. He knew that the investigation had only just begun; he had a long road ahead of him.

***

Unlike the morning, the rest of the day was monotonous. Nardi stayed at police headquarters all afternoon, going through paperwork searching for something useful. Unfortunately, because of the scarce information on the case so far, he found nothing of any value.

Later, having been home for a while, Nardi had just finished his dinner and was enjoying a coffee. Sipping at it slowly, (he looked like a sommelier savoring a good wine) allowed him to reflect and organise his thoughts. As he pondered between each sip he felt enlightened almost as if a light had been switched on in his head. After all, his job was not so different than that of a sommelier. While the latter uncorked wine bottles, judging color, aroma, limpidity, Nardi opened metaphorical boxes of hidden truths, evaluating their importance, solidity and objectivity.

He swallowed what was left of his coffee and headed towards his laboratory.

The room was full of clocks. Situated in a harmonic chaos were pocket watches, wristwatches, wall and table clocks, pendulum clocks and cuckoo clocks. Some of them were antiques with significant value and artistically precious, with gold, silver, and bronze filled cases. Others were obsolete objects, like music boxes, broken alarm clocks and old clocks whose workings had stopped many moons ago.

For Nardi mechanical watch-making was the only passion that had survived after his wife's death. He had had this passion since being a young boy, attracted to the mystery of the passing of time. A dimension that man would never be able to imprison or own.

His interest had turned into something more concrete when, as a child, he had started to open up watches, he wanted to know how they worked, before reassembling them again. Fascinated by the cogs in the wheel and the inner mechanisms, he had refined his technique until he had become an expert in the field. He knew all about mechanical watches. Their history, their features, their working principles and anything else that could be known. In other words, he was fanatical about them.

Sitting on a stool, he switched on the lamp in front of him. A warm light spread over the shelf where his tools were spread. Among other things, a pocket watch was on the table, left there from the night before. It had worked well for years but recently it had stopped counting the seconds and then the minutes, losing its perfect equilibrium.

Watching the hands, he noticed that the time spread had increased two more minutes since last time. He opened the case to check the balance wheel. It had lost its isochronism and didn't swing at the same time anymore. Even if the gear in its entirety looked perfect. The spiral, rotating around the axis, kept alternating rhythmically in one direction and then the other, exchanging the kinetic energy with the potential one that had been accumulated by the torsion spring. A rhythmic marching, where the anchor, putting its edges between the escape wheel's gears, prevented the quick release of the charge. Periodically freeing one tooth and then another, it allowed the gears to proceed step by step.

After examining the mechanism for several minutes, he understood where the problem was and, putting himself to work, he changed the compensation to correct the balance wheel acceleration. When he was done, he lubricated the gears to decrease the friction between the pivots of the axes and the other wheelworks that generated the motion. Then he closed the case, and stared at that little mechanical jewel with both satisfaction and melancholy.

The watch had been the last of a series of many gifts. His wife had given it to him for their wedding anniversary. Noticing how the hands had started to move again, with their irrepressible steadiness, he thought about how he was able to repair these mechanical objects and give them new life, but he hadn't been able to do the same for his wife. A premature demise had taken her away from him and all he had left were cherished memories, memories that he grasped passionately. They had had a very happy marriage but her premature death had taken everything he had ever loved. He'd seen himself deprived of both a wife and a child.

What made everything unbearable was the feeling of guilt that continued to torture him unceasingly. There wasn't a night that passed without him thinking about how pushy he had been with his desire to have a child. Although the doctors had stressed the risk of carrying a pregnancy to term, his wife had refused to listen to them. And Nardi hadn't done anything to prevent it. He had watched her die, aware that she had made the ultimate sacrifice for him, that her love for him was unconditional.

Absorbed by these regrets, he couldn't help but think about the murdered woman. The fact that she'd been pregnant had significantly reduced the professional detachment he usually had in following a case. Already he'd allowed this case to involve him, making him feel closer to the victim and the child who would now never be born. And empathy even, to the, as yet, unknown father.

Thinking about the father, Nardi wondered what he was feeling at that moment. He wondered if the man was regretting the past, just as he was at the moment, or if he was focused on the future. Maybe the killer was Mezzana, or maybe not. But in any case, Nardi didn't feel much different from him. At the end of the day, love and hate were the two weights that made the world's pendulum swing. Two parts of the same gear that gave the universe its balance and allowed it to carry on the perpetual motion that was human nature.

CHAPTER 39

After the unpleasant episode at the clinic, Lisa Colasanti had been taken to the safety of her own home. Considering what had happened, Nardi had deemed it inappropriate to summon her to the police headquarters. Instead, the next morning he went to her house to proceed with questioning her about events so far.

When he got to the mansion, he had to wait outside for a while until the automatic gates were opened, allowing him access to the grounds. He drove slowly along the drive, passing beautifully tended gardens and flowerbeds, before reaching the entrance to the building. Once there he switched off the engine and got out of the car. He went up the few steps that led to the front door.

He was just about to ring the bell when the head of the domestic staff opened the door. She escorted him to the living room and before leaving, she said: "Mrs. Colasanti will be with you in a minute."

"That's fine. Thank you," he replied.

While waiting for Mrs. Colasanti to arrive, he began looking around, realizing that the fanciful opinion he had of her was very far from reality. Order and harmony seemed to be the true essence of the house. Everything appeared to have its own place.

Almost perfectly organized, each piece of furnishing seemed to respect its neighbor's space.

On the other hand, when he considered his own chaotic life, he realized how their lives were worlds apart. He also realized that he would never be able to live in a place like this; he enjoyed the stability of his chaos.

"Good morning, Inspector. I'm happy to see you," Mrs. Colasanti said, entering the room.

"Oh, good morning," he replied.

"I can't ever thank you enough. If it wasn't for you, I wouldn't be here."

"Anyone would have done the same," Nardi said awkwardly; compliments always made him feel uncomfortable. "How are you feeling today?"

"I'm still a bit shaken. But at least I'm in one piece," she replied, inviting him to sit.

"Well, the worst is over. You'll need to try to forget about it, if you can."

"It's not that easy. That man was my best friend's husband. I can't reconcile myself with what happened just yet."

"You mustn't torture yourself. It wasn't your fault."

"I know. The truth is that I would like to be able to open my eyes and realize it was all just a nightmare."

"Unfortunately, it's an unpleasant situation. Especially when it's someone we trust that hurts us. You don't have any idea about what may have led Monti to do something like that?"

"Absolutely not. We have known each other for years and I could never imagine him doing anything to harm anyone."

"There must be a reason though. Think about it. Have you had any problems recently?" Nardi asked.

"No, none. Our relationship was the same as always. I don't know what was going on in his mind."

"Is there anyone else that may have something against you? Maybe someone who wanted to benefit from your death."

"I don't know what to tell you. I really can't think of someone who would benefit from…"

The woman didn't finish the sentence and for a few moments she looked pensive and brooding.

"What are you thinking about? Have you remembered something?"

"No. I mean, yes. Something that's just come back to me."

"And?"

"Before you entered the room, Riccardo... Professor Monti... well, he said something. I believe he spoke about someone who would make him pay if he had backed off, away from hurting me. I think he'd been threatened. Him and his wife."

"Did he say a name?"

"No."

"And of course you have no idea who he was talking about."

"Unfortunately, I don't. I'm sorry."

"Hum!" He muttered, appalled by the woman's words.

He couldn't think how to proceed now that he'd come to, what appeared to be, a dead-end in his quest for the truth.

Considering her to be a potential murder suspect, he had gone to her house hoping to find some inconsistencies in her story that would have betrayed her. But now everything was different. It was lucky that she hadn't received the same fate as Ms. Fogliani. Plus, the fact that they both worked at the center raised even more questions.

He wondered whether the two women had accidentally seen or listened to something they shouldn't have, making their presence a danger for somebody.

"Do you know if Professor Monti knew Ms. Fogliani?" He asked.

"I don't know. Why do you ask?"

"Oh, it's just a thought. I was just wondering..."

"Wait a minute!" She interrupted him. "I believe that Ms. Fogliani had had her mother admitted to his clinic. So I would say that it's possible. But why? Do you think he's the one who killed her?"

"Well, it's one hypothesis." Nardi answered.

"Oh my God! The man was a monster. And in all these years

I've never noticed anything."

"Please calm down. It's just a supposition," he said. "I think you need to rest so, I won't bother you any longer. But just one more question, if you don't mind."

"Go ahead."

"I heard that you and Ms. Fogliani didn't get along well. May I ask you why?"

"Well... It doesn't feel right to speak badly about her, especially now that she's dead, but that woman was subversive. Working with her was anything but easy, believe me. She never missed a chance to make my life difficult."

"Any particular reason why she behaved like that?"

"I told you. She was subversive. She enjoyed messing with other people's lives, questioning everything and everyone. Especially me."

"And that's all?"

"Sure. What else would there be?"

"Well, an insignificant detail, something you may think is irrelevant may indeed be vital. All information is precious." Nardi said.

"Unfortunately, I don't know what else to say."

Nardi appeared satisfied and allowed Mrs. Colasanti to lead him to the door. When he was about to leave, he turned around.

"Oh! I nearly forgot to ask," he said nonchalantly. "Where were you on Friday night?"

"Inspector...!" She exclaimed, surprised. "Am I a suspect?"

"Of course not," he lied. "Every time I have a case such as this, I always ask for alibi's for whoever is involved. It's a simple and quick way to eliminate someone from my enquiries."

The woman looked at him with an annoyed expression.

"I was at home," she affirmed.

"And someone can confirm it?"

"Only my maid. My husband was out."

He thought that questioning the maid was superfluous. The house was large and, if someone wanted to leave without being seen, it would be simple enough to do so. He kept his doubts to himself and finally took his leave.

***

The police station had been as hot as a hash-house kitchen for the past couple of days. A failure in the air-conditioning system had made the air foul, which, with the mixture of body odors, sweat and the subsequent lack of oxygen, made the mind sluggish and the eyes heavy. Going inside the building, Nardi was immediately hit by the smelly heat. He complained loudly so that someone would have to call the repairs people again. He was used to long waiting times, it was the same every time something needed fixing. Working in those conditions today though, was too much even for him.

Determined to not fall asleep, he stopped by the vending machine to get a coffee but, fishing in his pockets, he realized he hadn't got any change. Annoyed by the combination of events, he hit the vending machine a couple of times. He noticed Lanzi was close-by and had witnessed Nardi's frustration.

"Can I get you a coffee, Inspector?" Lanzi asked, walking forward.

"Yes, thank you," Nardi replied slightly embarrassed.

He let the sergeant buy two cups of coffee and, thanking him again, started to drink. After a couple of sips, he put the cup close to his nose and smelled what was left in there. The aroma of the coffee softened the foul odor that pervaded the space around him and, for a while, he felt relieved.

Just then, the deputy walked by. He was carrying some folders, and seemed to be in a hurry.

"Hey! Cataldo," Nardi called.

Hearing his name, the man stopped abruptly and turned around clumsily. "Yes, Inspector?"

"Do some research on Riccardo Monti for me, please. Look for anything that may link him to Ms. Fogliani."

"Sure. Let me take this stuff away and I'll start working immediately."

"While you're on that, look into the *VitaNuova* center as well, please. I want to know everything about the place. Who works there, who are the people staying there; everything that happens there. Check if they have everything in order. Anything out of place, you advise me immediately." Nardi said.

"Of course."

The deputy took his leave and both Lanzi and Nardi moved into Nardi's office. Nardi informed the sergeant about his meeting with Mrs. Colasanti and about the alleged connection between Riccardo Monti and Ms. Fogliani. He asked Lanzi for his thoughts and opinions so far.

"Well," Lanzi began, "If it's true that they knew each other, and knowing what has happened, I wonder whether they were having a secret affair. Maybe the thought of having a child made him lose his mind and behave erratically. Maybe Mrs. Colasanti had sensed something was going on and so Monti tried to get rid of her too. Her friendship with his wife made her a danger."

"Hum! I don't know. I'm not convinced." Nardi mused.

There was a knock at the door and Cataldo appeared in the doorway.

"Don't tell me you've done that already?" Nardi asked.

"No, Inspector. I just wanted to inform you. It seems that Rita Visentini is back in town."

"Who?"

"Ms. Fogliani's neighbor."

"Ah!"

The man turned to leave but Nardi called him back.

"Cataldo, tell me something," he said. "Were you able to track down the victim's sister?"

"Unfortunately not, Inspector," Cataldo replied. "A few officers have been to her apartment several times but she was never there. She isn't answering her phone and her neighbors couldn't tell us anything."

"Ok, thanks", Nardi said, dismissing Cataldo. Turning back to Lanzi, he asked himself if they would have any luck questioning Mrs. Visentini.

***

As soon as the front door closed, the daylight dimmed giving the interior a murky darkness. Lanzi began to move forward, not caring about the shadows. Nardi, on the on the other hand, preferred to see where he put his feet, and pushed the switch to light up the stairs. After a couple of attempts he realized that the electrical system was out of service. The first time he had been here the morning sun had lit the building and he had missed the fact that the lighting wasn't working. Going up the stairs he thought about the time of the murder; night-time. Considering the likelihood of poor illumination he concluded that it was probable that the woman hadn't even seen her aggressor's face. Maybe she had died asking herself who her killer was, Nardi wondered.

On the second floor police tape remained in front of the victim's apartment and would stay there until all of the investigations had been completed. Nardi and Lanzi continued to the third floor and knocked on Mrs. Visentini's door.

"Who's that?" they heard her ask after a moment.

"Police," the inspector replied.

The door opened a little, allowing them to meet the wary little eyes of an old woman.

"I want to see your badge," she said.

Lanzi showed her his ID and, after a careful scrutiny, the woman opened the door and let them in.

"I'm sure that you've heard about the unfortunate events," Nardi said after introducing himself.

"Yes, I did. Did you find out who did it?"

"If we had, we wouldn't have needed to come here to speak with you."

"Who are you investigating?" the lady asked.

"I beg your pardon, madam, but I am the one that will be asking questions..." Nardi responded.

"Do you at least have any suspects?" she probed.

The woman continued her questioning until, after a couple of minutes, she gave up and the policemen finally had her full attention.

"Did you see or hear anything unusual the night of the murder?" Nardi asked.

"You bet!" She exclaimed, resuming her ramblings. "Inside this building there are too many strange things happening. You don't know how many times I have written to the administrator, but he keeps ignoring me."

Mrs. Visentini's mouth was like a car with no brakes, running at breakneck speed. The two men seemed to be unable to stop her and quite a while passed before something interesting came out of her mouth.

"...and believe me, Inspector, I don't like to speak badly about other people, but I knew that sooner or later it would happen. Those two argued every day."

"Who are you talking about?" Nardi asked.

"Who do you think I'm talking about? Ms. Fogliani and her boyfriend."

"Mr. Mezzana?" Lanzi clarified.

"And who else?"

"Let me understand, madam," Nardi said. "Are you saying that you saw him the night of the murder?"

"Well, to be honest, I didn't see him at all."

Overly stressed, Nardi raised his eyes skywards, convinced that he was speaking to a clone of the bizarre man on the fifth floor. He thought that the building was indeed a home for crazy people.

"But I heard him. And I know his voice very well. I'm never wrong about these kind of things."

The two police officers exchanged a skeptical look, wordlessly expressing their doubts about the reliability of her statements. But when she spoke again, their doubts faded away.

"It was ten thirty-five," she said. "I remember it well because they were keeping me awake. And the next morning I had to leave early to go to see my daughter. He started to pound his fists on the door and when she let him inside they started screaming and fighting. I could hear objects flying across the room and I believe they even destroyed a mirror or something like that because I heard the sound of breaking glass."

Mrs. Visentini had rendered a perfect description and there were no doubts that she had been a witness.

"Are you absolutely sure that the voice you heard was Mr. Mezzana's?" Nardi asked.

"Oh, yes! Absolutely. I couldn't recognize him on the stairs because it was too dark. Or because of the car; it wasn't the one he usually drove, so at first I didn't even think it was him. But then I heard him very well, when he started shouting like a madman."

"Can you describe the car?" Lanzi asked.

"No, sorry. Cars all look the same to me. I just know that it made a terrible noise, and it was greener than a highlighter pen."

Lanzi kept questioning her, but Nardi had already shut her out, allowing his ideas to develop. Finally, he thought, the investigation is starting to take direction. It didn't take long before the gears in his mind were set into motion.

CHAPTER 40

Waiting for the final results of the medical tests and forensic analyses, the news that Mezzana was under investigation for the commission of a crime had not been divulged, until now. It was Mrs. Visentini's testimony that had persuaded the state's attorney to let the veil of secrecy fall and issue a subpoena. Summoned to be questioned about the circumstantial evidence that linked Mezzana to the case, he and his lawyer had arrived at the police station to meet those leading the investigation.

Nardi had been authorized to conduct the questioning. He'd ordered that as soon as the two men arrived they were to be escorted to the appropriate room. Determined to use every card available, he would let them wait a while before he went to meet them. He knew very well how tensions can increase in a room without windows and with only minimal furnishings. The stress of waiting for him to arrive could work in his favor. Being deprived of any stimulus, it would be difficult for Mezzana to ignore the severity of his situation. Nardi knew that the guilty often fell prey to becoming increasingly agitated and to lose their ability to string coherent answers together when being questioned, frequently contradicting their stories.

The same was true for the innocent, he thought, who, afraid of saying too much, gave the impression of hiding something. But Nardi had conducted so many interrogations he could now distinguish between truth and fiction.

When he entered the room with Sergeant Lanzi, Nardi sat at the table opposite Mezzana, a file in front of him. Not yet wanting to meet Mezzana's eyes, he opened the file and began leafing through the documents inside, feigning interest. Then, grabbing a pen, he started to beat it on the table with a steady, rhythmic beat that appeared to accentuate his stress. He continued with this act, allowing some time to pass before, suddenly, he raised his eyes, and observed the man opposite with a searching look.

Nardi would study Mezzana's physical reactions and verbal answers throughout the questioning but this initial reaction to Nardi's unexpected move spoke volumes about a person's frame of mind. Taken by surprise, the suspect wouldn't have any mental defense. His facial demeanour during those first moments would determine the best way to proceed with the questioning.

Mezzana's look showed a hint of nervousness, but not enough to raise any suspicions. Nobody liked to be questioned so Nardi let it go.

Nevertheless, he continued studying the man's behavior. While the sergeant wrote down Mezzana's details, Nardi observed all of his movements and noted the inflexions in his voice.

When they were done with the bureaucratic formalities, he informed Mezzana about the possible charges against him. He began to ask questions that appeared to be unnecessary and for which he already knew the answers. His intent was to determine whether the opposing party was willing to collaborate with him.

"A witness statement has placed you at the murder scene," Nardi said. "Specifically, at the time the crime was committed."

This was a lie, Mrs. Visentini had said she had heard the man's voice. Not that she had seen him. But that wasn't important. Making people believe that there was evidence against them, insinuating doubts in their minds, went someway to get them to back down or, at least, betray themselves. As much as the 'right to lie' was recognized by the suspect, a half-truth, if spoken wisely, could be as effective as a lie or even more.

A thin line separated what was true and what was false, and the law didn't allow for mistakes. But Nardi had always been good at reading people and getting to the truth.

"So?" He spoke again. "Can you confirm you were in the victim's apartment?"

The lawyer put a hand on Mezzana's shoulder, giving him the sign that he should answer the question.

"Yes!" The suspect exclaimed. "It's true. I went there. But only because I wanted to talk to her."

"Why did you lie when previously questioned?" Nardi asked.

"You showed up at my house saying that Rosa had been killed. I was shocked. Also, I was afraid I would be in trouble, I wasn't thinking about the consequences. But, I'll say it again. I went there only to talk."

"About what?"

"I had found out that she was pregnant and I wanted to know if it was my child. She refused to take the paternity test. So I went to her house to try to convince her to have one."

"And then what happened?"

"She kept refusing, as if I had no right to know. We fought. But when I left she was alive. I would have never hurt her. I wanted that baby. It would have been my chance to start anew. After my divorce, the judge denied me the right to see my son and you can't understand what it means to lose a child."

Nardi remained silent. He understood perfectly. He would have liked to say something, show his understanding, however, he forced himself to maintain his impartiality. Without letting his emotions show, he took two photographs out of the folder. They pictured the murder weapon at the crime scene.

"Do you recognize this object?" He asked.

Mezzana was bewildered. His face became very pale.

"That's my razor," he whispered. "But I don't know how it

got there. Someone must have put it there."

"There were just your fingerprints on it."

"What do you want me to say? I keep it in my office all the time. Anyone could have taken it. I don't usually lock the door."

Nardi was unrelenting in his questioning; dropping hints, pointing out contradictions in the entire deposition. Finally when concluding his grilling, he told Mezzana to ensure that he would be available for further questions, if needed and then he let him go.

***

The interview had unfolded without surprises.

Mezzana's declarations had clarified a few aspects of the case, but they didn't bring the investigation to any kind of turning point. The evidence against him was circumstantial, not enough to detain him. And, as much as the man remained the main suspect, Nardi was not sure about his guilt.

Holding on to these doubts he went to his office to update the prosecutor, Ms. Mellis. It was just a standard phone call plus he would make sure to send a copy of his report as soon as possible. He avoided going into too much detail, simply reporting the salient points of Mezzana's interview, omitting any unnecessary elements.

During the conversation, Lanzi came into the office. Nardi gestured for him to sit down. He also indicated that the call was almost done. He knew that Ms. Mellis didn't like to waste time in needless conversation. As soon as he had completed his verbal report to her, she dismissed him without any further comments.

"So, Inspector?" Lanzi started. "What do you think?"

"To be honest, I'm not convinced of Mezzana's guilt. The evidence seems to point to him at the moment, but he appeared sincere and answered our questions without guile. Moreover, he doesn't look like the type of person stupid enough to kill someone and leave the weapon that nails him to the scene."

"Maybe he panicked…"

"If it's true that he keeps the razor in his office, we would be talking about premeditation. He would have taken it with him with the intention of using it and in that scenario he would have been unlikely to panic." Nardi said.

"To tell you the truth, I wasn't able to get the measure of the man either. While he was speaking, he seemed to believe in what he was saying, yet, he contradicted himself more than once. Also, he lied to us the first time we spoke with him so we know that he's capable of dishonesty." Lanzi replied.

"Yeah, but maybe I would have done the same thing, if I was him."

"What do you mean?"

"He knew from the beginning that he would be the main suspect. He has known that since the day we went to speak with him. How would you react if you knew you were implicated in a murder?"

"I don't know. And I hope I'll never have to find out. Still, he hasn't said anything that would clear his name."

"We did discover something interesting though. If what he says is true about the woman's reluctance to take the paternity test, it would support the suspicions we had at the beginning. There was probably someone else in her life. Someone who now hides in the shadows and who could be the real murderer."

"In the meantime," Lanzi asserted, "we can't overlook the evidence against Mezzana, circumstantial or otherwise."

Lanzi was right. Nardi was underestimating the issue. Without realizing it, he was looking for any excuse that would confirm Mezzana's innocence even if he happened to be guilty. And behind this behavior, he was hiding his own desperate need to justify himself.

After reflecting on the situation for a while, he was about to reply to the sergeant's comment when Cataldo entered the room, this time not bothering to knock first. Nardi looked at him, astonished. The deputy was a shy and clumsy man, a victim of his own nervousness, and he had not behaved like that before.

"Inspector," he blurted. "They found the victim's sister."

"Why are you so agitated?"

"She's dead, Inspector."

"What are you saying?" Nardi asked.

"We've just been informed. Some kids found her in a park. And it seems like she's been dead for a few days."

Shocked by the news, Nardi turned to look at Lanzi, as if looking for an answer, but the sergeant looked as perplexed as Nardi. This was a new twist in the case rendering it more complicated, with knots intertwining instead of unravelling.

"It won't be easy getting to the bottom of this story," Nardi stated, withdrawing into his thoughts.

CHAPTER 41

The night had transformed into a living nightmare. Sleeping had become a challenge for Ivano and such was his agitation, sleep eluded him. His bed became a mass of damp, clammy sheets. His mind in a turmoil of confusing images that threatened to overwhelm him.

Little by little, Ivano imagined that he could see Giada's face emerging in front of him. He raised a hand to touch it and as he did so the vision diminished before fading completely into the shadows of his bedroom.

Bizarrely, this terrible nightmare took him back to that damned park. He could see himself running frantically along the small walkways towards the mansion, the surreal silence crowding in on him as he went. He was in a state of anxiousness, apprehensive of the vision materializing in front of him, something quite terrifying. As he tried to escape and run away, he could feel its presence, a malevolent phantom of his imagination threatening to engulf him. The paths seemed to become as one. He felt like he was going around in circles with more horrors waiting to embrace him at every turn. All he could do was run.

It seemed to Ivano that endless hours had passed in a terrifying loop, repeating itself, ceaselessly. But then, gaining some respite from his interminable nightmare, he remembered the hobo he'd spoken to when he'd arrived at the park.

Still in his nightmare state Ivano saw that the man wasn't seated anymore. He was standing at the end of the street, and looked like he was trying to tell Ivano the way to get out of the labyrinth. But, for some inexplicable reason, this image terrified him. All at once, the figure of the man had replaced that of fear. Looking both amiable and threatening at the same time, he conveyed something enigmatic. His mouth was immobile, yet a penetrating voice seemed to emanate from him. Ivano didn't want and couldn't listen to it. The non-existent, yet ear-splitting, sound was unbearable.

The man appeared three or four more times, insistent with his advice, but Ivano refused to listen. As if upset by Ivano's attitude, the man grabbed a cardboard box, dumped its contents on the ground, and then faded away as quickly as he had appeared.

The wretched man had thrown all of his coins at Ivano's feet. Ivano looked at them, suddenly captivated by a furious greed, and then, beaten by an insatiable need to possess all of that money, he started to pick them up one by one.

When he had gathered up the last coin, he raised his eyes and saw that Giada was there, close-by, sitting on a bench. He let the coins fall from his hands and, moved by an uncontrollable desire to hold her, headed over.

The sequence of his ordeal now began to flow in a series of erratic flashbacks. He was in front of her and they were looking into each other's eyes.

"The police came," he said.

"Did they catch us?" She asked, agitated.

"No, don't worry. They weren't there for us. They were there for your sister's murder."

An imaginary tape rewound one more time, and he was once more standing away from the bench. He felt that one part of him was living that scene, while another seemed to observe from a distance, as if he was just a spectator.

"Now that I've killed her, she can't hurt us anymore," he said, seeing himself in front of her again.

"You're an idiot. The original diary is in Della Torre's hands. So you haven't solved anything. You just made the situation worse."

"I did it for you. For us."

"You fool! There is no us. Get out of my life."

At first, the words didn't touch him; he felt that he was already far away; a onlooker observing what was happening. He watched Giada, and he watched Ivano, with the impression that he was witnessing a lovers' quarrel. Then he was back in the body that was standing in front of the girl. They were very close and, looking into her eyes, he thought that could see his own self reflected there. It was through her limpid eyes that he saw himself raise his arms and push her violently until she fell.

He could feel himself falling backwards as if in slow-motion, but it's Giada who was falling. The impression of being detached from the events playing out before him made it impossible to establish who was falling and who was standing. He remained there, passively observing the slow falling of her body, until he saw Giada's head hit the corner of the bench and he felt that something was breaking inside his own self.

Her body lay on the ground, her head smashed and the crimson of her blood painting the whole scene red. Suddenly everything stopped. All Ivano could hear was himself, screaming out in horror of what he had just witnessed.

Still feeling afraid, Ivano moved his hands to his neck. He felt his body shaking and soaked in sweat. He inhaled deeply a few times to calm his breathing and, with a great effort, he got out of bed, feeling the burden of that horrific scene laying heavily upon him.

He opened the windows before briefly using the bathroom to splash water on his face and then on to the kitchen to find a much needed drink. He grabbed a bottle of vodka and knocked back a few swigs. Staring into the void of the kitchen he thought back to the terrible nightmare he had just had. He couldn't get Giada's image out of his head. The memory of when he had pushed her violently towards her death had been worrying him for days. He had killed the only person he had ever loved; the only person that had probably loved him and he would never be able to forgive himself for that. He had killed her twice. First, by pushing her down and then, secondly, by taking off in a run and leaving her on the ground to die alone. Thinking back to those brief moments, Ivano felt overcome with shame. Instead of helping her, he had run like a coward. His now empty glass seemed to signify the absence of someone who would never come back.

As he pondered the images of the night Ivano put the glass in the sink, he wanted to hide it from his view. To him, it represented isolation and emptiness. Other images from the night began to resurface in his mind. He visualized the beggar throwing his coins to the ground. He saw himself picking them up one by one. He saw the man showing him the path to take, and he wondered what the meaning was behind these illusions.

Ivano was still searching for answers when, unexpectedly, he heard the doorbell ring. With his head swimming with emotions, he didn't even bother to wonder who it could be. He stood up and headed for the door. When he opened it, there stood the same guy he had met at the *VitaNuova* center. He recognized him immediately. He hadn't forgotten the sharp look of the policeman.

Before the man could say a word, Ivano instinctively closed the door again. His visitor was quicker though and thrust the door open with a shove of his shoulder. Ivano was thrown backwards by the force of the door swiftly opening. Recoiling from its thrust he grasped onto a piece of furniture so as not to fall down. Regaining his balance, he noticed that the policeman was now inside his house. At that point, Ivano threw himself at the man, savagely launching into a violent attack.

Although he didn't look young, the policeman was considerably more agile than Ivano had expected. It took a couple of failed attempts and retaliations before Ivano finally managed to punch him in the stomach with such force, that the man collapsed. Flexing his legs he bent over, breathlessly coughing, and covered his chest with his hands. As the policeman moved his position he began to pull his gun from his pocket. Ivano saw this action and quickly reiterated with a violent punch before the man could react. As the weapon fell to the floor, the man managed to kick it away from them both. Ivano tried to reach it but as he did so he was grabbed by the shoulders. His assailant had recovered and, catching Ivano by surprise, he threw an elbow to Ivano's chin. Immediately, a shooting pain went through him and he realized that he wouldn't be able to withstand another attack. Ivano stepped back in a desperate attempt to catch his breath. He reached the living room, thinking it would be a place of refuge, but as he turned he saw that the other man was already behind him.

They both stood still for a few moments, staring at each other until Ivano, on the opposite side of the table, tried to outsmart his opponent. Taking a step to one side, he launched himself in the opposite direction and reached the door, but the policeman threw himself on him, causing him to fall to the ground. A couple of seconds later, they were upright again. But Ivano wasn't fast enough. Turning around, he barely had time to see the fist that hit him in the face. He stumbled but reacted quickly when the man moved to attack him again. Bending over, he avoided the blow from the not-so-old guy, who lost his balance and fell. Ivano grabbed a container full of solvent and threw it at his face, hoping to stop his assailant in his tracks.

The policeman covered his eyes with his hands and began to groan with pain. His inability to defend himself seemed to trigger all of his fury. Like a madman he grabbed a chair and started to swing it through the air. Blinded, couldn't see what he was doing as he attacked. But now the fickle hand of fate stepped in to steer the fight in a new direction. The injured policeman directed a blow towards Ivano, who took a step backwards to avoid the impact. He landed at the windowsill with such force he couldn't stop himself falling through the window. He felt his feet lifting from the ground and his body falling back beyond the parapet.

Stunned with panic, unable to even scream, he started to fall. All he could do was look down at the road beneath him; the ground that he was speeding towards. He knew that the road would mark his demise. His terrifying fall began to move in slow-motion. It was then that he started to scream. And it was then that, once more, he woke up in the darkness of the night.

CHAPTER 42

Since the first murder, and the moment they had tried to get in touch with the victim's family, Nardi had noticed the difference between the last names of the two sisters. Although the detail had stirred his curiosity, it wasn't enough for him to dig more deeply into its meaning. At the start of the investigation he had considered Ms. Rubini as a relative they needed to inform and nothing more. Their name anomaly was an insignificant detail and had been ignored. But then Ms Rubini's fate had followed that of her sister's and so the issue of their different names became an element in the case that could no longer be overlooked. Researching into the sisters' lives had brought to light the divorce of their parents; how it had affected the estrangement between the two sisters, and how, some time later, Ms. Fogliani had taken her mother's last name. Nardi felt that he had, maybe, been negligent, stirring up feelings of self-reproach.

Convinced that he hadn't done all that he could have, Nardi asked himself whether stricter attention to detail could have prevented Ms. Rubini's tragic demise.

Her death had messed up every single investigative element they had collected so far. The long estrangement from her sister had been established, but the fact that they were almost identical had left Nardi puzzled. He wondered whether she was supposed to have been the real target and not her sister. Whether the attacker had been misled by their resemblance or if he had killed again, simply to muddy the waters.

According to the medical examiner, Dr. Padovani, the death could be considered accidental. But Nardi wasn't willing to make the same mistake again. This time he wasn't going to leave anything out. If there was something to discover, he would find it.

Nardi decided that it would be helpful to have a look in Ms Rubini's apartment. Accompanied by Lanzi, he went to her home hoping to pick up any clues that may have been overlooked during the first inspection.

Arriving there, he was about to enter the apartment when he hesitated, suddenly thoughtful. He had the strange feeling that he was violating the woman's privacy. He knew she was dead, he knew she wouldn't be coming home but he couldn't shift this uneasiness. He felt that he needed to be respectful during his search, more so than usual. Head down, he proceeded to the living room. He thought that if it wasn't for the coincidence that linked her death to that of Ms. Fogliani, they would never have needed to cross this threshold. The case would have simply been a bunch of paperwork to be buried under a million other papers. Most likely, it would have been archived as accidental death.

Absorbed in his musings, and staring at the floor, Lanzi spoke, breaking the Inspector's train of thought.

"I don't think there's much to look for here," he said, pointing at the mess. "It seems that our colleagues have done their job already."

"It's worth giving it a try," Nardi replied, looking around. "A home always holds secrets. Especially for someone with such a solitary existence."

"If you want my opinion Inspector, the only lead to follow is that of money."

"Someone's already taking care of that." Nardi replied.

Indeed, they hadn't been able to track down the source of the money in Ms. Rubini's bank account. Whoever had made the transaction had taken all necessary precautions. The forensic experts were still working on giving a name and a face to the mysterious benefactor.

"Knowing who made that transaction would be a big step forward," Lanzi insisted.

"I agree with you, but it's not our job to discover it. We can only wait for an answer."

"Then let's hope we get one soon."

"We will," Nardi concluded. "In the meantime though, we can't sit here twiddling our thumbs."

Nardi began to inspect the living room. He walked through the room in a rhythmic, almost mechanical, way. Up and down, side to side, he concentrated on each area before moving on to the next whilst allowing his natural gait to determine the direction of his gaze. He kept his sophisticated pace going for several minutes until the small writing desk caught his attention. The contrast with the dust surrounding it emphasized a well-defined clear space on the wooden surface, clean and bright. Something had been taken away recently and the size of the imprint, its square shape and the presence of a printer close-by suggested that it was a computer. Evidently, someone was interested in the woman's secrets, perhaps. He wondered what information her computer might have hidden within it.

"Hey Lanzi," he said. "Come, have a look at this."

The sergeant, who had been searching around in the kitchen, stopped what he was doing and came to the living room.

"Did you find anything?" He asked.

Nardi simply pointed at the printer and the empty shelf. "The computer!" Lanzi exclaimed, understanding immediately.

"Yeah," Nardi nodded. "It must have been stolen before the inspection team arrived."

"Do you want me to call someone to come here?" Lanzi asked.

"Yes. Call the station. They need to have this place inspected again from top to bottom."

"Let's hope that whoever took it left some fingerprints."

"I don't think we'll be so lucky. There's nothing to steal here. Whoever came here was looking for something specific. I'd say it was a professional. Whoever it was they were looking for something in particular and it seems they found it."

Nardi headed towards the hall, seeking out any further clues. His intention was to proceed to the bedroom but when he reached the hallway, he couldn't help but stop, captured by the beauty of the grandfather clock. It was a collector's piece with a decent market value. The woman probably didn't even know she possessed such a precious object. And its value was intrinsic, evident to collectors like him, but hardly detectable to an amateur.

Noting the poor state of the artwork, he felt a little sad. The device's artistic and mechanical perfection had been neglected over time. Deprived of any attention, the mechanism had lost its original gleam. It was in the threadbare wood, in the wear and tear of the overlays and in the signs of rust in every single notch. Even more clearly, it was in the lack of the pendulum's swing and in the stillness of the clock hands. Nine o'clock had been and gone, but the hands gave the time as six thirty-five. Drooping downwards, the hands had stopped moving, almost as if they had followed the fate of the clock's owner. Feeling sad Nardi touched the pendulum's glass door lightly before heading towards the bedroom. Suddenly he remembered the story behind that clock. He had read somewhere that those models were famous in the mid-eighteenth century for their secret hiding places. He turned back towards the clock, his eyes looking at the dial and the motionless hands. He stared at them for a few moments, thinking about what to do. Then, decisively, he removed the metal plate that kept the glass in place on the bezel and started to move the hands, arranging them in random combinations, hoping to find the correct arrangement. Despite moving them in various permutations, his efforts were unsuccessful.

"What are you doing, Inspector?" Lanzi asked, intrigued.

"I'd like to know that myself." Nardi replied.

"I know you're a fanatic for that stuff. But doesn't it seem a little out of place?" the sergeant dared to point out.

At that point, Nardi stopped what he was doing and, turning around with an annoyed look, he said: "The answer to our questions could be inside here."

It was reasonable that Lanzi didn't understand what Nardi was doing yet, but he couldn't stand that his professionalism was being criticised again. Regardless of that, at the moment, the only thing that mattered was to open that damn clock. He continued to play its enigmatic game for another fifteen minutes or so before giving up, disappointed. He lowered his head, feeling defeated. He then looked at the motionless pendulum and he understood. The mechanism had been still for a very long time. Nobody had recharged its energy. The hands didn't move, and the same went for all the other parts of the gear. He grabbed the butterfly key located in the bottom of the clock, inserted it into the correct charger port and rotated it until the pendulum started swinging once more.

As soon as the mechanism started up again, the seconds' hand resumed its ticking. The time between one second and the next was extremely long however. Nardi knew that the balance wheel was not working as it should be but, at that moment, its timing was irrelevant. The only thing that mattered was to generate movement.

Crossing his fingers, Nardi moved the hour and minute hands to mark twelve thirty, forming a perfect vertical axis. The second hand continued moving freely on its own and when it had covered a quarter of a rotation, creating a perfect perpendicular line with the other two hands, Nardi heard a small click. He was stunned, but pleased, to see a small drawer open, revealing a CD.

Nardi looked at the sergeant with a satisfied expression and said: "Maybe we're back in the game."

***

A little after nine thirty the two men arrived back at the police station. Drawn by their curiosity, they hurried into the inspector's office without acknowledging the rest of their colleagues. When Nardi sat down at his desk, Lanzi, forgetting etiquette for a moment, sat beside him. Nardi looked at Lanzi's excited face and understood that he felt the same. They knew that they had found something crucial to their case; they were both impatient to discover exactly what it was.

The computer was already on but Nardi stared at the disk for a few moments, nervous in case its contents weren't the key to their investigation.

"Come on, Inspector!" Lanzi snapped. "What are you waiting for?"

"Calm down," Nardi replied.

When he finally inserted the CD, a single folder appeared on the screen. It contained a series of *files* and he selected one at random. The image of Rosa Fogliani, dressed in her underwear, popped onto the screen. In another shot, Rosa was with a male figure. He had his back to the camera though, so it was impossible to determine who he was. The next picture carried a surprise within itself, however. The two people had been photographed in an unequivocal manner. She was standing completely naked at the entrance to the bedroom and the man, his face turned towards the window, could be clearly identified. "But...!" Lanzi exclaimed with surprise. "Is he who I think he is?"

"I think so," Nardi replied, also confused by what he was seeing.

Silence fell in the room as Nardi began to flick through the images at a faster rate. Each picture superimposing on top of the next, adding small details that made everything clearer and more defined.

"Well! We knew that the woman was having an affair," Nardi said. "It seems that we have found the mysterious man."

"Della Torre! Who would have thought?"

"In this job nothing can surprise you."

"Yeah, but..." Lanzi started.

Without finishing the sentence, the sergeant stood up and moved around to the opposite side of the desk and sat down facing the inspector. They remained silent, each lost in their own thoughts. Nardi couldn't help but notice how the evidence seemed to be piling up from within the rehabilitation clinic. In one way or another, everyone seemed to be connected to the center. From Lisa Colasanti to Rosa Fogliani. From Giada Rubini to Mezzana and Della Torre. Not to mention the weapon used in the first murder whose original location was there as well.

"Let's try to put things into order," Nardi said finally, thinking out loud. "Ms. Fogliani and Mr. Della Torre have an affair. When Ms. Rubini starts to blackmail him, he's forced to give in to the extortion. But even if, let's say, he decided to get rid of her, why would he kill her sister? It makes no sense."

"The fact that the woman was blackmailing them is evident. And that explains the bank account," Lanzi intervened. "But going as far as killing her... I don't know. Della Torre could have bought her silence without any problems."

"Still, he did have a good motive. And in certain situations it's easy to cross the line." Nardi said.

"Yeah. But what sense would it make? You said it yourself. Why kill the sister? At the end of the day, they were lovers and he wouldn't have gained anything." Lanzi replied.

Nardi recalled Mr. Mezzana's statement. According to his testimony, Ms. Fogliani had refused to take the paternity test.

"What if she had made Della Torre believe that he was the baby's father?" Nardi said. "For someone like him, that could have been a problem. Who knows? Maybe he just wanted to get rid of the child."

"It's possible, but I don't see him getting his hands dirty with something like that. Whoever committed the murder was an amateur who did everything alone. Someone like Della Torre would have hired a hit man." Lanzi suggested.

"You're right. But I do think that he was involved somehow."

The discussion between the two men was interrupted by Cataldo arriving.

"Excuse me, Inspector," he said. "I wanted to inform you that we found out who made the bank transaction."

Nardi and Lanzi smiled at each other.

"You won't believe it, but it seems it was Vincenzo Della Torre. The president of *Co.S.Mic!*"

"Yes, Cataldo. I understand. You can go, thank you."

"Actually there is more," the deputy continued.

"What is it?" Nardi asked.

"A large amount of money in favor of Riccardo Monti was also deposited from the same account."

"What?" Nardi asked, astonished.

"Yes, Inspector."

"Thank you, Cataldo."

After Cataldo had left the room, Nardi raised his eyes to the ceiling.

"Uhm!" he muttered. "Riccardo Monti."

"What are you thinking?" Lanzi asked.

"Uh?" Nardi replied. "Oh, nothing. I had been wondering about an action that didn't make any sense at the time. Now it's clear. Professor Riccardo Monti was paid to do what he did."

"Do you think Della Torre tried to have his wife killed?" Lanzi asked, incredulous.

"It's a hypothesis. After what we have learned, I wouldn't be surprised. What I don't understand is Monti's behavior and what caused him to take his own life."

"Maybe he didn't do it." Lanzi suggested.

"What do you mean?"

"Maybe someone wants us to believe that he killed himself, when in fact he could have been pushed to make it look like a suicide."

"Who knows?" Nardi replied, thinking back to that day.

He recollected the woman screaming beyond the railings, the subsequent chase and the tragic image of Monti, lying on the roadside. And finally he remembered the elegant man with the black Porsche. Besides himself, the Porsche owner had been the last person to cross the hospital's ward. Nardi couldn't recall the man's face. All that was impressed on his mind was the luxury car and the classy clothes. He asked himself who the man could be and whether he was the one to push Monti out of the window. Nardi continued to contemplate this scenario when, finally an overlooked detail came to him. He realized he had been an idiot to not think about it sooner.

Getting up from his chair, he said to Lanzi: "Go pay a visit to Della Torre and see what he has to say about this turn of events."

"You're not coming?"

"I need to follow another lead."

"What lead?" Lanzi asked.

"Ah! You go and speak with Della Torre!" He replied, ignoring the sergeant's question. "Do some research on him. We need to find out if he had a reason to kill his wife."

CHAPTER 43

Elena Monti had been shut away with her grief for days, crying alone over the death of her husband. That morning, she, as was usual for her, sitting on a recliner chair on the terrace, browsing through an old photograph album. All that was left of her marriage. She turned the pages slowly, prolonging the memories held within each snapshot. She looked back nostalgically, and admired herself in her white wedding gown, carrying a bouquet of stunning lilies and Riccardo, then young and so handsome, waiting for her at the altar, his face radiant with love. It had been a joyful day, many years ago, and had remained a vivid and pleasurable memory to her.

Elena needed to recall her past with her husband and looking at their photos was an emotional release at this time of immense grief. Such precious memories. Memories made up of the little things in life that molded the mosaic of an entire life together. She remembered some of their joyful, and a few of the painful, moments along with regret for the projects that they had procrastinated over for too long and that now would remain unrealized and meaningless. She longed to relive those days with him.

She could feel tears beginning to fall again and she wiped them away with her hands. She was surprised; she thought that she had no more strength to cry. She had poured out her pain on the day that Riccardo had died. She hadn't even wept when Lisa had come to visit her. Her broken heart was empty. Hopefully, given time, her heart would mend. In the meantime she would use the healing power of reminiscing on happier times and go to her photo album for inspiration and solace. She would have continued her in her reverie but for the interruption of her maid.

"Do you need anything, madam?" The maid enquired.

"No, thanks." Elena said.

"Do you want me to bring you something to drink?"

"I'm fine. Don't worry."

"I'll be in the next room if you change your mind."

Since Riccardo's death, the girl's behavior towards Elena had changed. She had always been polite. She had to be. But since that fateful day, her behavior, and the way she looked at Elena, was given with a compassion that Elena didn't like at all. She hated the idea of being pitied. It was that thought that prompted her to react.

She saw that the clock marked a quarter to ten. She had already spent a large part of the morning reliving the past and she now decided that it was time to move on. She forced herself to get up from the chair and go to her husband's studio. She needed to clear his paperwork and possessions. It was time to put her life in order, without her beloved Riccardo.

With no clear plan of where she should begin Elena looked around the room. It was generally tidy but she could see that his desk held stacks of folders, scattered documents and notes. She would start there. Moving to Riccardo's seat she plopped herself down and hesitantly put her hands on the table, caressing the worn wood. It was then that she realized that she had undertaken a task that was too difficult at the moment. She was emotionally vulnerable and wasn't ready to make the step just yet. Everything in the room was a reminder of Riccardo in one way or another. It would be hard to decide what to keep and what to throw away.

But she didn't want to give up. She knew that if she didn't make a start, she would sink into an abyss, along with the pain that tore through her heart. She put her feelings to one side and began grabbing at pieces of paper, screwing them up before throwing them into the rubbish bin. A liberating activity that she prolonged for a while until a letter, which was in plain view, caught her attention. It had been in front of her the whole time, but she'd ignored it because, unlike the others, it was addressed to her. Recognizing her husband's handwriting, she opened it apprehensively. There she found the last words of a man who was saying goodbye. She started to read the lines carefully and as she did so her expression became more and more incredulous. She couldn't believe what she was reading. For a moment, she thought she was dreaming. The room seemed to be spinning around her. Dazed, she dropped the letter to the floor and, with a confused expression on her face, tried to convince herself that her mind was tricking her.

CHAPTER 44

Nardi would have liked to hear Della Torre's interview in person. He was curious to see what he had to say about the whole matter. But at the moment he needed to listen to his intuition and act upon it. He'd returned to the *Santa Caterina* clinic to verify whether his hunch was well-founded.

There was a single entrance to the clinic which was monitored by a security barrier. He stopped the car in front of the barrier and waited for the security guards to let him in. The guards were engaged in a discussion and appeared to be ignoring him, almost as if they hadn't noticed his presence. He was not in a hurry to get in. He had gone there to look for confirmation of his theory. And then he saw it, right in front of him. In fact, above his head, two security cameras were installed to record every vehicle that passed in or out of the complex. He thought back to the elegant man whose face he couldn't recall. But then he remembered the black Porsche; locating such a prestige vehicle should be easy, he thought.

But for now the CCTV recordings could wait. The videos wouldn't be going anywhere. Nardi needed first to go inside the building to have a look around. Monti's case had been considered a suicide and had been treated as such by the officers. A thorough investigation had not been conducted and so now it was up to him to find any possible clues that led to the truth.

Eventually one of the guards glanced outside the cabin and, finally acknowledging Nardi's presence, lifted the bar and let him through.

The space where he had parked his car the first time he visited was empty, so he decided to park there again. He'd never been the superstitious type but this time he was striving to believe and keep all of his options open, whatever it took; he needed luck to be on his side for once.

He got out of the car and headed towards the entrance but after a few steps he stopped and reflected for a minute. He decided to go to the spot where Monti had landed. When he reached the other side of the building he stopped, and stared at the ground. Some traces of blood, which had now become one with the asphalt, preserved the memory of that day. A day where events had happened quickly and in a confused way. The attack, the chase, the suicide; everything had happened too fast, and some details had probably gone unnoticed.

Lost in the abstract world of hypotheses, Nardi continued staring at the patch of ground, tinted with red stains, until, visualizing the image of Monti lying on the ground. He turned, searching for something that would reveal the event from a different perspective. In an effort to widen his field of vision Nardi stepped a few meters away from the place of death. Looking back up at the window from where Monti had fallen, he established that the point of impact was three to four meters away from the building, maybe more. It was too big of a distance to fall for someone who had thrown himself from the window. It was clear that somebody had pushed him violently.

With all that had happened at the time, and overwhelmed by the series of events that had involved him, he hadn't noticed that detail. But now he had checked it for himself he knew it was proof that Monti had been killed.

Wasting no time, he went inside the building to check the

room from where Monti met his demise.

He walked the same route he had taken with Sabrina Colasanti, but when he reached the floor, he became confused. He had chased the man from one corridor to the next but now it was difficult to find his bearings. Eventually, he finally reached his destination. The room was empty, just as it was the last time he was there. Clearly nobody had set foot in there since that day. If any trace of what happened had been missed, it should still be there, he thought.

Looking around, Nardi noticed plain decor and assumed that this simplicity would make the task easier. He started trawling the room, hoping to find something. A little later, he noticed a button hidden behind one of the bed supports. He picked it up with a piece of paper, being very careful not to touch it. It could be evidence and he had no intention of contaminating it. Maybe it was just a simple button, but his gut told him differently. If Monti had been thrust out the window, surely he had tried to get a foothold to escape death. And maybe in a desperate attempt to do so, he had grabbed his aggressor's jacket, tearing off the button. In that case, even if he hadn't been able to save his own life, he had at least left a trace of his killer.

Nardi spent a few more minutes searching for anything else that could prove useful. He soon realized, however, that there was nothing more to find. So, his next task would be to find the identity of the mysterious man with the Porsche. He went to the administrative offices, introduced himself and asked to examine the videos recorded over the previous few days. The receptionist contacted the head of security who, raising no objections, ordered the inspector to be taken to the correct room.

One of the security guards escorted Nardi to the monitoring room. Once there, the guard excused himself with a handshake leaving Nardi in the room with the security monitoring team.

"Good morning," Nardi said, addressing one of them. "I am Inspector Nardi. I need to see a few recordings, please."

"Yes, of course," the officer replied. "Which ones are you interested in?"

"Those recorded the day before yesterday."

"Could you be a little more precise?"

Realizing that his request was a bit too generic, Nardi specified the time range he was interested in.

While the man started to search for the requested material, Nardi glanced at the monitors. He noticed that even the parking lot was observed. With a bit of luck, he was about to see the face of the man with the Porsche.

After skimming the recordings until he reached the time indicated by the detective, the young officer slowed the images down and the two of them started to check the various cars that had entered the clinic within that time range. Nardi didn't remember the exact time of his arrival, so had given the officer an approximation. A few minutes more and there was the Porsche on the screen.

"There! There it is!" Nardi blurted, as soon as the car appeared on the monitor.

The car was right in front of the clinic, its number plate clearly displayed. Nardi wrote it down immediately on a piece of paper and then asked to see the recordings of the parking lot.

Unfortunately, the man's face was not visible. The shots were high-angled and the man had kept his face looking downwards. Nardi remembered the button and asked to compare the images recorded when the car arrived with those taken when it left. Unfortunately, the man was facing the camera only on his arrival. When he left, he was framed from behind. "Damn!" he snapped, annoyed by the situation.

"Wait, Inspector," the officer said after a little while. "Look! He turns around here. When he gets in the car."

Once again detecting his face was impossible, but at that moment all that mattered to Nardi was having his hypothesis confirmed. He had the image enlarged as much as possible and when he saw that a button was missing from the man's jacket he was ecstatic. "It's him!" Nardi said with satisfaction.

The officer didn't know what the inspector was referring to. But he was satisfied with the outcome, happy because he had helped the inspector. Nardi shook the officer's hand and after thanking him, left.

Once outside, he paused in the corridor to call the police station. He asked Cataldo to check the number plate while he remained on hold. After a few silent moments, the deputy's voice came back to the phone.

"Inspector?" he asked.

"I'm here. Tell me everything."

"It's a Porsche Boxster…"

"I don't care about the car. I want its owner's name."

"Oh, yes… It belongs to a man named Gianni Spada."

"Perfect. Please do a search and see what you can find out about him."

Nardi was about to hang up the phone but realized that the man's voice was croaking on the other end of the line. He moved the phone back to his ear and said: "I beg your pardon, Cataldo. I didn't hear. What did you say?"

"That I have already heard this name. Hold on one second. I'm checking if it's the same person."

"What are you talking about?"

"Yeah! Here it is! I knew I'd seen it somewhere else."

"Cataldo! Are you planning on filling me in or are you going to keep this a secret?" Nardi yelled, impatiently.

"Oh, yes, Inspector. I'm sorry. It's about that bank account. This man is on the list of names as well. It seems that Della Torre made several transactions to this man. Both in the past and more recently."

"Oh, now that is interesting," Nardi responded.

Saying goodbye, he ended the call and headed towards the exit. His head felt bombarded with so many twists, turns and coincidences in this case, a case that had started with just one murdered woman and had now expanded into so much more.

The fact that Monti had been killed was beyond question. And the identity of the murderer was also clear. What didn't have a logical explanation was the reason for the whole ordeal. Why would Della Torre want to get rid of him? Nardi tried to think of a valid motive, but in the end, it didn't matter anymore. At this point, they had enough evidence to incriminate him. Everything else would be revealed during questioning or the trial.

CHAPTER 45

Della Torre had been a customer of *Verde&Verde*, a company who specialized in garden maintenance, for years. On Mondays, an operator would go to the mansion to mow the lawn and tidy the hedges. And as it happened every Monday the company van was on its way and about to pass through the house gates. However, today's driver was not an employee of *Verde&Verde*; it was Spada. He had snuck into the vehicle warehouse earlier that morning and waited patiently for the usual operator to arrive. The man had been taken by surprise being attacked while opening the door. Without leaving him any time to realize what was happening, Spada had knocked him out with a violent blow to the head. He had then tied and gagged him before locking him in the back of the van. Wearing the man's work clothes, Spada replaced the picture on the ID card with his own and started the engine.

When he arrived at the mansion, he went in unnoticed. The van was the same as always and nobody paid too much attention to the fact it was a different person driving. After years spent working for Della Torre, this was the first time he had been to his house. The moment the gate opened he was mesmerized. He gazed, with admiration, at the elaborate flower beds. Enchanted by the stunning elegance on display, he thought that one day, he would like live in a place like this as well.

He drove to a small garage and parked the van outside. Following detailed instructions, he knew exactly where he needed to go and how to get there. Della Torre had planned everything personally, charging Spada with completing the task that Monti had left unfinished.

Spada, pulling the peak of his cap down over his face and wearing dark sunglasses, kept his face hidden. He could see that the external areas of the house were well protected with a comprehensive CCTV system covering every zone of the property. So he moved very carefully; he couldn't afford to leave any trace of his being there. He had a detailed map of where the cameras were located and, despite having memorized it, he took it out of his pocket to check. The plan gave the locations of where the cameras were installed. It also indicated the rotation time of each camera. He knew that he had just fifteen seconds to clear a blind-spot before being picked up on a camera. Fifteen seconds. It wasn't long, but it should give him enough time to sneak into the garage that wasn't monitored. Once inside, he would be able to take his time to do the work he had been tasked with.

The plan was to sabotage the brakes on Lisa Colasanti's car. Della Torre knew that she would be going out that morning and wanted it took look like an accident. To get to the main street, she would have to go downhill on a road with several dangerous turns. The brakes would stop working and Lisa wouldn't be able to handle the vehicle. Declivity and gravity would take care of the rest. The car would accelerate faster and faster before finally crashing.

It was nearly ten thirty. From the information Spada had been given, Lisa would leave by eleven. He gave himself a fifteen minute safety margin, which would give him fifteen minutes to complete the task.

Sabotaging the brakes was a very simple job, and it wouldn't take him long. But he knew that every second was precious. As always, he had planned everything in great detail but he couldn't foresee unexpected events. The traffic on his way to Della Torre's house had been re-routed causing a significant loss of time for him.

He risked paying a high price for that delay, but worrying about it now was useless. He opened the trunk in the back of the van and took out his work tools.

By then the operator had recovered his senses. Squirming in his need to free himself, he tried to yell for help. But he was gagged. His cries were in vain, no one would hear him. Without paying him too much attention, Spada took out a pair of shears and some gloves. He glanced back at the man while closing the trunk. He had tied him up and blindfolded him so that he wouldn't recognize Spada. The guy was not a danger and once the job was over, Spada would leave the van somewhere with the man inside. Eventually someone would look for him.

On the pretence of actually doing some gardening, and wearing the gloves, he walked up to a hedge and started to snip at it, randomly. He could look at the camera rotations without being noticed. He needed to move within the fifteen second timeframe into the garage. Once in there he had to quickly disable the brakes before making sure that he was within the fifteen second phase for his exit.

***

Going back to work was the best medicine. With her husband's encouragement, Lisa was absolutely certain it was the best way forward. Therefore, that morning she would start again and pick up her life once again.

She had advised her secretary the night before that she would be returning to the office. The secretary hadn't been told details of Lisa's absence but seemed to be relieved by the news. Lisa could hear the sincere joy in the woman's voice and this had reassured her that her decision to return was the right one. It appeared that she had been missed and this lifted her spirits. This could only mean that she did a good job, she thought, and that she was important to the center. For the first time, she realized she was a point of reference for many people. And this realization had made her happy.

However, starting back to work again wasn't easy. She had decided to work just a half day to start with. She would go there a little before lunch to regain confidence with the environment and later in the afternoon she would return home.

It was past ten thirty and she would have to leave shortly. After spending the morning rummaging through her closet, she still wasn't ready. She was looking for something special to wear to help boost her confidence; if she looked stunning and poised then she would feel assured and confident within herself. She was selecting dresses randomly just to toss them on the bed a little later, discarded as useless. She just couldn't make up her mind.

Becoming more and more anxious at her inability to find something suitable to wear she went to the window to take some fresh air. She stared, unfocused, trying to clear her mind, but she was soon distracted by the noise made by a gardener who was trimming the hedges. Obviously, the agency must have replaced the usual operator, as she was sure she'd never seen this man before. Staring at him indifferently for a moment, she began looking at the various hues of green contained within the hedge; calming colors. This was the inspiration she needed. Quickly returning to her closet she started looking for clothes that would emulate the color combination. She searched until she found a greenish tunic and decided to wear it. Sure, it wasn't the most appropriate garment for work but she didn't care. She had made her choice. She turned to face the mirror and, putting the dress close to her body, she admired herself for a few seconds. Finally satisfied, she smiled to herself and she thought that today nothing could go wrong.

***

More than ten minutes had passed, but Spada was still snipping leaves in the garden. One of the cameras had located him and paused, so he had started working at full gallop, trying to look as credible as possible. Someone was observing him so he needed to keep his act going for as long as possible. This gardening detail was an unpleasant situation that had wasted some precious minutes for him. He now reduced his pruning to the bare minimum. He didn't want to arouse any suspicion but at the same time he was aware that time was passing quickly and he needed to be certain that he would have sufficient minutes to complete his task and leave. Glancing sideways he saw that the camera lens was still zoned in on him. He didn't understand why. He hadn't done anything to draw attention to himself. Clearly, someone in the security personnel was having some fun at his expense. Despite the cameras being automated they could also be manoeuvred manually and, until the person behind the camera got tired of using Spada as a diversion, he couldn't move from his hedge cutting.

Determined not to show any signs of agitation he moved his arms so that his sleeves moved up from his hands. Then, still holding onto the shears and pretending to cut, he managed to glance at his watch. His eyes widened in despair as he saw that it was already a minute past the time that he needed to be inside the garage. What should have been a safety margin was now non-existent. He glanced once again at the camera and realized that he'd lost control of the situation. Whoever was manoeuvring the device didn't have any intention of changing its angle. Foreseeing his own failure, he sighed with resignation. But then, after a long silence, he heard a barely perceivable buzz again. The camera had finally resumed its rotations.

Instinctively, Spada checked his watch again.

Fourteen minutes to eleven.

He could still make it.

He waited for the camera to complete a whole rotation in his direction before starting the countdown in his head. Fifteen, fourteen, thirteen… three, two, one… Zero! The camera was fully turned in the opposite direction and he darted away.

Stopping every fifteen seconds, he moved intermittently zigzagging his way forward, using the various blind spots to cover his tracks. He took one minute and fifteen seconds to go past the four devices that separated him from the garage and, once inside, he checked the time again. He felt like he was walking on a razor's edge. He had very little time left.

Five cars were parked inside. He's been told that Mrs. Colasanti usually took the same car. Wasting no time, he reached the correct vehicle and, with a rapid and firm movement, he sliced through the brake pipe. He made a slight side cut so that the oil would seep out a little at a time. Halfway down the hill, the liquid in the tank would run out and the brakes' pump wouldn't be able to activate the small pistons and press the brake pads against the disk.

He had almost finished working on the car when his mobile phone vibrated. He didn't want to answer; it was a few minutes past eleven o'clock and the woman could appear at any moment. He took the phone from his pocket, determined to refuse the call, but he saw Della Torre's name on the screen. He must have a good reason for calling Spada at that delicate moment. He'd better answer it, he thought.

"Yes?" he whispered.

"Stop," Della Torre said sharply. "Suspend everything and leave."

"What? The job's done already."

"Damn it!"

There was a moment of silence. Spada didn't understand what was happening.

"Where are you? Have you left already?"

"No. I'm still in the garage. But the job's done."

"Then make sure that my wife doesn't get in the car."

"It's too late. There's no time left…"

"Do as I say!" Della Torre yelled. "The police have just been here. They're suspecting me of something. I'm too exposed, so find a solution right now. Do whatever you need to, but don't let her take the car."

"Alright," Spada said, finishing the conversation.

He took a nervous look at the gate. He was sure that shortly he would be face to face with Lisa Colasanti. There wasn't time to do anything to remedy the cut pipe, nothing satisfactory anyway. Thinking quickly and without any hesitation, he approached the vehicle and slashed both front tires. He then made his way carefully, moving back towards his starting point. Once there he picked up the shears and continued the hedge snipping task he'd started earlier.

A minute later, the woman appeared. She walked past Spada and glanced at him as he touched the visor of his cap to greet her. She walked on, indifferent to his gesture, and entered the garage. Finally, when he heard the roar of an engine, Mrs. Colasanti reappeared driving a car that was not her own. He stood looking at her while she drove out of the grounds. He thought that she must be really lucky.

She didn't know that once again she had cheated death.

CHAPTER 46

Nardi was revved up. He felt that he was reaching the final hurdle of solving the case and his impatience to get on with it was evident to everybody he came into contact with. As he set foot in the station, he saw the deputy running towards him. "Did you find any information on that guy?" he asked before the other man had a chance to speak.

"What? Oh, yeah! But I wanted to tell you…"

"Great! Tell me everything."

Cataldo turned and rushed into his small office with the small windows along the wall. He found what he needed and came out with a folder in his hands. He gave it to the inspector and said: "Something happened…"

"Ah!" Nardi interrupted him again. "What about the other research I asked you to do? Any information on Giada Rubini?"

"I did as you asked. I'll bring it to you immediately. But first, you should know…"

"Later, later. Now take everything to my office. Thanks."

"Hey, Inspector!" Lanzi arrived at that moment. "Finally you're back."

The sergeant had a strange expression on his face. He looked like he was waiting for the inspector to say something. Maybe he was just curious to know what Nardi had found out at the clinic. But his hesitant demeanor, which wasn't like him at all, left Nardi a little puzzled. "What's happened?" he asked. "Why that face?"

"What?" Lanzi replied. And turning to Cataldo he said: "You haven't informed him yet?"

"I tried to tell him, sergeant, but he didn't let me speak."

"Tell me what?"

The expression that had been on Lanzi's face until that moment disappeared and was replaced by a more serious and solemn one.

"It's Della Torre. He's been killed."

"What did you say?" Nardi asked, astounded by this news.

"It's absurd, I know. I had just talked to him."

"How did it happen? Do we know anything yet?"

"Oh, we know more than that. We already have the killer. They are in an interview room, giving a full confession."

Nardi was speechless. He didn't know what to say. For some strange reason he thought about Mrs. Colasanti. The woman had faced her own death. She blamed herself for Monti's death. And now she would have had to deal with something harsher: her husband's death. A husband who had wanted her dead.

"Don't you want to know who did it?" Lanzi asked.

"Uh? Sure. Tell me."

"You won't believe it, but it was Monti's wife. She says she wanted to avenge her husband."

"What?"

"Yeah. And to think I passed her in the corridor. I had just left Della Torre's office when I heard a shot. I found her with the gun in her hand. A gun registered in her husband's name."

"How did she know that Della Torre was involved in this story?" Nardi asked.

"Her husband left her a letter. It seems he had already decided to end his own life."

"What letter? What are you talking about?"

"Come with me. I'll show you."

The sergeant started to move, but the inspector grabbed his arm.

"Have you already informed Mrs. Colasanti?" Nardi asked.

"Not yet."

"Good. I'd like to take care of that personally."

"As you wish."

The two of them moved into a room close by. Lanzi indicated the letter on the desk and Nardi, more curious than ever, started to read it.

Farewell, my love,

I know that when you read this letter, I won't be here anymore.

I'm writing to ask for your forgiveness. It's too late now to fix all the mistakes, but it's never too late to ask for forgiveness. I couldn't do it while looking into your eyes. Forgive me, my dear Elena. I don't want to hurt Lisa, but I have to. Please believe me! I'd rather die. But Vincenzo threatened to kill both of us. I know he wouldn't hesitate to do it but I can't let you pay for my mistakes. So I'll do what he wants and then I'll leave this world. I could never live with such a burden on my conscience. Maybe you'll think that this is a selfish and cowardly gesture, and maybe it is, but I don't have any other option. I hope one day you'll be able to understand and forgive me.

Forever yours,
Riccardo

Nardi's reaction wasn't immediate. He kept staring at the letter feeling certain that something wasn't right. He noticed that that the letter wasn't handwritten, and realized that it probably hadn't been written by Riccardo Monti at all.

"Did she say how she found it?" he asked Lanzi.

"It seems she found it in her house. Why?"

"It must have been placed there intentionally," Nardi said. "By someone who wanted Della Torre dead. Whoever did it must have foreseen the woman's reaction."

"What makes you think that?"

"Have you ever written a letter?"

"Sure, why?"

"And how did you do it?" Nardi asked, showing Lanzi the letter. "With pen and paper or in front of a computer screen?"

"Of course!" Lanzi exclaimed. "I hadn't thought about it not being handwritten. But that does not mean…"

"Trust me! It couldn't be any other way because Monti didn't take his own life. He was murdered," Nardi stated.

"What?"

"Yes. You were right. I had confirmation at the clinic. And do you know what the best part is? It was Della Torre who called the shots."

The sergeant frowned. It was clear that he couldn't put the pieces of the puzzle together.

"Come," Nardi said. "Let's talk about it in my office."

Lanzi gave a detailed report about the events that had followed the meeting with Della Torre.

At the same time, Nardi updated him about what he had discovered at the clinic.

"We need to find this Spada," Nardi said, handing the dossier to Lanzi.

Nardi's thoughts now focused on other aspects of the case. He considered the last piece of information that he had been given about Ms. Rubini. He browsed through the paperwork looking for something that would help him make sense of the events that had occurred. The two men were silent while they reviewed the evidence that they had gleaned so far. Finally, a detail caught Nardi's attention. A name that had cropped up during the investigation. "Does the name Ivano Terravalle tell you anything?" he asked Lanzi.

"I don't think so. Why?"

"It seems he testified in favor of Ms. Rubini. She was suspected of her father's murder. And I am sure I've already heard this name."

"Maybe you read it in some reports."

"Yes, maybe…" Nardi said.

Searching through the mound of papers on his desk he

scanned them all, searching for the name.

"Here it is! It's him," he finally said.

"Who is he?" Lanzi asked.

"He's on the *VitaNuova*'s personnel list. So not only has he known Ms. Rubini for years, he also worked with her sister. And guess what? It seems he was hired shortly before this sad story started."

"Do you think they were accomplices in the blackmail thing?" Lanzi pondered.

"I don't know. It's probable. There are too many coincidences. Anyway, I am more and more persuaded about one thing. We went in the wrong way from the beginning."

"What do you mean?"

"Linking Ms. Fogliani's murder with what happened to Mrs. Colasanti, we asked ourselves the wrong questions. We should have treated the two cases separately."

Lanzi was about to give his opinion when Cataldo ran into the room. The door was open and he walked forward, quickly.

"Inspector, the forensic lab's latest report just got here," he said. "Here it is."

"Thank you." Nardi said.

When Cataldo left, Nardi remained silent for a few seconds, waiting for the sergeant to continue with his opinions on Nardi's theory. But he seemed more interested in knowing the latest news, so Nardi let it go and looked at the report.

"They found traces of a substance on the weapon," he said to Lanzi.

"What kind?"

"Turpentine essence. A solvent for varnishes. It's toxic when inhaled or ingested, when it comes into contact with the skin and the eyes… and a bunch of other useless technical information."

"I don't think so. This would explain why the only fingerprints on the handle were Mezzana's."

"What are you saying?" Nardi asked.

"They recommend using gloves when dealing with corrosive products, right? So obviously whoever took the razor from his desk was wearing them."

"The gloves are a plausible hypothesis. But we're talking about a rehabilitation center. Who would use a solvent…?"

Nardi's intuition kicked in and he left the sentence hanging while returning to examine the *VitaNuova*'s personnel list. The list reported the tasks of each employee and despite having given it a superficial search for names previously, he was sure he had read more about Terravalle. When he found confirmation of this, he smirked and said: "Do you know what our man is in charge of?"

"Excuse me, Inspector, but I'm lost. Who are you talking about?"

"Oh, sorry, of course," he said, realizing that he had kept his thoughts to himself. "I'm talking about Ms. Rubini's friend. It seems he's a painter or something similar. He works at the center as an art therapist."

"Well, it's not overwhelming evidence, but at least it's a starting point." Lanzi replied.

"A starting point? The man knew both victims. Working at the center, he had access to Mezzana's studio. And the substance found on the razor leads to him as well. I'd say it's definitely a starting point."

"Do you want me to send someone to arrest him?" Lanzi asked.

"We'll go as well, I think," Nardi said.

Nardi was convinced that soon he would see the face of the true killer and finally be able to close the case.

This notion filled him with some satisfaction, that the end was in sight.

CHAPTER 47

It was almost lunch-time when two police cars, and Nardi's, stopped in front of the *VitaNuova* entrance.

Nardi left an officer guarding the exit and had a couple more take up surveillance of the external perimeter. He then headed towards the administrative office, followed by Lanzi and two other police officers. Once there, he addressed the secretary, abruptly.

"We're looking for Ivano Terravalle," he said. "Where can we find him?"

"Why? What did he do?" she asked after hesitating for a second.

Nardi remembered the woman's reaction the last time he'd been there. When she'd got the news about Ms. Fogliani, she had burst into tears. But this time he wasn't bringing her any news and he didn't have the time to reply to her questions.

"Where can I find him?" he repeated brusquely. "Can you tell me or should I ask someone else?"

"Well… Right now he should be in the painting room," she said.

"And where is that?"

She opened her mouth to speak, but she stopped. She thought for a second, then said: "It's a bit difficult to explain. I can take you if you wish. It's quicker…"

"Yes, thanks."

The woman left her workstation and, moving to the other side, she signaled for them to follow her. Nardi started to walk with her; Lanzi and the officers followed. They continued along, not saying a word. Only the secretary would, every now and then, slightly turn her head to look at the inspector, as if she wanted to say something. He returned her gaze with a reassuring smile.

Taking a turn into yet another corridor, Nardi remembered that Mrs. Colasanti's office was next door to the administrative office. But despite him speaking quite loudly they hadn't seen her; she hadn't even looked out of her office to see what was happening. Knowing that the woman had been absent from work for quite a while, he asked the secretary: "The director hasn't come back yet?"

"Oh, yeah! Today. She's left her office for a minute, otherwise you would have seen her."

"Oh!" he commented.

"Here we are. It's the next corridor."

"Great. You can go now. Just tell us which door it is."

"The second one, on the right."

"Thank you again."

The woman headed back to her office, turning to look back a couple of times. When she finally disappeared around the corner, Nardi commanded the officers to not let anyone pass and, along with Lanzi, he headed for the painting room.

The door was open and Nardi stuck his head in without being noticed. The man was alone in the room. He stood by one of the windows, with his back to the door. Nardi signaled for Lanzi to come forward.

"Ivano Terravalle?" the sergeant said as soon as he entered.

When the man turned around, Nardi recognized him immediately. It was the same guy he had come across in the corridor the last time. Obviously, he must have recognized him as well, because suddenly he turned and jumped, rotating with the agility of a cat, out the window.

"Stop!" Lanzi yelled. And with the same nimbleness, he climbed over the parapet and ran after the man.

Nardi, on the other hand, was not the athletic type. Reaching the window, he lifted himself up with great effort. Once outside, he tried to keep pace with Terravalle and Lanzi but his efforts were in vain. Monti's chase had been a joke compared to this and even then, he'd ended up breathless. But right now, he wished he could keep up with these two men, yet they were much younger than him and so it was a one-sided contest. He saw them moving further and further away from him, both becoming smaller as the distance increased. Terravalle moved to the back of the building with Lanzi following hot on his heels. They both disappeared from Nardi's view yet he carried on running. In that moment, he didn't think about anything. The only thing his head told him to do was to resist the breathlessness and keep going.

When he reached the far end of the building, he saw the two men again, the distance between them getting shorter. Lanzi was in good shape physically and had been able to close the gap between himself and his prey. It looked like Terravalle was heading towards the parking lot where a railed fence separated a tract of internal road from the space reserved for cars. When Nardi saw him reach the fence and start to climb he thought that, surely, he should be able to do the same. In an effort to keep up he continued on, relentless in his need to catch Terravalle and assist Lanzi. He felt motivated at the sight of his sergeant, who was now climbing the railings, hot on the heels of Terravalle.

The moment Nardi got there, he tried to imitate the acrobatic abilities of both Terravalle and Lanzi, but he could barely lift his body from the ground. He was no more than thirty or forty centimeters up, the distance that separated him from the ground. His arms were paralyzed. His muscles wouldn't push him any further. He exerted himself until he was exhausted and had to let go. Unable to move because of the strain, he observed the chase from his side of the fence. In the distance, he saw the other two officers arriving to help Lanzi. They were still quite a way off, but unlike Nardi, they were on the right side of the fence.

Terravalle halted at a car and took keys out of his pocket. Obviously, he hadn't chosen that winding route by chance, he knew exactly where he needed to ensure his getaway. Unable to do anything to stop Terravalle's escape, Nardi felt anger boiling up inside of him. He wanted to pull down those damned railings and run. Instead, he was forced to observe passively, as the man jumped into the car and prepared to drive off.

He would have managed it too had Lanzi not grabbed him and forced him out of the car. The two men struggled to overcome his assailant; this was a fight that both were desperate to win. Finally, the other officers arrived at the scene and helped Lanzi bring Terravalle down. Pleased with the result Nardi yelled Lanzi's name. "I'll see you on the other side," he said, lifting up a hand to compliment his man.

The sergeant brought two fingers to his forehead as a confirmation, then started walking behind the group.

With some effort, Nardi set off back to the *VitaNuova* building. He felt exhausted. Worn out by a run that went beyond his ability, the pain of cramps hit his calves with every step, but nonetheless he eventually reached the main entrance. He looked back to where he'd just come from, swearing it had taken an eternity to get from one side of the building to the other.

Terravalle had been locked in one of the police cars and was glowering at Nardi from behind the glass. As usual, an event out of the ordinary had fostered a small group of spectators from the center. Nardi would have happily ordered them to be kept at a distance, but he'd rather save the breath he had left. He hadn't fully recovered yet and, feeling the pain hitting his legs again, he was forced to sit down on the small set of steps at the entrance to the building.

Just then, Lisa Colasanti came outside as well. Like the others, she must have been drawn by all the drama unfolding. "What's going on?" she asked, seeing the police cars. She hadn't asked her question to anyone in particular, and nobody answered her.

"Inspector," she said when she saw Nardi sitting close-by. "What's wrong? Are you unwell?"

"No, don't worry. I'm just a bit exhausted."

"Can you tell me what's happening?"

He lifted his eyes and sighed. He didn't feel like talking to anyone, but he felt obliged to answer the director.

"We arrested Ivano Terravalle. One of your employees. He could be the one responsible for the homicide."

"Terravalle?" she replied, her expression changing.

"Yes."

"And why would he have killed those poor women?"

"I don't know. We don't have a motive yet."

"Oh my God!" the woman exclaimed, bringing her hands to her face. "To think that I was the one who hired him."

"I hope you won't blame yourself for this too."

"No you don't understand. I insisted on having an art-therapist in our center. If I hadn't done that, none of this would have happened."

Nardi looked at the woman, feeling discouraged. His task was becoming harder and harder. He didn't have the courage to tell her that her husband had died and that he had plotted against her. But he had to do it. With extreme effort, he got up from the steps and said: "Can I talk to you in private? I need to inform you about matters that concern you personally."

"Sure. Let's go to my office."

"You go ahead. I'll see you at the station," he told the other police officers.

He really didn't want to go to her office and he wished he didn't have to impart this awful news but, he realised that it could only come from him and so, moving his aching limbs, he followed her into the building.

***

Speaking with Mrs. Colasanti had been harder than expected. Nardi had never faced such a situation before. His job was to find the criminals. Informing the victims' families was not part of his job. However, in this case he had felt obliged to take care of that responsibility personally.

When he finally returned to the station and he was sitting comfortably in his office, Nardi kept thinking over the upsetting scene with Mrs Colasanti, the moments of his deep uneasiness, and wondered at the reasons behind his disquiet. He had to admit that he liked the woman. He had liked her since he'd first met her. Maybe it was her insecure demeanor, or maybe the sense of vulnerability that she emanated. But what had led him to speak to her personally was something more profound. He had made the mistake of getting emotionally involved. And that had also affected his professional objectivity. He had acted in anything but a professional way, he thought, giving in to distractions that would prolong the investigation. Thankfully the entire case had reached its conclusion. Terravalle was already in the interrogation room waiting for him and soon he would go there. But first, Nardi wanted him to sweat a little, to become agitated and be ready to spill his story.

When he left his office, he found Lanzi outside the door. He complimented him once again on his apprehension of Terravalle. He had already done this several times since they had returned to the station but Nardi reckoned that Lanzi deserved all the credit for the arrest.

"Do you think he'll talk?" the sergeant asked after the umpteenth handshake.

"Oh, yeah," Nardi replied. "From the way he ran away, I wouldn't say he's a very calm person. He'll break down at the first difficulty."

"I see you have no doubts."

"We'll soon find out if I'm wrong," Nardi concluded. And he gestured for the sergeant to follow him into the room.

Once inside, they found the court-appointed lawyer sitting looking quite bored with the whole scenario, while his client, elbows on the table and face in his hands, pulled at his hair as if he wanted to rip it out of his head. Nardi thought that the questioning would be easier than expected. He was so sure about this that he didn't even play any of his usual tricks. Using no device at all, he asked Lanzi to take down the man's details. He then informed Terravalle of the charges against him and of his rights. When all of this had been completed Nardi asked him to tell his side of the story.

Terravalle took some time before talking. When he finally managed to speak, his fear was apparent in the tone of his voice. He began to explain his side of the events that had led to his arrest. But it soon became clear his testimony in defense of his actions was an incoherent mass of contradictions that wouldn't stand up to scrutiny in a court of law.

"What kind of relationship do you have with Giada Rubini?" Nardi asked, now starting the real questioning.

"I don't know anyone by that name."

"That's not how it seems to us," Nardi replied showing him a paper. "Do you recognize this signature?"

The man glanced at the sheet and, afraid of exposing himself, remained silent. The lawyer examined the document, but didn't say anything.

"According to that report, eight years ago you testified in her favor, exonerating her from a murder charge."

"Oh, yeah. I had forgotten about that."

"So you knew her."

"Well… yes. But I had forgotten her name. It was a long time ago."

"Strange. Very strange. Working alongside her twin sister didn't awaken any memory in you?" Nardi queried.

Terravalle seemed unable to answer. His anxiety was clearly visible in his demeanor. His hands were shaking, grasping his pants at the thighs. His eyes were two wild spheres looking up and around, perhaps searching for a way out of this situation. He thinned his lips together to still an impending nervous twitch. All separate elements that made up the whole: he was panicky as hell. Nardi grabbed the photo of the weapon used. The same one he had showed Mezzana.

"Do you recognize this object?" he asked.

"Why should I? It's not mine."

"We know that. But some traces of a substance were found on it. Turpentine essence. You use it regularly."

"So what? You can buy it anywhere. Many people use it."

"Sure. But not everyone that uses it was in contact with the victims. You knew them both, however."

"Say something, dammit!" Ivano yelled at the lawyer.

"I don't think there's much to say," Nardi replied, ready to shoot the final blow. "There are two witnesses. One saw you with Giada Rubini and the other saw you entering Ms. Fogliani's apartment complex the night of the murder."

He was bluffing, but Terravalle didn't know that. He was sure that those words would be enough to break any last defense; the man had almost reached his breaking point.

The lawyer began to speak but he didn't have time to say a word as Terravalle started crying hysterically. Determined to end the torture, he launched into a confession, releasing himself from this ordeal. The court-appointed lawyer kept telling him to not add anything else. But this instruction was in vain. Terravalle, in full flow now, kept on talking, confessing to Rosa Fogliani's murder, his responsibility for Ms. Rubini's death and the fact that he'd known her for years.

There was no need to ask any further questions. Wanting to render a full confession, the man spoke about the two sisters and the dark points that enveloped their past. He explained how destiny had played with their lives and how he'd been a passive witness. He spoke about his relationship with Giada Rubini, about how they had lost contact, only to meet again eight years later. He talked about the woman's intention to avenge on her sister, about the hatred she had harbored for years, and about her plan to blackmail Della Torre.

Finally, silence fell once more in the room.

Nardi was satisfied. All the outstanding issues had now been resolved.

"Okay. I think that's enough," he said, standing up.

Lanzi put the deposition on the table for Terravalle to sign. Then both he and Nardi left the room taking the written confession with them to the inspector's office.

"You were right," Lanzi said, sitting down.

"About what?"

"About the fact that he was going to talk."

"Ah," the inspector replied, sitting down as well.

"Well, it sounds like an improbable story."

"No more than the others."

"Anyway, we can consider the case closed."

"Yes, I think so."

Nardi sank back into the chair and started to read the statements over.

"Don't you need to call the prosecutor?" Lanzi asked.

"What?"

"Prosecutor Mellis will want to be informed, won't she?"

Nardi remained silent. Just then he wasn't paying too much attention to the sergeant's words. His mind was focused on the series of questions and answers written on the report. There was still something that didn't feel right.

He read the entire document over a couple of times before his eyes set on a specific sentence.

"You knew them both, however."

He'd been the one to make that statement. It was a response to Terravalle's answer. However, he hadn't fully understood the significance of those words at the time. Only now, connecting the sentence to the whole story, he realized that the detail was valid for everyone. He realized that he'd been tricked like an idiot.

"Why did she use the plural?" he said out loud.

"Who?" Lanzi asked.

Nardi didn't answer. Thinking about the problem, he brought one hand under his chin. After a few seconds, he abruptly started to search for Monti's letter. As soon as he found it, he read it over again. And then, like pieces of a jig-saw puzzle everything fell into place.

"Inspector?" Lanzi asked again. "Who are you talking about?"

"Do you believe in coincidences?"

"No. Why?"

"Well, me neither," he replied. "And this story is full of them."

With those words, he stood up and left the office.

CHAPTER 48

Nardi glanced at the clock on the dashboard while getting out of the car. A few hours had passed since he had last spoken with Mrs. Colasanti; however, if someone had asked him, he would have said the opposite. He could swear he had lived that scene only a few minutes earlier. And now he was in front of the woman's house, ready to meet her once again, but for very different reasons.

Covering the few steps that separated him from the house, he rang the doorbell and waited for someone to come. The housemaid opened it a few moments later. "Good morning, Inspector," she said. "I'm sorry but Mrs. Colasanti has retired to her room and doesn't wish to have visitors. She has just learned about her husband's death. I'm sure you understand."

"Yes, of course," Nardi replied. "But this is not a courtesy visit. I'm afraid you'll have to disturb her and ask her to come down."

The woman frowned, giving him a deprecatory look. She stared at him for a few seconds, before moving from the door and letting him in.

"Will you please wait in the living room while I call madam?"

"Sure."

Nardi went inside and started to look around. He had the impression that he'd never been in that room before. His opinions had changed and, with it, his way of assessing things.

The first time he had been there his eyes had contemplated a domestic space that was kept in obsessive order, but now he couldn't stop staring at the mobile bar. He knew Mrs. Colasanti's story and her past as an alcoholic. The glass strongbox, which in the beginning he had considered simply as something bizarre, now seemed to indicate someone with a sharp mind, able to foresee danger and anticipate events. He had always been good at judging people, but this time he'd been wrong. Mrs Colasanti had tricked him well.

When she finally entered the room he looked into her eyes. They didn't belong to someone who had been crying.

"Hello, Inspector," she said. "To what do I owe this unexpected visit?"

"Don't you think that's a useless question?"

"What do you mean?"

"Well... I guess that at this point we can simply lay the cards on the table."

Mrs. Colasanti took a seat on the couch and, with a shrewd expression on her face, said: "Please, have a seat."

"No, thanks. I'd rather stand."

"So, Inspector... Can you help me understand?"

"Oh, I'm sure you understand perfectly. But, it's only fair that I speak first."

Nardi's tone was vague, but the woman didn't say anything. Keeping her eyes fixed on his, she moved her lips and offered a shy smile.

"I'm impressed," Nardi began. "You were really good at planning this whole sham but unfortunately you spoke a little too much."

"I don't know what you're talking about. But I'm curious. So, please, go ahead."

"Sure. It's the reason I'm here," he replied. "Very few people are able to fool me, yet you succeeded. Like I said, you were really good. However, this morning you gave yourself away."

"Let's see... What did I allegedly do?"

"Trying to look surprised about what had happened, you spoke of *poor women.*"

Nardi left the topic in abeyance intentionally. He turned to observe the woman's attitude. She didn't show any hesitation though.

"You asked me why Terravalle had killed those poor women, remember?"

"So?"

"I never told you that there had been more than one death, nor did I speak about the existence of another woman. Yet you knew a detail very few people were aware of. And this is because it is you that's been behind this whole dreadful crime. You planned everything. Admit it! You knew everything from the beginning. And far from any suspicion, you kept plotting from behind the scenes." Once again, Nardi stared at the woman looking for any signs of humiliation; he saw only indifference and boredom. He continued with his accusatory statement. "Before coming here, I went to the center and spoke with Mr. Bernini. He told me a very interesting detail. Ivano Terravalle never sent a job application to you. You presented his candidacy and pressured for the job to be offered to him."

Mrs. Colasanti's lips lifted on both edges and the smile on her face grew wider.

"Very good, Inspector," she said. "I didn't think you would ever find that out. So, I wasn't wrong about you, after all. When I first met you I thought you were smart. You have all my respect. And this time for real."

The woman's attitude was not that of a hunted person. On the contrary, she seemed amused by what was happening. Nardi stared at her provocatively and, facing him she imitated that challenging gesture.

"Well, are you going to talk or are we to continue playing these little games?" he asked.

"I didn't want to deprive you of the pleasure of finding the truth by yourself. But since you have asked me, I'll be glad to speak."

"I'm listening."

"Before I start... Please, have a seat," she said, indicating with her hand.

"Alright," he replied, sitting on the armchair.

"See, Inspector... Everything started with the suspicion that my husband was having an affair. Something that I couldn't accept. Hoping that I was wrong I hired a private investigator. Unfortunately, my assumptions were well-founded. When I found out about his relationship with Ms. Fogliani, I felt humiliated. So I ordered for her to be investigated as well. I don't even know why. Back then, I wasn't looking for anything in particular. Anyway, I found out about her past and about the fact that she had a twin sister. I was intrigued, and I asked him to dig deeper. And, unexpectedly, a whole world of hidden truths came out. Something I didn't expect to happen. But it did. Giada Rubini hated her sister. Maybe more than me. In the report that my investigator produced Terravalle, and his connections to the two women, was mentioned as well. And, by chance, he was an art-therapist and was looking for a job. Great coincidences? A sign from destiny? Who knows? I couldn't miss such a chance. To get rid of that woman, I only had to give the go ahead and then watch, while everything unfolded on its own. So, I asked the center's general management to introduce art-therapy and at the right time I presented Terravalle's candidacy. I was sure that his meeting with Ms. Fogliani would be enough to trigger the mechanism. And everything went exactly as it should have."

Nardi had listened to her in silence for the whole time she was speaking. She had confirmed his hypotheses. Except for few little details, everything had happened just as he had imagined.

"So, Inspector!" Lisa said. "Have I satisfied your curiosity or is there still something else you want to know?"

"Only one more thing. Did you know that Ms. Fogliani was pregnant?"

When she heard that question, Mrs. Colasanti's expression changed completely, but Nardi started talking again.

"Oh, don't worry," he said. "It wasn't your husband's, if that's what you're thinking."

"No, I didn't know that," she finally replied.

"Well, now you do," he said, showing his reproof.

For a few moments, they just looked at each other with mutual disdain, absorbed in their own thoughts. The silence between them gave the room a deceptive calm, each waiting for the other to speak again.

"Just out of curiosity," Mrs. Colasanti finally said. "What's the real reason you bothered to come here? I don't think you want to incriminate me for recommending the hiring of an employee. You know better than me that you can't charge me with anything that happened. You have no proof against me. So I wonder why you came here. Did you want to see my reaction in person? Or was it to satisfy your ego? Maybe the pleasure of telling me to my face that you had figured it out? Tell me, Inspector. Which one of these?"

Nardi remained silent. The woman was right. He couldn't charge her with the crime and they both knew it. Ms. Fogliani's murder would never go to trial. Well, not one with Lisa Colasanti as a defendant. It would have been archived among the many unsolved cases if it hadn't been for Terravalle. He would be the only one to pay for the crimes while the real killer would get away with it.

"Well, if that's all," Lisa resumed talking, "I guess we're parting ways here." With a satisfied expression, she lifted her arm mid-air and added: "How about we say goodbye with a handshake?"

He stood up, pretending to ignore her jeering provocation, and, his head bowed down, he headed towards the exit without breaking the silence. He was halfway to the door when he turned around abruptly. His demeanor had changed and on his face was an amused expression.

"Oh! How stupid!" He exclaimed. "I almost forgot the most interesting part."

"I don't know what else there is to say."

"When I said that you gave yourself away... I should have specified that you committed the same mistake twice. One too many, I might add."

It was clear that Mrs. Colasanti didn't understand what he was referring to. He saw her frown with uneasiness. She clearly didn't have the courage to ask any questions, so Nardi continued talking.

"You would have gotten away with it, if you hadn't faked Monti's letter." he said.

Lisa's attitude grew more exasperated. Her shocked expression was emphasized by the paleness of her skin. She parted her lips slightly, maybe in an attempt to protest against that statement, but no sound came out of her mouth.

"You and I were the only ones who knew about that death threat," Nardi continued. "But what you didn't know was that Monti didn't take his own life. Your beloved husband had him killed. Moreover, whoever left that letter must have done so after Monti's death. And since that moment, according to Monti's wife's testimony, you were the only person to set foot in that house, except for the maid."

"I don't know what you're talking about," she said, gruffly.

"Come on! At this point, lying is useless. You understood that your husband wanted you dead. Maybe you were willing to live with a man who cheated on you, but surely you couldn't remain by his side after discovering that. You knew that sooner or later he would try it again, so you decided to be the first to act. And you didn't hesitate to take advantage of your friend, instigating her to commit the crime in your place."

At that moment, the doorbell rang. As the maid passed by, Mrs. Colasanti glanced at the door.

"You're talking nonsense," she replied. "Why would my husband have wanted to do something like that? He loved me, like I loved him. That stupid affair didn't mean anything."

"Your husband had millions and millions of reasons. We did some digging. Almost all your wealth is in your name. With your death, he would have inherited everything."

"You can't prove what you're saying. These are just..."

Lisa didn't finish the sentence as sergeant Lanzi and two officers appeared in the room.

Nardi had called him after speaking with Bernini, informing him of the situation.

"Inspector," Lanzi greeted him.

"I was just wondering where you all were," he replied, beating a finger on his watch. Then, answering the woman, he said: "I don't have to prove anything. That is not my job. I just gather evidence. Everything else, I leave to the judges. The court will determine whether you're guilty or innocent. Just know that the fingerprints of two people were found on the letter. I'm sure that along with Mrs. Monti's fingerprints we'll find yours as well. I wish you could pay for Ms. Fogliani's murder, but I'll have to be content with charging you for involvement in your husband's death instead."

Unable to reply, Mrs. Colasanti sank down on the couch and Nardi, utterly satisfied, offered her his hand, repeating the mockery of a little earlier.

"If you haven't changed your mind."

She looked at him with hatred. A malevolent expression appeared on her face, disfiguring her usual attractive countenance. Nardi remained unmoved, as if to underline the facts before her. He had been tricked, and he now wanted to point out who was victorious between them both. He lowered his arm, and looked around the room. He felt disgusted by such sophistication and all that had been hidden behind its elegant façade.

"Take care of her," he told the sergeant. "I don't want to spend another minute here."

"Don't worry, Inspector."

Nardi was about to leave when Mrs. Colasanti unexpectedly spoke again.

"What if it had been you?" she asked.

"Uh?" he replied.

"What if you had been in my place? How would you have behaved?"

"I can't answer that. My wife never cheated on me."

"Yeah. I used to think the same before I discovered the truth," she concluded, becoming silent again.

Nardi didn't answer. He tried to not show it, but that last sentence had hit him deeply.

Looking at what was left of a defeated person, a person annihilated by jealousy, selfishness and by her own past, he couldn't help but notice the similarities that they shared. Their lives had been lived as polar opposites but they weren't so different. Just like her, he had lived most of his life certain of everything until fate had stabbed him in the heart, destroying everything he held dear. No, the two of them weren't so different. They were victims. Although in different ways, misfortune had tricked them both.

Looking for confirmation of these thoughts, he glanced at the woman one last time. Their eyes met. Hers resigned to a life of regret. He could almost see himself in her eyes, feeling the same despair and helplessness. But there was now one major difference between them, he could move on with his life unlike Lisa who would suffer a tortured soul for the rest of her days. He opened his mouth to speak but there was nothing he could say. Putting his hands in his pockets, he shrugged his shoulders and with Mrs. Colasanti's words still swirling in his head, he headed towards the exit.

He couldn't wait to leave that place. He needed the purity of the air outside. He stopped on the threshold to enjoy the now fading sunset. The earth's beauty and its continual rotation never failed to revive him. He had the impression that the sun, in its endless journey towards tomorrow, brought with it all the doubts and answers of existence. Staring at the beautiful landscape and the lights flickering in the city below, he felt relieved, almost free to go back to living as he had done before. These musings were short-lived. They lasted long enough for him to think that even though this case was finally closed, the sun would rise again. And he would go back dealing with his usual demons. He knew too well that these shadows from the past would never leave him; he was the one who wouldn't let them go.

He was thinking about his wife and his son. But then reality stabbed him in his calves and his reveries were lost, for now. He was paying for the frantic chase with Terravalle earlier that morning. He took out his keys and headed towards the car, wondering if he should take a day off to rest up and restore his energy. Convinced that a good sleep would renew his vigour, he let go of the idea, got in the car and started the engine.

Leaving the mansion, he looked in the rear view mirror. He saw behind him the handcuffed figure of Mrs. Colasanti being led out of her home. She would suffer for the rest of her days, a tortured soul who could have played her game so differently and kept everything. Nardi was gratified that he'd solved this crime but he knew it wasn't quite over.

Spada's image was taunting him. That man was still walking free. Who was he, where did he come from and how dangerous could he be? These were questions that Nardi had yet to answer. He knew that with some fake documents, Spada could easily disappear, and the thought that he had had him within close reach was a bitter pill to swallow. Nardi wondered if he would ever come across him again.

It had been a hard twenty four hours and now feeling heat and exhaustion clouding his mind, he lowered the windows to refresh the inside of the car. Going at a good pace, he immediately felt the outside air hitting his face and, wanting to block every emotion crowding in on him, he pushed on the gas, allowing the wind's energy to blow all negative thoughts away. Tomorrow would come soon enough, he thought. His life would go on with more cases to solve, more lives to infiltrate. But just now he needed to drive away from the shadows haunting him; his wife, his son. He needed to stop punishing himself and to forget everything and everyone for a while.

BOOKS BY JACQUES OSCAR LUFULUABO

INSPECTOR NARDI MYSTERY-THRILLER SERIES

- *SHADOW OF PUNISHMENT*

- *ENIGMA OF THE MISSIONARY*

THE LAST SPIN

ABOUT THE AUTHOR

Jacques Oscar Lufuluabo is an Italian author. He was born in Rome, where he still lives and works.

After his studies he specialized as a copywriter and in the comic strip industry, in the meantime collaborating with local newspapers. Then he attended the Omero School for creative writing and TV-fiction screenplay.

Presently, he has published numerous short stories for anthologies and magazines, some of which have been awarded prizes in literary competitions. *Shadow of punishment* is his debut novel.

www.joloscar.com

Made in the USA
Monee, IL
21 June 2024

60307183R00166